Down the Dark Path

Also by Gordon Anthony Bean:

Dawn of Broken Glass
Bloodlines

Down the Dark Path

Gordon Anthony Bean

Off the Beaten Path Press

Windham, New Hampshire
www.otbp-press.com

DOWN THE DARK PATH
by
Gordon Anthony Bean

Off the Beaten Path Press
Website: www.otbp-press.com

Cover and interior design by:
 Pam Marin-Kingsley
website: www.pammarin-kingsley.com

Paperback ISBN: 978-0692732717

Copyright Acknowledgements

From a Whisper to a Dream©2008 by Gordon Anthony Bean. First appeared in *Sinister Landscapes* by Pixie Dust Press.

Out of the Corner of His Eye©2013 by Gordon Anthony Bean. First appeared in *From Beyond The Grave* by Grinning Skull Press.

Knob Lake©2015 by Gordon Anthony Bean. First appeared in *Forgotten Places* by The Horror Society Press.

Printed in the United States of America

This book is dedicated to Greer and Alexa
whose light keeps me off the dark path.

Table of Contents

Introduction

As a writer, the two questions which I am always asked are why I choose to write horror and where do my ideas come from. Like any writer of dark fiction, there are many reasons why I am compelled to weave dark and twisted tales. I suppose that horror is a genre that awakens my primal fears and satisfies something deep in my psyche. Of course, I might just have a dark side and find it easier to let the demons out on paper than in real life. The honest truth is that I love horror and couldn't imagine wanting to write anything else. To coin a phrase: it's in my blood. Our genetic blueprint is mapped out for us and we are nothing more than slaves to generations of internal programming. In other words, I am hard wired to write stories that keep the reader on the edge of their seat.

From the time I first saw Frankenstein on television as a young child, to seeing the brilliant Alien as a pre-teen, there has always been something about horror that captivated me.

That love of horror translated to what I read as well. As a kid, I devoured everything by Stephen King, Dean Koontz and Robert McCammon, among others. Of course, I needed more and writers like Clive Barker opened darker and more forbidden doors and exposed me, the reader, to the seamier underbelly of life. Writers like Ed Lee, Richard Laymon and Jack Ketchum showed that horror could have teeth and that boundaries were meant to be pushed and, in many cases, broken.

Movies were another medium where horror was evolving and being pushed to the limits. I spent countless hours in the welcoming darkness of the local movie theatre immersing myself in the latest horror offering to grace the silver screen. Slasher films that were so prevalent in the seventies and eighties (shout-outs to the Halloween and Friday the 13th franchises) gave way to films like Saw and Hostel and brought a whole new sub-genre aptly nicknamed torture porn. Extreme horror films popped up, many from Europe and Asia paving the way to give the viewer something more shocking than they had seen before. Films like Inside, A Serbian Film, Audition, Haute Tension and Oldboy crafted some of the most disturbing images ever caught on cinema, and once again showed that horror wasn't something that could be easily compartmentalized.

As horror has evolved, so has my appreciation for the genre. I'm not sure where the light switch was thrown and the metaphorical bulb came on prompting me to write horror, but it was many years back. I had stories to tell and like most authors, had to put pen to paper and craft and then fine tune the story.

The stories in this collection are a sampling of my short fiction over the last decade. I am not a prolific short story writer, preferring to spend what little free time I have available to me working on novels. The stories that are included in this anthology have been edited and, in some cases, completely rewritten from their original form. Therefore, what you hold in your hands is pretty much new work.

So, where do I get my ideas? I've thought about telling people that I have a minor demon locked in a cage in my closet and he writes my stories if I promise to bring him small children to snack on, but most people do not respond well to sarcasm. Suffice to say, ideas come from several sources.

I first came up with the idea for the story *From a Whisper to a Dream* from a nightmare I had one night. Usually, my dreams are vague or indistinct but, in this case, the story was seared into my brain with crystal clarity. When I awoke, I had to get it down on paper before I lost it. I'm glad I did because it was my first published short story in the modern gothic collection *Sinister Landscapes* and was the inspiration for my second novel *Bloodlines*. The story is a surreal look at transition between life and death. To this day, I still feel a chill when I think of the two brothers observing the soul eaters approaching the mysterious house. I hope that you, dear reader, will as well and want to continue the story in *Bloodlines*.

I wrote *In Her Skin* in one sitting. I've never written an extreme horror story, so I decided to try my hand at it. Of course, I added my own personal touch, threw in a background in physiology and made the story uniquely mine. I wanted a story that was both horrific in its pacing, but also with an ending that left the reader feeling like they've been sucker punched. I like to think that I really get to explore the notion that underneath the thin veneer of civilization that we project, we are all nothing more than savage beings.

Music often serves as inspiration for my stories. The idea for *Climbing the Corporate Ladder* came from a song by Pennywise called Perfect People. As I listened to the song, the outline of the story began to form. Having worked in downtown Boston, I always thought that people tended to dress alike and in many ways, act alike as if driven by a hive mentality. It seemed that every office building had a collection of interchangeable employees, as if there was a grand design as to how the workforce should be laid out. This story was a real departure for me as I stepped outside of my comfort zone, bringing in elements of classic science fiction to blend in with the horror. The end result has a 1950's sci-fi feel to it, reminiscent of a Matheson era *Twilight Zone* story.

The idea for *Legacies* came about as I was considering ending a friendship due to the person's increasingly erratic behavior. Severing ties with a friend can be a painful and difficult choice. It made me think about friendships that last for life and, sometimes, over the years, you get exposed to a few of the skeletons that are inevitably in their closets. Throw in a pinch of introspection and a healthy dose of horror and the story was born.

The story *My Thoughts are With You, My Beloved* comes from an idea I had for writing a love story about unrequited love. Of course, what a horror writer considers as a love story might be something else entirely.

I was home alone one night working on my debut novel

when I felt like someone was in the room with me. I turned and, of course, no one was there, but it got me thinking. What if there really was someone there? That idea terrified me. The concept of shadow people has been around for many years and is terrifyingly real to many people. Could there be some truth to it and, if so…what do they really want from us? *Out of the Corner of His Eye* was born from that incident.

I used to work for a tech company that was based in Helsinki, Finland. I loved the country and really enjoyed the people and the culture. On one of my visits, a Finnish co-worker and I were talking about music and he told me that the band Children of Bodom was named for the infamous Lake Bodom murders. I was intrigued and read up on the story and the folklore around it. What I read stuck with me and one day out of the blue the idea for the story *The Kids in Black and White* popped into my head. I knew that I had to write my version of the story. The strong backdrop of true events lends a sense of credibility to a very dark story. It will make you think twice about visiting a famous murder site, especially at night.

Several years back, I tried my hand at flash fiction. I wanted to see if I could pack a punch in a very short story of around five hundred words. *Of Lights and Shadows* was that story and, yes, it shows that you don't need to write lengthy prose to be damn scary.

The genesis for *Grey* was fairly straightforward. I wanted to write a zombie story but did not want to rehash the same old thing. I decided to do the story from the perspective of the dead.

I traveled to South Africa for work at the time that Ebola was ravaging Liberia and Sierra Leone. Even though I was far away from the spread of the disease, an incident at the airport in Johannesburg gave me an insight into how serious the outbreak was. While at the airport getting ready to go through customs, a government agent had me stand before a scanner to read my body temperature and then carefully looked at my eyes prior to giving me the go ahead to leave. I was feeling a bit under the weather that day and was concerned that they might refuse my request to return to the United States and instead hold me in some kind of quarantine for an indeterminate time. Thankfully, I was given the green light to travel out of the country. I wrote *The DRC* on the long flight home.

A part of life which we all must deal with is death. We watch our family members grow old and in some cases die. After my aunt passed away last year from cancer, I was thinking about my own mortality and how after we are gone, all that is left are memories and some possessions we have accumulated in our homes. This is always followed by the difficult task of packing up what's left of a person's life, trying to decide what to get rid of and what to keep. As I thought about these things, the idea for *Timepiece* came to me.

Readers who are familiar with my work know that I frequently look to various cultural beliefs and mythology for inspiration for my stories. My debut novel, *Dawn of Broken Glass*, delves into Jewish mysticism and includes a terrifying and very deadly Golem. My second novel, *Bloodlines,* incorporates Egyptian mythology, including Anubis and the judgment he passes on the dead who stand before him. In *The Congregation*, I center the story around Jewish culture and look at how faith can make a difference, even in a synagogue at the end of the world.

A basic part of life is having loved, then lost. In some cases, the loss can be reversed and relationships can reconcile. In other cases, a loss can be due to death and we are forced to move on, never being able to get true closure. Once again, my story was influenced by music. In this case it was a great song called Heart's Desire by the Finnish symphonic metal band Dreamtale. I began thinking about how far someone might be willing to go to get their true love back once more and wrote an outline for a story that became *Heart's Desire*.

As someone who has been married for close to twenty years, I have seen my wife's moods running the full length of the emotional spectrum. Any married man can affirm, when his spouse is having her monthly period, hormones are running rampant and rapid mood swings can follow. What started out as a light-hearted look at relationships went down a much darker path by the time I got through with the story. *Her Time of the Month* is a story of a husband's utter devotion to his wife.

When I was a kid, I was a huge fan of the old EC Comics line of horror. The stories were dark and campy and a lot of fun. I wanted to try to do a story in that vein. *The Puppeteer* was my homage to that era.

Shadow Play was originally written as the first chapter in my forthcoming novel *Shadowspawn*. I decided to take the novel in a different direction and, as a result, *Shadow Play*, while still entertaining, did not enhance the continuity of the story. I'm presenting it here to you, dear reader, in its entirety.

The next story in the collection was inspired by a song by Chris DeBurgh. The Traveler told a dark and haunting tale of revenge. It wasn't much of a leap to add my own twisted touch to the song and the resulting story was *The Horseman*.

A year ago, The Horror Society put out a call for short stories using the theme of abandoned places. I decided to go back to my roots and find an abandoned location in my home province of Quebec. While I didn't find something to my liking from Montreal, an abandoned mine in northern part of the province offered a great opportunity to weave a story around the cultural tension between local Quebecers and people from the First Nations. Throw in a dark and terrifying secret in the mine and weave in racial undertones and the story *Knob Lake* practically wrote itself.

So, pull up a chair, but don't get too comfortable. The darkness awaits. Monsters, human and otherwise, lurk in the shadows and beckons you *Down the Dark Path*.

Gordon Anthony Bean
05/20/2016

Man is fully responsible for his nature and his choices.
- *Jean-Paul Sartre*

From a Whisper to a Dream

The two brothers stood at the window of the old house, looking out at the vast expanse of property that made up the estate. The elder of the two looked at his younger brother and wondered how they had come to be there. Everything felt right, like they belonged, yet he couldn't shake the feeling that something was very wrong.

The room that they were in was hot, almost cloyingly so and there was a musky dampness to the air. The furniture was Victorian and seemed to be covered by a thin film of mildew which emitted a faint, unpleasant odor. A gold candelabrum, mottled with green, sat atop a rotting mahogany desk. The candles were all lit and cast a depressing pallor over the room.

The window from which the brothers looked out was streaked with grime, giving the outside a sepia-hued appearance that made the brothers feel like they were trapped in an old movie.

Anthony, the elder of the two, looked over at Bryant who sat motionless since the moment of first awareness. He just sat there, pale against the fading light by the window. Motes of dust floated about his head, settling on his face and giving his pale skin an iridescent sheen.

"Bryant," Anthony asked, noting how his younger brother slowly turned his head, as if waking from a long dream, his eyes taking on a glint of awareness, "how did we get here?"

"As opposed to where," Bryant replied as if it were the most natural thing to say yet, somehow, it made sense to Anthony. He walked to the door of the room and turned back to face his brother who continued staring out the window.

"I'm going to look around. Want to come?"

Bryant turned to face his brother and replied, "I think I'm supposed to be here. You'll find me later when they arrive."

"When who arrives," Anthony asked, feeling uneasy at the vague response his brother offered.

Bryant looked up at his older brother. The effect of the flickering candles and the waning light outside seemed to make his eyes take on a menacing hue. "Why, those who will eat our souls." He then turned back to the window and resumed his trance-like vigil.

"Are they here already?" Anthony asked his brother. His brother continued staring out the window and Anthony knew that no further response would be forthcoming.

Anthony left the room and entered the long, dimly lit hallway. The walls were adorned with portraits of those family members long dead, yet still bore an air of the familiar. Several doors lined the hallway, but Anthony knew there was nothing behind them for him, at least not at this time. The doors housed other secrets, other truths which Anthony did not wish to address. He knew that he had to go down to the ground floor. There was nothing for him on the top floor this day. As he walked towards the stairs, the hallway behind him slowly lost color and seemed to fade off into mist, becoming more intangible the further away he went.

Anthony descended into the liquid darkness, wishing he had had the foresight to bring one of the many candles which adorned the room where his brother waited. He heard his heart beating, amplified in the still darkness. At the bottom of the stairs, he came to a landing with doors to each side and a long hallway heading out into the shadows. From under the door on the left, a bluish-white light flickered and pulsed.

Anthony felt drawn to his left and grasped the cold metal handle. He pushed the door open. The room seemed to embody the general malaise of the house. The floor was scuffed and worn and mostly covered with a threadbare Persian rug that must have been quite exotic in its day. The wallpaper hung down in damp, lifeless rolls, exposing the yellowed underbelly of the walls. As upstairs, the furniture was old, Victorian and damp with mildew. In the far corner of the room sat an orange Naugahyde couch that seemed out of place with the rest of the house's furnishings. In front of the couch was an old model RCA television with rabbit ears perched precariously on top. The set was on and showed a screen of bluish-white light which pulsed in synchronic bursts and hissed with static. On the couch, two people sat unmoving, staring at the screen, as if enraptured.

Upon closer inspection, Anthony noticed that the two figures were his parents. His mother turned to him and cried, "How can I watch anything? I can't even see." Anthony noticed, with horror, that his mother did not have any eyes. She just had hollowed indents where her eyes should be. She clawed at her face, digging deep furrows in the dry skin. Blood welled up in the cuts and ran down her face. Anthony's father turned towards him and Anthony had to take a step backward. His father's once fine features were mashed together, a jumble of broken bone and shredded flesh. "Help your mother, will you, son," Anthony's father gurgled through his ruined face. "Things simply haven't been the same since the car accident."

"Why are you here?" Anthony whispered, unable to look at either of his parents.

"We need to be here when they arrive," Anthony's mother said matter-of-factly, as blood oozed from where her eyes should be.

"Who?" Anthony screamed. "Who are you waiting for?"

"No need to be so testy, son," Anthony's mother continued. "Of course, we mean those who will eat your soul." She grinned, a wide, lopsided grin, her teeth bright red from the blood which flowed from the side of her mouth. "So," Anthony's mother hissed as she patted the couch, "sit down and join us. We can wait together."

The television shut off, leaving the room in an impenetrable darkness. Anthony heard his parents slowly rising from the couch and heading towards him. He turned and ran from the room with his parents in hot pursuit.

Luck guided his hand and he found the door and shut it hard behind him. From the other side of the door, the scraping and pounding on the wood, mixed with taunts from his parents, became almost too much for him to bear. Anthony was in a panic. He could head back upstairs to his brother, down the hallway, or through the adjacent door. Anthony chose the door and slipped through quickly.

Anthony stood on the other side of the door, his back pressed to the wood as he struggled to regain his composure. He was assailed by the musty and damp smell of the earth. Candles burned on shelves lining the walls which were thick with dust and grime. He began walking and realized that he was in a tunnel, the floor being nothing more than earth and rocks. Each step he took seemed to be as if he were in a kind of stop-motion photography, moving in a series of jumps.

Eventually, Anthony found himself before a massive oak door. The handle, set in the dead center, was a brass claw with long and gnarled fingers which seemed to beckon him closer. Anthony raised his hand to the handle and it grasped him firmly about the forearm and pulled him through the wood.

Anthony found himself outside the house on a stone step facing an old rope and wood bridge that crossed a deep chasm to an older, long abandoned section of the house. He turned, contemplated returning to the house, and found that the door had no handle or other visible means to regain his entrance. He realized that he would have to cross. As he took his first tentative step, the bitter wind assailed him. Looking back to the house once more, he wondered why there were no windows on this side of the building.

With each step he took, the bridge swayed and shook in the gusting wind, threatening to toss Anthony over the edge into the yawning black abyss. Anthony was numb with cold by the time he reached the other side and stood before a small, featureless black door.

He placed his palm against the door and found himself falling forward. He frantically attempted to grab on to something, but was unable to find purchase. Anthony plunged downwards, spinning head over foot until he came to a crashing stop on the cold, tile floor. Pulling himself back to his feet, he saw that he was in a kitchen, long since abandoned. He shivered and hugged himself, striving to shake the chill from his bones. He saw his breath in short plumes of frost and noticed a fine surface of ice coating every surface. Against the walls was a series of stainless steel sinks and counters, all covered with dried blood, thick and coagulated in parts, sparse in others. The floor was the standard black and white tile pattern of an industrial kitchen, and was streaked with grime and blood spatter.

Anthony looked around, noting the shelves with discarded cans and jars, their contents long since turned rancid. Past the cutting tables and prep area was a door which led deeper into the old section of the house. Anthony did not wish to leave the relative safety of the kitchen but knew he had to continue if he wished to find his way back to the main section of the house.

Before they come. The thought came to him and he cringed.

A shadow crossed his field of vision and vanished in the direction of the door, fleeting and ethereal, yet it evoked a fear unlike any he had ever experienced before. It brought to mind a lost memory which lingered on the periphery, not allowing enough time to coalesce into meaning.

At the door, something seemed to freeze Anthony in place, as if strong hands were warning him against proceeding. *Something bad happened here*, he thought, yet he could not recall what it was, simply that he was filled with a sensation of dread. Beyond the kitchen was a short hallway which opened up into a small classroom. The classroom contained two dozen small desks, all in a late stage of rot and decay. The blackboard at the front of the class was cracked and sections seemed to have fallen and shattered on the floor below. Behind the missing sections of the blackboard was nothing but darkness, an inky void stretching out to the depths of nothingness.

Next to the blackboard on the left was a door which led further into the old house. To the right was another door that led to the cloakroom. Anthony paused for a moment, wondering how he knew this. The room seemed to throb and pulse and Anthony wished he were anywhere else. He needed to get back, and fast. Events were being set in motion to which he was more than simply a spectator. The room seemed to be getting grayer, as if the color were slowly being leeched away and with it went any warmth left in the room. Anthony paused to note the surreal quality of the situation. The room had bled color until it was a black and white copy of the original, yet Anthony retained his normal appearance. He studied his hands, still flesh toned, yet they, too, were slowly losing their color and were slipping into shades of black and white.

A thump from behind the cloakroom door caused Anthony to stop suddenly. He heard a scraping noise, as if a stick were being dragged across cement. Fighting the urge to run, he advanced on the cloakroom and swung open the door. A small boy, dressed in a school uniform, sat there, in the darkness, his hands tied firmly behind his back. A thick plastic bag was placed over his head and tied tightly around the neck. The boy wheezed and struggled with his bonds, his eyes bulging as he struggled for air. His face was ashen, and his eyes were rimmed with dried blood.

"Help me," the boy wailed, eyes wide with fear.

"I can't," Anthony replied in a whisper, slowly backing away, "no one can."

"You heard me screaming," the boy roared, his voice getting louder and more menacing, "You all did."

"I was only six," Anthony sobbed, backing away towards the door.

The little boy stood and screamed against the bag. "But you won't let me die. And now I must die for eternity!" Then the door to the cloakroom slammed shut, leaving Anthony alone in the darkness. He sank to the ground, clutching his knees as he rocked back and forth and screamed for forgiveness.

After what seemed an eternity, he got himself to his feet and brushed the dust from his clothes. The house was dark and silent. Dust filled the air and thick cobwebs hung from the ceiling in a myriad of patterns. He left the room and found himself in another room, right off the classroom. This room was clearly a nursery, long since abandoned. The room smelled old and lay undisturbed, as if nothing had lived here for years. Cobwebs were visible on all the walls and ceiling and a thick blanket of dust covered the floor, furniture and even the crib. Anthony knew what he would find in the crib and yet he peered over the side anyway, needing to see. The stink of decay assailed his senses, so he cupped his hand over his mouth to allow himself to breathe the fetid air without getting any of the dust in his lungs.

The crib was filled with dust and rotting toys. As soon as Anthony got close, the dust shifted and the baby sat upright. Dust clung to its clothes and fell from the grey and leathery skin. A visible wound in the baby's forehead puckered and oozed pus. It opened its eyes, all milky white, and pointed a finger at Anthony and screamed. Anthony ran from the room, not once daring to look back. He ran down a maze of hallways, ignoring closed doors until he came to the end of the house. Where there should have been a wall was instead nothingness. It was as if the house simply ceased at this point. Floor, walls and ceiling ended on this swirling void of emptiness. Anthony looked back from where he had come, whispered a silent apology, and leaped into the void.

He stood once again at the threshold to the first room, looking in at his brother. He silently walked over to where his brother sat, still staring out the window, his features waxy and ashen.

"Bryant," Anthony probed, gently placing a hand on his brother's shoulder.

Bryant's eyes snapped open and, without turning, he replied coldly. "They are coming; those who will eat our souls." Bryant gestured to his brother to look out the window. He pointed to the far edge of the lawn. "There," he said, "they're here."

Anthony leaned forward and wiped the filthy glass with his hand in a feeble attempt to make it clearer. Through the grimy glass he saw two shapes lumbering across the lawn towards the house. The larger shape was black, covered in a fine and silky fur that looked wet and shiny. The other shape was smaller and silvery grey. Both creatures had stumps for arms and legs, a misshapen bulge for a head and no other discernible features. Their bodies moved and undulated like two large sacks of meat, folding over and back again to manage enough momentum to effectuate movement.

As the two shapes moved across the lawn, Anthony hissed through his teeth, his eyes wide with fear. These two shapes were aberrations of nature and he knew that allowing them entry to the house could mean his and his brother's death.

Anthony grabbed his brother by the arm and dragged him downstairs. Once down the stairs, they headed straight down the hallway and found themselves in a small sitting room. Elegant antique furniture filled the room which, unlike the rest of the house, was illuminated by the warm, flickering glow of a hearty fireplace. On the table between two chairs were two large brandy snifters, half full. A beautiful armoire held a series of framed pictures, which were surrounded by scented candles in copper candlesticks. The room felt alive and Anthony sensed a newfound vigor. He was about to suggest some plan of action when he sensed movement behind him. Both Anthony and Bryant turned and stood facing the two shapes they had seen moments earlier approaching the house.

"We must kill them, brother," Bryant said, "because they will devour our souls if they win."

"What happens if we defeat them?" Anthony asked.

Bryant sighed, "I don't know. I don't think it has ever been done."

The shapes shambled forward. The grey one moved towards Bryant while the black one moved to corner Anthony. It stood there, simply undulating before him. It shimmered and it changed, taking on the appearance of Anthony's wife. It moved closer and reached a long, slender hand out to caress his cheek. Anthony shuddered and felt his skin bristle with the sensation of numbness. His wife seemed to shimmer before him and he felt drawn into her aura. She smiled at him, her lips red and sensual and he longed for her embrace.

Anthony looked over at Bryant and saw his brother stand helpless before the grey creature who held him in a kind of trance. Bryant smiled and moved towards the creature. Anthony watched in horror as the creature's head split open. It seemed to elongate and then leaned forward to completely engulf his brother. Without a sound, Anthony saw Bryant get devoured. The image of his brother's demise shattered the glamour which held him in sway and his wife became the creature once more. He turned and, with all his might, lashed out at the shape. It fell back with an ungainly motion. Anthony grabbed two of the copper candlestick holders from the armoire behind him and plunged them deep into where the creature's eyes would be. It howled and fell back to the ground, and thrashed about before it lay still. Once dead, its form reverted to Anthony's wife, with two copper pennies in the sockets where her eyes should be.

The house shook and rumbled; pieces of dust and plaster fell from the ceiling. The walls shook and groaned as if alive. Then it all went dark.

Anthony stood by the grave in the rain. All other mourners had long since left for the dry havens of their cars. The sky was dark and mottled with purple and threatened even heavier rains for the next few days. Anthony looked down once more at the temporary marker placed at the foot of his wife's grave. The permanent stone wouldn't be ready for a few weeks yet. Such a tragedy, people whispered, but he knew the truth.

Of course, how could he have known at the time what a choice he'd be required to make? The soul eaters were what they were, and he had the rest of his life to reflect on what had transpired and how he had chosen.

The house had been in his family for generations, growing with each new owner, and he knew it always would be in his family, long after he left this world. The house was eternal and bound his family together, in life and beyond. One could say his family's heart and soul kept the place alive. He knew he'd see his brother again, back at the house, as he would his parents. After all, they were part of the house. Of course, he wondered what would have happened if, instead of fighting fate, he'd left the front door open, and welcomed her in, when she came across the lawn. He supposed he'd never know.

In Her Skin

The man looks at the naked woman lying face down on the stainless steel surgical table. Her arms and legs are splayed and are shackled to hooks built into each corner of the table. She lies there motionless. A small, barely audible moan escapes her lips. Her eyes move beneath closed lids, but she does not stir.

The bare bulb overhead flickers and, for a brief moment, casts the entire room in a suffocating darkness. He looks up at the bulb and curls his upper lip in disgust. The man observes his surroundings, both familiar and yet as if he was seeing them for the first time. The room was perfectly designed, he decides, noting how the flue of the table aligns itself perfectly with the drain located in the center of the bare cement floor. There is a bookcase against the far wall, long unused and is covered in a thick patina of dust. The shelves are filled with several jars containing objects floating in milky opaque liquids, all recent additions. A variety of medical instruments lay open on a tray that hangs off the surgical table. The man gently removes a scalpel from the tray and rotates it slowly between thumb and forefinger, letting the light catch and dance on the razor sharp steel.

He brings the scalpel's tip to the back of the woman's head just below the hairline and applies a gentle pressure, sinking the blade deep into the skin. He draws it slowly downward to the base of her neck. The blood wells up from the cut and he gazes lovingly as her life blood oozes from the open wound. A rich, coppery smell fills his senses and awakens something primal in him. He feels his breath catch in his chest, unsure whether it is from terror or excitement.

She sat before him at the breakfast table. Her mouth was tightly drawn as she glared at him with thinly veiled contempt.

"So you got fired again," she hissed through clenched teeth.

The man wiped his brow. He wanted to explain, but the words would not come. There was a good reason, of course. Like the last time and the time before. Each time the reason was valid. Of course, she never wanted to hear it. He hung his head in shame and didn't say a word. He knew he should say something to defend himself, but years of marriage told him his wisest move was to just keep quiet.

"Damn you, Jim, don't you see that you're tearing us apart? I have to work two jobs just to keep up with our bills. And then, when I get home, I'm the one who has to tend to our daughter while you attempt to write your great American novel." She stood up and wiped the tears from her eyes. "Can't you see how your instability is killing our family? For God's sake, put yourself in my shoes for once. You couldn't possibly handle the life I'm forced to live. You wouldn't last one day in my skin." She turned and stormed out of the room.

"Jenny, wait," Jim called to his wife. Her only response was the slam of their bedroom door. Jim sat down hard on the couch and buried his face in his hands. Life shouldn't have to be so hard.

He gently applies a soft sponge to blot the excess blood from the incision in her neck. He then takes the scalpel and continues the incision down from the top of the neck to the base of her spine. Blood pools in the small of her back and, even though he had thoroughly applied enough topical anesthetic, the woman begins writhing on the table in agony. Though she is securely shackled by her hands and feet to the table itself, her erratic thrashing is causing the free flowing blood to spray all over the man in a fine mist.

"Stop it," he cries and punches her as hard as he can in the back of her head. She lay still and he feels a moment of panic that he had hit her too hard. It isn't until he sees her erratic and shallow breathing that he feels his panic slowly begin to subside.

It had been a very bad day. He had been unsuccessful, once again, in finding work, having spent the past six months unemployed. As well, his manuscript had been rejected by yet another publisher and the comments were clearly harsher than they needed to be. After what best could be called an uncontrolled meltdown, resulting in some broken household items, he sat down and proceeded to get completely and utterly drunk.

He was awakened by his wife standing over him, her face red with rage. "Where were you, you son of a bitch?"

Jim looked up stupidly at his wife. His head was pounding and he felt both disoriented and nauseated. He tried to speak, but his mouth felt thick and all that emerged was meaningless gibberish.

"You forgot our daughter, Jim," his wife screamed at him. "The aftercare center called me at work because you never showed up to get her. I had to leave my shift at the restaurant to come pick her up. She was terrified, wondering why you weren't there for her. Do you realize that not only will this cost us another thirty dollars for the late pick-up, but I think I might have gotten fired for leaving in the middle of my shift with no one to cover for me? We don't even have enough money to get by now. With you out of work, we simply can't afford my losing this job."

"I'm sorry," Jim managed, "I had a bad day and I lost track of time."

"I have bad days all the time, but don't get stinking drunk and wreck our home. I'm keeping this family together by the smallest thread, Jim. I get no help from you. Not one bit. Do you not understand? I can't do it all. I do everything around here. You need to get your act together, and soon, and start pulling your weight. I honestly think we'd be better off if you just went away."

He looks at the woman lying so still on the table. He notices that the chill of the room has raised the goose bumps on her skin. The fine blond hairs on her lower back stand erect. He leans close and gently licks the bloody incision from the base of her spine up to her neck, savoring the coppery tang of her blood. He grows excited as he admires his work. With a smile, he grasps the scalpel once more, a little tighter this time. He gently cuts laterally from the cut at the base of the spine, making the incision nearly a foot long per side.

The room seems to close in on the man and he takes a rag to wipe the perspiration from his brow. Though the room is quite cold, he finds he is perspiring more than he thought possible. With a quick glance at his watch, he sees that it is nearly two in the morning. The task is taking a lot longer than he planned.

He grabs the scalpel and draws it down over her firm buttocks to the back of each of her long, shapely legs. He makes an incision down her right leg, then her left, finally coming to a stop in both instances at the heel.

Jim felt that things were finally turning around. He had gotten a job interview as a permanent substitute teacher at the local high school. Sure, the pay was far less than what he had earned as an editor, but it was an honest job with honest pay. Even better, it offered a stability that had been lacking from his life for a very long time. He arrived on time, in his best suit and tie, and as far as he knew, answered all the questions intelligently. When they told him that they were interviewing other candidates and would let him know by the end of the following week, he felt his chances were good and had a gut feeling that he would get the job.

Jim picked up their daughter a bit early at aftercare and went straight home to prepare dinner. While his daughter watched Spongebob Squarepants, he set about preparing supper for the family.

Midway through the dinner preparation, his daughter stated that she was bored and wanted Jim to play with her. He tried to explain that he was busy and that he would play with her when he was done. Of course, to a six year old, that simply was not good enough an explanation and she kept pestering Jim to play with her. He finally had to turn his back on her as she cried and screamed and demanded attention. She grabbed his arm just as he was moving the fry pan off the grill and it caused him to drop the pan and all its contents on the floor. Without thinking, Jim swung at his daughter and backhanded her across the face.

When Jenny got home and saw the bruise on her daughter's cheek, she became enraged. She started screaming and crying and finally told Jim to pack up his things and get the Hell out.

Jim pleaded with her, even got down on his knees to beg forgiveness and explained that it was an accident, but his wife was resolute.

"We're better off without you, Jim," Jenny had said through the tears. "I should have done this long, long ago. I'm tired of working so hard to support our family when all you do is drag us down through your many accidents and repeated failures. I do everything and you don't see it. All you do is drink and kid yourself that you'll ever be a writer. You won't, Jim. You have no talent. The small bit of charm you had when you were younger is gone. It faded along with your looks. And today, after what you did to our daughter, is the final straw. You're a loser and I want you out."

Jim felt the rage boil up within him. It was supposed to be a good day and yet it had ended up like all the others. Today, though, his wife's words cut to the core and he saw his vision getting red. He grabbed the phone from its cradle and slammed it down repeatedly on his wife's head. She collapsed soundlessly in a heap, her eyes rolling back in her head as she fell. He picked her up and carried her downstairs to the basement. It didn't take long for him to get the room ready. He supposed that, subconsciously, he knew that it would have come to this sooner or later. After all, he had been acquiring all the tools necessary for the task at hand over the last few weeks.

Jim stripped his wife and shackled her face down to the table. No turning back now.

Jim tightens his grip on the scalpel once more and makes vertical cuts out from the spinal incision just below the shoulder blades. He deftly slices through the skin on the right arm down to the palm then proceeds to do the same to the left.

He glances at his watch. It is now quarter past three. He barely has two hours left. Jim slips his left hand under the skin just below the shoulder blades. He eases his hand slowly under the line of incision, gently lifting as he does. The skin slowly lifts from the body, the fascia connecting the two easing apart silently, fine as gossamer. Jim stares at it, marveling at how well put together the human form is. He gently moves his hand all the way up her back under the skin until he comes to the base of the neck. He then slips his hand in further, continuously lifting and pulling the skin back as he does. Sliding his hand back down the line of incision, he manages to peel the skin completely away from the body over the entire left side of her back. Jim then slides his right hand under the skin and repeats the process on the right side.

He wipes his brow with his forearm, careful not to get any skin, blood or connective tissue on his face. The sweat drips and blurs his vision as it gets into his eyes. Wiping his hands with a towel, he turns back to his wife. She is still bleeding and her breathing is getting shallower. Jim knows time is running short. If he doesn't hurry and finish, she will expire here on the table and that simply wouldn't do. He unfurls some gauze and gently applies it to her back, where the muscles and bones lay exposed, with the flaps of skin hanging open like a casually tossed dress shirt. Within a few minutes her back is covered with the gauze.

Jim then proceeds to peel the skin off her waist and rear, pulling the skin back and downward from the incisions. He then sets to work on the left leg, gently easing the skin off the sturdy muscles until he comes down to the foot. He bites his lower lip, a troubled expression crossing his face. He decides he really doesn't have any better options, so he peels the skin off the foot like a sock. It comes away with a wet, slopping sound as he pulls some connective tissue and flesh along with the skin. Wiping his hands again, he takes more gauze and wraps it around her waist and left leg. He liberally applies antiseptic and enough topical analgesic to keep the pain levels down, but he worries that she will wake if he doesn't hurry.

Jim is about to start on the right leg when he hears screams from upstairs. He runs up, taking the stairs two at a time. Once upstairs, he rushes to his daughter's room. She is sitting up in bed, crying.

"Is everything okay, honey?" Jim asks his daughter, trying to ratchet down his jackhammer heartbeat.

"I have to go to the bathroom, daddy," his daughter says in a small voice. "Will you take me?"

Jim nods wearily and helps his daughter out of bed and to the bathroom down the hall. When done, he brings her back to her room and gives her a hug before he helps her back into bed.

"Did you hurt yourself, daddy?"

"Why do you ask, sweetie?"

His daughter points to his hands which are stained brownish-red with the dried blood from his wife. Jim smiles weakly. "I had an accident, but everything is okay. In fact, I think things will be great from now on. Now, go to sleep. It's late." Jim tucks her in and when he is sure she has fallen back asleep, he turns and heads back downstairs to the basement.

Jim checks his watch. It is now four-fifteen. He knows his daughter will be up within two hours. The time for delicacy is over. He doesn't have the time to be exact. Better to get it finished and cut a few corners than to have his daughter awaken while he's still working.

He eases his hands under the skin of the right leg and repeats what he had done with the left. When he gets to the foot, he yanks it off quickly. It doesn't come off as easily as the left foot and the skin from two of her toes rips and stays attached to her foot. Jim curses loudly, slamming his hand down on the surgical table in anger. The scalpel and gauze both fall to the ground.

Cursing and feeling his anger escalate, Jim picks up his tools, wipes the dirt off the scalpel, and turns back to his wife's prone figure. There's no time to sterilize the scalpel again. He'll have to continue as is and hope that infection doesn't set in. Jim checks her pulse and, while shallow, it still is steady. He quickly wraps the gauze around her left leg and tries to ensure that the bleeding is slowing in all exposed areas.

Jim then peels the skin off her left, then right, arms using the same technique as he did on her legs. After wrapping them in gauze, he takes a step back and surveys his work. Aside from the mishap with the toes on the right foot, he's doing a great job.

Jim slowly unties his wife, loosening the bindings on her arms and legs. She makes a soft mewling noise but doesn't awaken. He grabs her by the hips and flips her over, and positions her gently on the table. The way the empty skin hangs on her body is a bit unnerving as only her torso and head still have skin attached. The rest of his wife is covered in blood-soaked gauze.

Jim leans over his wife and grasps the skin on her right side. He pulls it back and it comes away easily across her taut belly and small breasts. It clings a bit by the inner thighs and, for a brief moment, there is a flash of panic that he will cause the skin to tear as he eases it away from her *mons pubis* and genitals but, in the end, it comes away easily enough.

All that is left to do is the head. Jim applies gauze and analgesic to the rest of the body, doing what he can to staunch the flow of blood. He finally gets the bleeding under control. He rolls his wife over and slips his fingers under the skin at the base of the skull. He inches his fingers in deeper and deeper until the skin is loosened along the back of the head. Jim slides his hand back out and grips the scalpel firmly, and then makes an incision down the skin at the back of the head. Putting the scalpel back on the surgical tray, he peels the two flaps of skin from the back of the head upwards and over and pulls his wife's head free of the skin. Jim drops his wife's skin on the floor, ensuring that she is bandaged with gauze from head to foot, and liberally applies the remaining topical analgesic.

Jenny awakens to a million screaming nerve endings sending pain messages nonstop to her brain. Her eyes are open and, with horrified awareness, she realized that she can't blink. She sees that she is in a dark room with a single bulb hanging overhead. It dawned on her that she was in the basement of their small Cape house. She tries to move but found that she is firmly tied to a support beam, her arms secured behind her back. Her feet are tied, as well. She also feels a belt around her neck holding her fast to the beam behind her. She could barely move her head. She tries tilting her head forward to look down at her arms and legs to see why they hurt so badly but she couldn't budge even an inch.

"Jim?" Jenny croaked, her voice dry and cracking. "Are you there?"

"I'm here, Jenny." Jim replied softly, his voice barely a whisper. He stood off in the shadows and, while Jenny could not see him, she seemed to feel his presence.

"Why am I tied up, Jim?" Jenny asked softly, careful not to enrage him again. She felt wrong, somehow. Everything hurt and her head felt groggy, as if she were drugged.

"Well, Jenny," Jim replied, his voice raising a bit in volume, getting thicker and a bit muffled sounding, as if he were talking into his arm, "I had to tie you up. You see, I've grown tired of you saying I can't handle things or that I'm a drain on the family." He took a step towards her, his footsteps making a soft squelching noise. He stood on the periphery of the light, and, while Jenny could not see him clearly, his silhouette seemed wrong somehow.

Jim took another wet step towards her and stepped out of the shadows into the light. Jenny screamed as she saw her husband standing there, wearing her skin over his own. Seeing him staring out through her eye holes and speaking through her mouth was simply too much to bear. She felt her sanity rapidly slipping away. Jim raised his right hand to his cheek. In his hand he clutched a large carving knife with which he caressed the curve of his cheek. He then lowered his hand and pointed the knife menacingly in her direction.

"You see?" Jim hissed through her mouth, "You said I couldn't handle a day in your skin. Well, what do you think? I think your skin suits me just fine. Fits like a glove."

"What are you going to do to us?" Jenny pleaded. "Please, Jim. I don't want to die."

Jim grinned wickedly through her mouth and ran his tongue over her lips, relishing the strangeness of the feeling. "Well, it's like this. There can only be one of you, and I've decided that it will be me. So, first, I'm going to gut you like a fish for all the years of misery you've given me." Jim glanced longingly at the knife, gently rotating it his hand. "Then I'll go visit our darling daughter upstairs. After all, a girl needs her mommy, right to the very end."

As Jim advanced on his wife, Jenny started screaming until everything was cut off in a splash of red.

Climbing the Corporate Ladder

"Screw the perfect people, fuck they all look the same"
– Pennywise, *Perfect People*

It was a Tuesday when the world officially went to hell for Darryl Pritchard. There wasn't any indication that things would go seriously to shit. After a week of grey, threatening skies with an oily rain, the sun was finally shining and the skies were a bright and comforting blue.

The day started like any other for Darryl. He got up way too early, exchanged a few frosty words with his wife, none of which he really heard, and suspected that she didn't either. He got his daughter ready for school while his wife got dressed and hurried out of the house, running late as usual for the bus she needed to catch. He then showered, shaved, and headed to work for another day toiling for a dysfunctional boss whom he hated with a blind passion.

After an uneventful drive, Darryl pulled into the parking lot and walked into the nondescript, windowless building which housed the corporate offices of Booth Industries. He hurried quickly past the front desk, hoping that the snippy bitch of a receptionist was otherwise busy with her nails or lipstick. She never failed to offer some offhand criticism about his clothes, hair or even his weight. All because he had made the monumental mistake of nailing her during a drunken office Christmas party three years ago, she seemingly made it her mission to never let him forget it. She wanted more, but he was married and was not going to leave his wife for the office tramp. She threatened to tell his wife but, in the end, she relented and instead decided the best revenge was a slow and torturous one of daily abuse.

Sally sat at her desk and smiled broadly when Darryl approached. "Good morning, Darryl. How are you this fine morning?" She handed him his mail as he stood there dumbfounded.

"Uh, I'm good. Thanks for asking, Sally." Darryl grabbed his mail and hurried to his office. As he made his way through the warren of cubicles, everyone he passed greeted him warmly.

Daryl reached his office and turned on his computer before he sat down at his desk. He was just about to start going through his daily pile of e-mails when Jerry Kirk, the divisional CEO, showed up at his office door.

Darryl suppressed a groan. Kirk was a ballbuster and only showed up at one of his staff's offices to either load on work or to offer scathing criticism. Darryl braced himself. If Kirk was at his office this early, it was bound to get ugly.

"Pritchard," Kirk said, his deep baritone voice booming, "How are you doing this fine morning?"

"I'm good, Jerry." Darryl paused. He was not one for small talk. He was a Finance guy. He did his work and crunched the numbers, but he rarely socialized and was simply not comfortable with the interpersonal side of the workplace. After what seemed like an eternity of uncomfortable silence, in which Darryl loosened the collar of his shirt and wiped the perspiration from his brow, he added, "So, what brings you to my office this early on a Tuesday morning?" He hoped his tone came across as light and pleasant. Kirk had a reputation for suddenly flying into a rage and had fired more than one worker on the spot.

Kirk let out a booming laugh. "You're always so serious, Pritchard. If I didn't know you better, I'd swear you were always like this." Kirk reached into his pocket and handed something to Darryl.

"What's this?" Darryl asked.

Kirk smiled. "Hockey tickets for tonight. The Bruins are hosting the Canadiens. I thought you might want to go, considering what a huge fan you are. I know how hard you've been working lately and wanted to show you my appreciation."

Darryl looked at the tickets. The seats were incredibly good and very hard to get. They were at center ice and only a few rows up. *What had just happened?* Kirk was always putting him down in front of the management team and made his dislike of Darryl no secret. He took the tickets and thanked Kirk who just patted him on the back, made some remark about keeping up the good work and walked away.

Darryl put the tickets in his pocket, grabbed his laptop, and walked across the office to Marketing where his buddy Sean worked. On the surface, no one could have possibly predicted that the two men would become such close friends. Darryl was neat and fastidious and considered quite dour, whereas Sean was a large, slovenly guy with a big booming voice, a love for food and a complete disregard for authority. Where Darryl wore khakis and dress shirts, and was clean shaven with hair neatly groomed, Sean was a good thirty pounds overweight, dressed in ripped jeans and tees and typically wore sandals on his feet. He wore his hair long and kept up a thick bushy beard. What sparked the friendship was their passion for horror films. It was a strange friendship, but it worked and the two men could be found together every lunch hour talking animatedly about the latest horror movies. Darryl knew if anyone had an idea as to why Sally and Kirk were acting so out of character, it would be Sean.

Darryl arrived at Sean's office and was about to knock when he noticed that Sean was seated at his desk, the back of his chair facing outwards.

"Sean, can I bother you for a minute?"

Sean slowly turned his chair around and Darryl nearly dropped his laptop. Sean was clean shaven and had a short, conservative haircut. Even more surprising was the smart and stylish slacks, shirt and sport coat combination. "Good morning, Darryl. What can I do for you?"

"Uhhh, never mind," Darryl replied, backing slowly out of Sean's office. "I wanted to ask you something, but it slipped my mind. I'll catch you later." He turned and headed straight for the men's room. He put his laptop on the counter and began splashing cold water on his face. The morning was getting a bit too surreal for his liking.

Darryl looked up at his image in the bathroom mirror. His features looked drawn and gaunt, and he had deep bags under his eyes. He rubbed his eyes and froze when he realized that the image in the mirror hadn't moved. He shut his eyes and looked at the image again. He raised his right hand and so did the image. He gently leaned forward and touched the glass, watching intently as his image did the same. As his fingers touched the fingers of his mirror image, he felt an electrical surge go up his arm.

Darryl pulled his hand back and put his fingers to his mouth. They hurt like Hell and felt like they were burnt, and he swore there was the residual smell of cooked flesh lingering in the air. He looked at his hand, closely examining the fingers. They were definitely tender to the touch, but there wasn't a single mark on them.

Darryl walked back to his office and sent an e-mail to Nate who headed up Human Resources. He'd known Nate for years and it was Nate who actually brought him on board at Booth. The two men had been friends since childhood and other than a few falling outs over the years, largely due to Darryl's competitive nature, the two were still quite close. They often got together with each other's families and their daughters were about the same age and were already becoming good friends. The e-mail was brief, but asked if Nate could come by to discuss an important issue.

Nate showed up at Darryl's office a few minutes later. "What's up, Darryl? Not like you to be so cryptic this early in the day."

Darryl ushered Nate into his office and closed the door. He took a seat at his desk and motioned for Nate to sit down. He looked at Nate for several minutes, not saying a word until Nate finally stood up and demanded, "What is going on, Darryl? I don't have all day for games."

Darryl breathed a sigh of relief. "I apologize for all the secrecy, Nate. I just needed to be sure it was you. Please sit." Nate sat back down.

"What's going on and what do you mean 'if it was me?'"

Darryl paused. "Does everything seem okay to you?"

"I'm not sure what you mean, Darryl. Define 'okay' for me."

"You're going to think I'm crazy, Nate." Darryl paused, "Some people here seem…off. Sally, Jerry Kirk, Sean and others have all been acting really odd."

Nate looked at Darryl. He seemed stressed, and perhaps tired, but Darryl was always a sensible guy who never made rash decisions, so whatever he was worried about was worth listening to. "What do you mean by odd? I got in early and have been in my office all morning working on the sales compensation packages. I haven't spoken to a soul all day except for you."

Darryl stood up and walked to the office door. He peered out the skylight, making sure no one was hovering nearby. He sat back down and faced his friend. "Okay. I walked in this morning and Sally was really friendly to me. She acted like we didn't have any history at all."

"For Christ sake, Darryl," Nate said, "I know you slept with her. The whole damn office does. Spare me the euphemisms."

"Fine," Darryl replied, trying to keep the anger out of his voice, "Sally has been a nasty bitch to me ever since I got drunk and did her at the holiday party. I was drunk and stupid and she's made my life a living Hell ever since. Are you happy now?"

Nate smiled. After thirty years of friendship, he could still rile Darryl. Seeing as how Darryl constantly competed with him, and usually won, Nate took some small consolation that he still could manage to get under Darryl's skin. "Okay. So Sally was nice to you. I'll admit that is a bit odd. But maybe she's finally letting go. It has been three years."

"I thought of that," Darryl said. "If it was just Sally acting like a human being for a change, I could believe your point. It didn't end there. After the exchange with Sally, Jerry Kirk came by my office. Want to guess why?"

Nate frowned. He knew Kirk's hatred of Darryl better than most. As head of HR, he had received more than a few complaints by Kirk against Darryl and knew that the CEO was in the process of building a case to have Darryl fired. "What did he say?"

"That's the thing. He didn't say much." Darryl paused. "He just came in, told me I was doing a great job, and handed me hockey tickets for tonight. It was like we were actual friends."

"Really?" Nate asked. "That was it?"

"Apparently it was. I decided to go see Sean to get his take. When I got to his office, I found Sean in khakis and a shirt, short haircut and all."

"Okay, Darryl. I can believe Sally finally forgiving you and maybe even Kirk acting like a human being for once. But there is no way Sean will ever cut his hair and go corporate. We allow him to get away with it because he's such a brilliant SEO marketer. Thanks to him, our sales and average order value have both gone through the roof. For results like his, they are willing to allow him his eccentricities."

Darryl walked to his office door. "Go see for yourself, Nate, and then come back here."

"This better not be some kind of joke, Darryl that you and Sean have cooked up. I don't have the time for it."

"Just go look for yourself, Nate" Darryl growled, "then tell me I'm crazy."

Nate left and came back a few minutes later. "All right, Darryl, something is very wrong here. I went and saw Sean. I even asked him why the change in appearance. He actually just smiled and told me that he wanted to be a better fit on the team. If he didn't look so earnest, I'd swear he was pulling my leg. So, what should we do?"

Darryl looked at Nate. "Right now, we don't do anything. We act like there is nothing wrong. We don't stand out and we don't draw attention to ourselves. Keep an eye out for anything unusual and at the end of the day or tomorrow, we'll regroup. As of now, all we know is that there are at least three people here who are acting very much out of character."

"Okay, that makes sense," Nate replied. "Text me if anything changes."

"You do the same, Nate."

The rest of the day passed without incident. Darryl pretty much kept to himself, sequestered in his office. He texted Nate and got similar feedback. They decided to catch up first thing in the morning. At five, he packed up and headed home, careful not to engage anyone for more than a few brief words in passing.

He did not notice the dozens of people sitting silently in their cubicles watching him leave with great interest.

Darryl took the back roads home. He wanted time to sort through the events of the day. Nothing seemed menacing in any way, yet things seemed off kilter somehow. Something was wrong. It was more than the odd behavior at the office. It was as if he were being watched, yet every time he seemed to sense someone watching him, he'd turn around only to find that no one was there. He was either slowly going mad or something was up. Darryl had spent the last thirty-five years of his life living as conservatively as possible. Sean used to joke that he was the sanest person he had ever met. He trusted his instincts and realized that if he ruled out madness, what did that leave him?

He was so engrossed in his thoughts that he almost didn't see the little girl who ran out in front of his car. Darryl hit the brakes hard and the car came to a screeching stop. He got out and ran to the girl who was lying in front of his car.

"Oh my God!" Darryl cried out. "Are you okay?"

The girl stood up. She looked about six or seven and had long blonde hair tied back in a ponytail. She wore a Justice shirt, which was covered in peace signs, and jeans which were likely from the same store. Darryl had shopped for his own daughter enough to know the brand. Her eyes were red rimmed and wet from crying. A thin string of mucus bubbled from one nostril.

"She's not my mommy," the girl cried, tears welling up in her blue eyes. "She looks like her, but she's not her." She started shaking uncontrollably.

"Shhh, you're safe now, sweetie," Darryl said, trying to calm the frightened girl. "What are you doing out here all by yourself?"

"It's my mommy," the girl said again. "She's acting funny." She shook with heaving sobs.

Darryl hugged the small girl and felt her initially stiffen, and then relax, in his arms. "What's your name?" Darryl gently asked.

"Emma," the girl said softly, then added suspiciously, "What's yours?"

"It's Darryl, honey. Why don't you tell me what's wrong?"

"Okay. Every night after supper, me and mommy do my homework together and then we play my favorite CD and sing and dance to a few songs before bed. Mommy always laughs when she dances and then she tucks me in to bed at night. Tonight, after supper, mommy told me to do my homework. I asked her to help and she said that I needed to do it myself so I could learn. I asked her about at least playing the CD and she looked at me and said that I wouldn't be able to study with it on. Then she said that she also didn't like music and that it hurt her head and to stop asking her. Mommy wouldn't say that. She loves to sing and dance."

Darryl looked at the small girl and asked, "Where do you live, Emma? You can't be out here all night."

Before Emma could answer Darryl saw a tall, blonde woman come running towards them. "Emma," she cried out, "there you are."

Emma tried to position herself behind Darryl. "Please, mister, don't let her take me. Please." She looked up at Darryl with a look of utter terror etched across her features.

Darryl stood up to face the woman. He noticed that she was tall and slender, and immaculately dressed. He also saw that other cars had stopped and that they were drawing a crowd.

"Oh, thank God she's safe," the woman said. "She ran out of the house after supper and I've been looking for her ever since." She extended her hand which Darryl noticed was perfectly manicured. "Ellen Kennison."

Darryl shook her hand. "I'm Darryl Pritchard. Emma ran out in front of my car. Thankfully, she's okay."

"I'm just glad she's safe." Ellen leaned over to her daughter. "Come on, honey, let's get you home."

Emma looked to Darryl. "Please. I don't want to go."

Darryl put his hands on her shoulders. He felt her trembling. He looked around and saw Emma's mother and a small crowd anxiously watching, seeing what he would do. "Emma," he said slowly, "she's your mother. See? She was worried about you. But it is late. You need to go home with her." Emma looked at him with a look of complete resignation. She lowered her head and slowly walked over to her mother who took her by the hand and led her home. The crowd began to disperse, as well and Darryl felt relieved. He hated just handing the girl over to her mother without at least making sure that she was safe, but what choice did he have? He climbed back in his car and drove the rest of the way home feeling as if he had condemned the girl to some horrible fate.

Darryl pulled into his driveway feeling incredibly low. He walked into his house and his dog, Lucky, a hyperactive black lab came running over to him. Darryl scratched the dog behind her ears and called out. "Hello? Is anyone home?"

"In the kitchen," his wife replied. Darryl walked to the kitchen to find his wife and daughter sitting at the kitchen table.

"What's going on?"

"We're doing Annie's homework," his wife added. Darryl noticed them both smiling. Usually homework time was one of endless screaming. Tonight seemed...calm.

"Hi, dad," Annie said softly.

"No hug?" Darryl asked. His daughter usually ran over and hugged him so tightly that he couldn't breathe. Tonight she just stared at him.

"Really, dad," Annie replied and left it at that.

The rest of the night was uneventful. They ate dinner, put Annie to bed at eight, and watched television until ten when they both went to bed. It had been a long day and Darryl was asleep almost as soon as he crawled into bed.

Darryl was awakened by the creak of their bedroom door. He looked up in time to see his wife slip out. He glanced at the clock radio on the dresser next to his bed. *Where was she going at two-thirty in the morning?* He was about to call to her when some instinct made him hold back. He got out of bed and quickly got dressed. He ran downstairs as he heard the garage door open. From the window in the den, he saw her SUV back out to the driveway. He hurried to the garage, got in his own car and followed his wife out to the street. The thought that his daughter was home alone in bed didn't even cross his mind. Keeping his lights off, he stayed a good distance back so he would be sure his wife didn't see him.

They drove down the main road which bisected the town and then she took a right at the Center school. She followed that road for another two miles until she came to the elementary school. There were dozens of cars already parked and Darryl saw people walking hurriedly into the doors that led to the gym. His wife exited her car and did the same.

Darryl pulled over on a side street and texted Nate. *Something big is going down at the elementary school in my town. I'm following up.* A few minutes later, he got a reply from Nate echoing a similar message.

Darryl got out of his car and looked over at the school. There was a faint luminescent green glow coming from the windows of the gym. Other than that, the school was dark and if it weren't for the dozens of cars parked around the school, he would have sworn it was deserted. He stayed to the shadows and crept closer to the building. He decided his best bet in getting in unseen would be around back. He crept slowly among the parked cars, careful not to make a sound as he moved.

At the rear of the school, he saw that the doors to the gym were wide open. The luminescent green glow seemed to pulse from within and lit up the rear parking lot in intermittent bursts. Darryl inched closer and crept in the shadows along the walls. He moved silently towards the doors, took a deep breath, and peered in.

Inside were a couple hundred of the town's residents standing in concentric circles around an oily grey obelisk that hung down from the ceiling of the gym. They stood there, still as statues, arms extended forward, as if reaching for the obelisk. The obelisk itself was grey and slick, with a smooth, glistening, greasy surface. It was attached to the metal beams which lined the gym's ceiling and seemed to pulse with thick veins that emitted luminescent green bursts. A low hum emanated from the obelisk and the people closest to it started to sway slightly. As the hum grew louder, the people in the next circle out started swaying. Within a few minutes, the humming was loud enough that Darryl felt his teeth ache and his head begin to throb. All the people in the gym were now swaying in unison, as if linked by a single consciousness.

The obelisk began to ripple and a long, grey pseudopod pulsed out and moved towards a middle aged woman who stood there transfixed. The pseudopod stiffened and thrust itself forward, driving into her open mouth and down her throat. The woman sighed as the oily grey tendril probed deeper and deeper down her throat. Dozens of other pseudopods extended from the obelisk, each one finding their designated targets. In less than ten minutes, everyone in the gym was connected to the obelisk by a grey tendril and was sighing contentedly as a luminescent green fluid was pulsed into them. They seemed transfixed by what was happening and Darryl felt emboldened enough to make his way into the gym.

Darryl moved slowly into the gym, trying to keep to the shadows, and spotted dozens of friends, neighbors and acquaintances from around town. It was clear that whatever was affecting people at his work was happening here in his small town. He realized with an increasing panic, that this nightmare could be happening everywhere.

He walked around people, standing there and swaying to the thing in the center of the gym, in apparent ecstasy, careful to give them a wide berth. Finally, he saw his wife. She stood there like the others, head arched back ever so slightly as the obelisk's tendrils pumped the glowing green fluid into her. She seemed oblivious to his presence or anything else around her.

Darryl grits his teeth and moved to the edge of the gym where the sporting equipment was stored. He grabbed a hefty aluminum bat and strode purposefully towards the obelisk. Letting out a primal scream, he swung the bat for all it was worth. It hit the obelisk and, for a second, nothing happened. Then the obelisk stopped humming and the green light winked out. At once, every person turned towards Darryl, their eyes snapping open simultaneously and glowing green. As one, they pointed to him and hissed in a furious rage.

Darryl turned and ran, pushing people aside as he did. They reached for him and, as one, turned and ran after him.

Darryl reached his car and raced home as fast as he could. He wasn't worried about being pulled over. He suspected the town's entire police force was part of the crowd in the gym.

He pulled into his driveway and ran up the stairs to his daughter's room.

"Annie," Darryl cried as he shook his daughter. "Come on sweetie. It's time to wake up."

Annie sat up. "What's wrong, daddy?" she asked. "Where's mommy?"

Darryl turned to his daughter. "Annie, some bad stuff is happening. Your mommy and a lot of the people in town have changed. They are not themselves anymore. We need to get out of here, right now."

Annie looked terrified. "Daddy, you're scaring me. What happened to mommy?"

"Annie, she isn't herself. I can't explain it to you any better. But you need to get up and get dressed. We have to leave now." Darryl pulled Annie from her bed and frantically found clothes for her to wear. He got her dressed and they rushed downstairs to the kitchen only to find his wife and several dozen townspeople already there and waiting for him.

"Get out of my way," Darryl roared. "I'm taking my daughter and we're getting the fuck out of here. So help me, God, I'll kill you if you try and stop me."

"Daddy," Annie whimpered in a meek little voice.

Darryl turned and saw his daughter standing there holding a pan in her little hands. "Annie, what is it? Can't you see we have trouble?"

"Of course, daddy," Annie replied softly, "but it isn't 'we' who have trouble. It's you." Annie swung the pan upwards and connected squarely with her father's head. Darryl felt everything spin and then go dark.

Darryl awoke on his bed. He tried to move but found he was strapped in. He saw his wife and daughter standing to his right. To his left were most of his neighbors. "What's going on?" he demanded. His voice was dry and cracking. His head was still ringing from where his daughter had hit him.

Darryl's wife smiled. "It's really simple, Darryl. It's assimilation. We cannot live without hosts, so we go world to world finding races we can assimilate. Through you, we have physical life. Your bodies are strong and allow us a long and healthy lifespan. Unfortunately, with every world we assimilate, there are always those who reject the process. It is unfortunate, but those individuals have to be destroyed."

"So what happens to me?" Darryl asked. He needed to keep them talking to try and find a way out of this nightmare. "It's clear I'm not one of you."

Annie looked at her father and smiled. "Most of us got changed during the last week. We were carried to your population through the rains. It got on your skin, and we got absorbed into your bloodstream. From there, it was only a matter of hours until we grew large enough to overtake your neural system and effectively remove what makes you who you are. Some residual memories remain, but those fade with time."

Darryl looked at his wife and daughter and all the neighbors assembled around his bed. His sense of loss was palpable. "Do with me as you wish, I just don't care anymore."

Darryl's wife took a small metallic canister from her pocket and popped off the top. She pulled out a small, oily translucent worm. It was about six inches long with several long feelers which ended in sharp hooks at both ends.

Darryl saw the thing and tried to move, but his bonds were too tight.

His wife smiled. "This will hurt, but it will make you one of us. It carries the host and will bring it to where it needs to take root. We'd rather not be forced to destroy you. You're so much more useful if you simply accept your fate. After all, there are so many of us and so few of you." She lifted the worm-like thing and dangled it over his left eye. The creature extended one of its hooks and latched it to Darryl's eye right by the tear duct. He screamed in agony as the worm pulled itself behind the eye and burrowed into his brain. He kept screaming until he passed out from the pain.

The next day, Nate went to Darryl's office at Booth industries. He walked in and closed the door. Darryl looked up at him, his eyes bloodshot, his face an ashen grey.

"You look terrible, Darryl," Nate said, "Are you okay?"

Darryl grinned. "I feel right as rain, Nate. How about you? Did you find anything out last night?"

"I did. I know pretty much my entire town is afflicted with this possession, including my family. But I've learned to act like them and can blend in. Are you sure you're okay, Darryl?" Nate asked again. "What happened at the school last night?"

Darryl told Nate everything that had happened up to the point where his wife put the worm to his eye.

"Jesus, Darryl. So how can you still be you?"

Darryl pulled open his office drawer and took out a small glass tube. A small grey worm-like creature covered in blood was in the tube. "Seems I'm not that compatible with the little bastards," Darryl said grinning. "But it worked out okay. The few hours that thing was in my brain caused a link to them. I hear their chatter in my head. They are a hive mentality and my time in the hive seems to have left it imprinted on me."

"That's incredible," Nate said. "So what are you going to do?"

Darryl smiled. "First, I turn you in." Darryl pushed a button on his desk intercom and calmly said to his assistant, "Please call security immediately."

Nate stood quickly. "You miserable bastard. Why would you betray your own race? Damn it. We're friends, Darryl."

Darryl looked sadly at his friend. "I know and that makes it all that much harder. You see, they are watching me, too. Turning you in will convince them of my allegiance. Also, since I'm stuck in this world for perhaps another five decades, I might as well make it worthwhile." There was a brief knock at the door and two burly men walked into Darryl's office. He pointed to Nate. "He's not one of us. Take him for processing." He leaned over to Nate and said in a low voice that only Nate could hear. "You know me, Nate. I'm always willing to do the jobs no one else wants in order to rise up the corporate ladder."

Barb Pritchard stood by the hospital bed. Her daughter Annie was by her side. She looked sadly at her husband who thrashed about on the bed, alternating between screams and peals of laughter.

A tall man with grey hair and angular, hawk-like features

walked into the room. "Mrs. Pritchard? I'm doctor Kane." He extended his hand which Barb shook. She introduced her daughter.

"What happened to my husband, doctor Kane?"

Kane sighed. He took a minute to appraise Mrs. Pritchard. She was a tall brunette in her mid-thirties. She had long black hair and, while she had a few extra pounds, he saw that she was quite attractive and seemed to have an inner strength about her. "Your husband was brought in a few hours ago. He was found in his car by the side of the road. The front end was clearly damaged in an accident. The air bags had deployed but, aside from that, there was nothing to indicate a collision of any kind. Your husband had bruises on his body and was bleeding from his eyes and nostrils."

Barb looked horrified. "What happened to him?"

"That's just it," Kane replied, "we don't know. There are minor cuts and bruises, but no broken bones or any internal bleeding. A CAT scan revealed no cerebral damage. The only thing we can't explain is the erratic brain waves. His alpha waves are low and uneven and the gamma waves are spiking through the roof. So, while he appears calm, his mind is going a mile a minute as if he's trying to solve some huge problem. We also can't seem to wake him."

"So what can we do?" Barb asked, the tears forming in her eyes.

Doctor Kane put a comforting hand on Barb's shoulder. "Right now, all we can do is wait. He's not showing any of the signs of a coma or catatonic state. His brain waves are unlike any we have ever seen. We'll keep him comfortable and under observation and perhaps he'll come out of this. Hope and prayer have never been known to hurt, either."

Barb shook doctor Kane's hand. "Please call me if anything changes. I need to get Annie home, but I'll be back later."

Kane smiled. "I'll see you later then, Mrs. Pritchard." As Barb walked away, she didn't turn back. If she had, she would have noticed Kane smiling, or the small, worm-like thing that moved beneath his left eyelid.

Legacies

The day started like any other, I suppose. I awoke and went about my daily routine, cognizant of the constant aches and pains which seemed to be becoming increasingly more intrusive. I suppose I should consider myself lucky. I am spry enough at eighty-three and, while there are few parts of my body that are pain-free these days, I pretty much have my shit together. All my senses were in fine working order and, with the exception of occasional bouts with my back acting up and forcing me to a bed for a day or two, I'd say I was doing pretty damn good. I could walk a good distance, didn't need a cane and had the constitution of a man a good decade younger. I also boasted a full head of hair and still could charm the old crones down at the senior center.

I guess an outsider might consider me a bit of a surly loner, but that couldn't be further from the truth. Sure, I was unmarried and, in fact, never had been married. I didn't want someone in my life, but more on that later. I cherished my space and solitude was simply a part of life. Not that I was queer or anything like that. Let me set the record straight that I loved women. It's just that I hated the complications that came with them. I didn't like people around me getting close and getting into my business. Some folks keep secrets. I was one of them and didn't need mine to come unburied. The past was where they belonged and the past was where they would stay.

So that's where life found me that morning when the letter came. I recognized the handwriting immediately, even after all those years. The penmanship was slightly effeminate, with broad sweeping strokes. Yeah, the letter could have only come from one person. I swear I must have frowned something fierce and probably cursed a bit, too. Sure as Hell glad no one was around when I did.

With a slight tremble to my hands, I opened the envelope. Inside was a small card with the following written in that familiar self-important handwriting:

David Joseph Wallis
Saturday, June 7
Church of Christ
Houlton, Maine

I dropped the card and felt myself grow numb. I walked over to the liquor cabinet and poured myself two fingers from a bottle of Macallan 25 that I kept for special occasions, took it down neat in one shot and poured myself another. This one I sipped, savoring the smoky flavor as I rolled the whiskey around in my mouth. DJ was dead, and that meant that there were only two of us left. I bent down to retrieve the card and stared at it again, almost as if I were willing it to be different. The seventh was in two days, just enough time for me to book a flight to Portland and reserve a car and hotel. Oddly enough, I didn't even like DJ all that much and certainly never cared for that fool woman he took as his wife, but that's water under a bridge long since left to the ravages of time, I suppose.

Hell, it's been nearly two decades since I last saw Mike and, if I never saw his smug face again, that would be just fine. Too much time has passed and the dark secret we shared has done more than enough damage to ever right this ship. I guess Saturday will be the last time we see each other until one of us drops dead and the other says his final good-byes and makes his long needed peace with his God.

Ah, fuck, I'm getting melodramatic. I swear I feel myself tearing up. One would think after seventy years the memories would have subsided, but they haven't. After all, one never really forgets an event that triggers the loss of the innocence of one's youth.

It was seventy years ago, nearly to the day. Don't need to name the year but, Hell, you can do the math. FDR was the president and well into what would be a very long tenure in office. My dad drove an Oldsmobile Coupe and I thought it was the toughest thing on the road. Dad had this job with the government that must have paid extremely well as we had a huge Victorian home, a shiny new car and all the most modern appliances on the market. Considering that the economy was still in a recession and not that long after the Great Depression, things were actually pretty good. Looking back, there were so many families who went hungry or packed up and left town in the middle of the night for greener pastures, but it never really registered for me. You see, I had been insulated from all that since we had what we needed and I did not dwell on the circumstances of others. Remember, I was a kid. When you have food in your belly, you don't think of those who don't. It's as simple as that. The downside is I hardly ever saw my dad. More times than I can remember, he left for work before I awoke and was still not home by the time I was ushered off to bed by my mother. On the few occasions he was actually home, it was like he wasn't really there, anyways. He never spoke about what he did at work and often flew into a rage when my mother pressed him about it. After a particularly vicious backhanded hit by dad during a heated argument, mom never again asked dad about work, or anything else for that matter. Something changed within her after that and I often saw her quietly sobbing when she thought no one was around.

My best friend in the world was Stan Peterson. Like me, his dad worked for the government, but I suspect his job was significantly less important than my dad's, as his family had nowhere near the creature comforts we enjoyed. Stan had a twin brother named Mike, although one would never have guessed they were even related. They were fraternal twins and, while Stan was tall with dark hair and eyes, dusky skin and a gangly, skinny build to the point of being scrawny, his brother Mike had lighter hair, fair skin and ice blue eyes. One thing about Mike which always stuck with me was how awful his temper was. The guys all called him Golden Boy because his brother told us how Mike wet the bed until he was ten. Looking back, it was our passive aggressive way of getting revenge for all of Mike's shit. He was so self-absorbed, he actually thought we called him that because he was his parent's favorite while his brother was the family pariah.

I always considered myself the smart one in the group. I was the guy who figured things out and often had all the answers. Of course, the one thing I never understood was how someone like Stan could ever get a girlfriend. To all our amazement, one day he actually did. Laurie Meloni was the most attractive girl in class. She was tall and slim, with a build that showed off her fine female lines even at thirteen. Her hair was so black it almost appeared to be blue when you looked at it in the right light. What set it off even more was the cream complexion of her skin with a slight bit of freckling on the bridge of her nose. Her most striking feature was her deep green eyes. Every guy in school was crazy for her, even the older ones, yet she constantly shot down every attempt to ask her out. I have to admit even I got my courage up one day and asked her to see a movie with me, but she shot me down as easily as any of the others. She was awfully nice about it and I'm not one to hold grudges even though at the time my pride was hurt. Stan's brother Mike was a different story altogether. He asked her out before she started up with Stan and she politely rebuffed him like she did with everyone. Instead of just letting it go, he spread rumors that she would give it up to anyone and called her the most spiteful names he could think of behind her back every chance he'd get. So, while she never knew the venom Mike spread about her, she did get the sense that people were whispering about her behind her back. It was a crying shame because she was a good girl. She had just crossed paths with the wrong guy.

That was likely how she ended up with Stan. One day, while walking home from school, he saw her sitting on a park bench, her head buried in her hands and her shoulders trembling as her body shook with her sobbing. Stan walked over, sat down, and must have said the right things because by the next day, they were dating. Of course, this little development angered Mike even more. He beat Stan within an inch of his life two days later and then regularly after that. I think if it weren't for Laurie, Stan's life would have been simply unbearable. She brought some good into what must have been an awful existence. He had few friends, was socially awkward, and seemed happier being alone.

Rounding out our group of friends was Jack, DJ and Alex. Jack Nolan was Mike and Stan's neighbor and had befriended the brothers when they were all little kids. I had only met them a few years earlier when my dad moved us all to that godforsaken little pit of a town in northern Maine, so I didn't have the same history with the guy. He was okay, as far as I could tell, a bit strange, but still fine to hang with for short durations.

DJ, or David Joseph as his mother used to call him when he was in trouble, was a genial and goofy fat kid. A bit of a simpleton and a little off as far as I was concerned. He got his thrills hurting animals and, while I never had proof, I was pretty sure he was involved in the sudden disappearance of his neighbor's kittens. The only reason he hung with our group was he was a real toady to Mike, who seemed to enjoy having someone worship the ground he walked on, so he invited DJ whenever we went anywhere, no matter the occasion.

The last guy in our group was Alex. Alex was the runt of the litter. He was a small boy with no athletic ability. He embodied the stereotype of the skinny, weak kid and was often a target for some of the bullies in school. I guess we saved his bacon so often that he was just absorbed by our little group, as if by osmosis. Still, no one complained too much and that was that. It didn't hurt that Alex always brought us candy bars and other snacks he took from his house.

So, life was pretty normal for us. Well, as normal as it could be growing up in northern Maine at the tail-end of the thirties. We rode our bikes, we talked about girls, and we even stole gum, candy, comics, you name it, from the local convenience store. One day, in the middle of August, we were all sitting around my backyard, having finished a scrub game of pepper when DJ raced over on his bike with news that would change our lives forever.

DJ had his mouth full of at least two Snickers bars when he climbed off his bike and said that he knew where we could see a bunch of dead bodies. Now, DJ was known to be full of crap and most of us barely listened because he would usually go off on some tangent and ramble on about nonsense. But something in the wild look in his normally dull eyes made us pause.

"What do you mean, DJ?" Mike asked. With DJ, he liked to take control and make sure the pecking order was maintained.

"I overheard my dad talking last night with my mom in their bedroom."

"How'd you hear anything, DJ?" Jack asked. "Did you have your ear to their door so you could catch them doing it?"

DJ blushed, as he knew he was caught, so he just nodded. "So I like to listen," DJ whined and pointed a chubby finger at Jack, "and I suppose you never listened in on your parents?"

Jack smiled. "I guess I'm not a pervert like you, Davey-boy."

DJ balled his pudgy hands into fists, like he was actually thinking of throwing a punch at Jack when I stepped in and pulled him back.

"Calm down, DJ. Tell us what you heard," I spoke softly, trying to bring him back from the brink. I knew if he lost his temper, we'd never hear what he had to say.

DJ seemed to calm down a bit, took another huge mouthful from his candy bar, and continued. "My dad was in his room talking to my mom. Well, actually he was crying. He kept saying that it was a sin against God and that the dead should be allowed to rest in peace. The rest was hard to hear as his sobbing got louder and louder. So I got a bit spooked and went back to my room. The one thing I did hear was that the bodies were stored at the base."

Right off the bat, we knew his story had some element of truth to it. DJ's dad worked at the military base with my dad as well as Stan's and Mike's and, while our fathers were military men, his dad was a scientist.

We debated if we should check out DJ's story and see the dead bodies. We speculated about whether they would all be cut up with their innards spread out over some kind of operating table. Our imaginations must have gotten the better of us because we decided that we absolutely needed to see the dead bodies. Jack even wondered if some of them would be women and whether we actually would get to see them naked. In the end, not going was no longer an option. We got on our bikes and followed the trails through the woods so we'd arrive around the back end of the base. The front had a guard tower and we knew that we'd never be allowed in. None of us wanted to be seen anywhere near there because we all knew that our fathers would tan our hides something fierce if they found out. It was pretty far out, but we really had nothing else to do and, honestly, it seemed like a real adventure.

Less than an hour later, we arrived at the base, dripping with sweat. I thought DJ would keel over from the ride. He was gasping and wheezing and looked a little green. Heck, that was probably the most exercise he'd done that entire year. Around the base was a stone wall, ten feet in height and, though it looked pretty high, there were enough gaps in the stones and mortar that we could use as handholds to help us climb over. Jack went first, scaling the wall as if it were the most natural thing in the world. I went next and, while I'd like to have a memory of having an easy time getting over, it proved to be challenging enough. Next up was Mike who made it over as easy as Jack. When he landed on the other side, he smirked at me as if to let me know that he had an easier time getting over than I did. Next up were Stan and Alex who climbed at the same time. Both had some trouble getting over but, in the end, managed as well with some encouragement from us. DJ had the most trouble and kept falling back on his fat ass. Finally, Mike had to climb back up to the top and help pull DJ up and over the wall.

Inside the wall, we noticed that we stood at the periphery of what looked like a well-tended park. The lawn was manicured and there were plenty of trees offering enough shade to make the place quite pleasant. This park extended as far as we could see. What struck me as odd, even then, was how quiet and still everything seemed. Not a bird flew overhead and not a single insect could be seen or heard. It was if the life had been sucked out of the park and that the trees and grass were only a façade of normalcy.

We began walking into the park, noting the unreal stillness in the air. Stan, I believe, was the first to speak since we all had scaled the wall. "Where are the soldiers?" he asked. "In fact, where is anyone? Shouldn't there be buildings and people?"

"I was thinking that myself," I replied. "I know my dad comes here every day, so there must be buildings somewhere. Maybe the base is bigger than we all thought and we can't see the office and labs due to the trees. Since we're already here, we may as well look around." Everyone seemed to agree.

We walked deeper and deeper into the park, noticing that the trees were getting a lot more plentiful, and that their leaves seemed to make a pretty good roof overhead, covering the park in darkness. With the sun blocked out, the still air felt cooler, as well. I remember watching Alex hug himself as if to keep warm and noticed that he kept glancing back the way we had come. I may have been only thirteen, but it was obvious he was scared and wanted to go back but didn't dare risk losing our approval, so he plodded on.

After walking a bit more, Jack stopped and held up his hand to let us know that we should wait. "Do you guys hear that?" he whispered. We all came to a stop and craned our necks forward as if that would help us. I then heard a low sound that I thought might be the wind until I realized that the air was perfectly still.

"I don't like this," DJ wailed, "I think we should go back."

"Hey," Alex called out, pointing deeper into the park, "what's that?"

Off in the distance was a small stone building. We walked over to the building which was no bigger than a tool shed. It was a squat, ugly square brick structure without windows. The door was solid metal and held closed by a shiny padlock.

"Someone go and find a rock," Mike said with excitement. DJ ran off and, after a few minutes, came back with a rock as big as a grapefruit. He handed it to Mike who started hammering the rock against the padlock. After a few minutes, the lock clasp snapped open.

"Open it, Jack," Mike said.

"Why do I have to be the one to open the door?"

"Because I said so," Mike said in a menacing tone.

Jack looked around to each of us, looking for some show of support or solidarity. When he realized that none was coming, he shrugged and cautiously opened the door. Surprisingly, the only thing inside was an empty room with a set of stairs going down to a landing which had another door.

"What do you think is in there?" DJ asked nervously.

"Probably the bodies, dummy," Jack added, his courage back up.

So we all went down the stairs and approached the other door. Stan put his ear to the door, but it was also metal and he told us that he couldn't hear anything. We all argued for another ten minutes about who would open this door until Mike finally got fed up and did so himself.

Inside, the room was dark. Mike lit some matches which gave us enough illumination to spot a light switch on the wall. With the room well lit, we all paused at what lay before us. It looked like a morgue, or I suppose what we would have assumed a morgue would look like. There were perhaps three dozen steel tables and, while some of them were empty, the others looked like they had bodies covered by white sheets on them. The air was cool and dry and it carried a smell of rot and decay with a faint antiseptic smell. It reminded me of the hospital room my grandfather had been in when he died.

"I told you," DJ exclaimed proudly. "See. There are the bodies like I said. They are under the sheets." DJ ran over to the nearest table and pulled the sheet back, exposing the body beneath. We all stood there staring at the corpse. It was a woman from town who had died the week before. Her skin was greyish green and seemed to give off a stink of mold and decay and something else, a sweet smell that I couldn't identify. She was completely naked and, although she was clearly morbidly obese, she was the first naked woman any of us had ever seen.

Jack went to the next table and pulled back the sheet. He cursed when he saw that the body on the table was a naked old man, all gray and wrinkled, the skin mottled with patches of blue. We spent the next few minutes running from table to table pulling back the sheets, hoping to find a young and pretty female body to look at. Sure, we knew they were all dead, but we were thirteen year old boys and doing stupid things was what we did best.

After a while, I was all set to leave. The thrill of seeing dead bodies had gone. Also, the cloying smell and the lingering feeling that something wasn't right made me start heading for the door. I was nearly out of the room when it happened. DJ decided to touch the breast of one of the female corpses. When his hand touched her skin, her eyes snapped open to reveal eyes that were clouded over and filmy, rimmed with red and black, yet still very much alert. The woman growled and reached up to grab him.

"Holy crap," DJ cried, falling backward and knocking Alex over onto another table causing both Alex and the corpse to fall to the floor in a tangled heap. The corpse sat up and grabbed Alex and pulled him close. Alex was screaming and thrashing about, trying to break the dead man's grip. Meanwhile, the low moans and growls from the two corpses who were awake were having a similar effect on the others. I saw that all around the room all the remaining bodies were sitting up and then awkwardly climbing off the steel tables to shamble toward us.

The dead man who held Alex leaned in and bit him on the thigh, pulling back a chunk of Alex's flesh in its teeth. Alex howled in pain and begged us to help him. I ran over and pulled him free. Now I certainly am not a hero, not by a longshot. I suppose at that time that I was not thinking about consequences. I just saw a friend who needed help, so I acted. I guess it was enough because I pulled him free and we all ran for the door with the dead following right behind us.

We turned and ran back through the park in the direction of the wall. The dead were close behind us, shambling after us faster than I would have thought possible. I was sure I recognized a few of them, but my mind would not allow itself to wrap around the fact that these were people from town whom I knew had died, some of them months earlier.

Jack was first to get back to the wall and scaled it easily. I reached the wall and was shocked to see several of the corpses right behind us. I looked for a handhold on the wall and had to dodge an old woman and a short, fat man, both obviously very dead, and both reaching hungrily for me. I still managed to get by them and climbed the wall faster than I could possibly have believed. Even with his bleeding leg, Alex reached the wall next, but tripped just before he could get a handhold. He got back up and started climbing with the dead directly behind him. I reached down and he grabbed my hand. As I started to pull Alex up, a dead woman lunged forward and clamped her mouth around his ankle. Alex screamed in agony, but I had him firmly in my grip and pulled him up. He came free of the woman with a tearing sound and I looked down to see her face smeared with the bright red blood that had flowed out of Alex's fresh wound.

As I was helping Alex up, Stan, DJ and Mike reached the wall. Stan got there ahead of the others and started up, closely followed by Mike and DJ. Directly behind them were the rest of the shambling dead whom we had inadvertently awakened. I helped Alex over the wall and watched him drop down on the other side when I heard a soul-wrenching scream behind me. I turned back to see Stan falling off the wall and landing in the middle of several of the creatures. Our eyes locked and I saw his pleading look before the dead tore him to shreds, feasting on his flesh and blood.

Mike made it the rest of the way up the wall without incident and, without a word or even a glance at me, jumped down to the other side. DJ and I followed and soon we were riding our bikes back as if the hounds of Hell were nipping at our heels. The only sounds made were the constant cries of pain from Alex and DJ's incessant sobbing.

We got back to our street and headed straight for the tree house in Jack's yard. We were in panic mode, all screaming at once and nobody allowing any of the others to get a word in edgewise. We knew we had been expressly forbidden to go anywhere near the military base and that we all would get the beatings of our lives from our fathers. There was also the matter of Stan's death. We knew if we went forward with the truth, the military would cover it up and we'd all be taken away...maybe even back to the base itself, never to be seen from again. As much as we hated to do it, we all swore on our lives that we'd never speak of what had happened to anyone under any circumstances. We agreed that, if asked, we'd say that we had no idea of Stan's whereabouts and, if pressed, to say he must have run away because he was unhappy with his home life. In retrospect, it was a damn flimsy story, but we were a bunch of scared kids and it was the best we could come up with at the time. We got some iodine from Jack's house and poured it over Alex's two wounds. We cleaned them as best we could and made him agree that he would tell his parents that he had been attacked by a stray dog while bike riding.

Under threat of repercussions by the others, we all agreed to our pact. Alex excused himself, saying he was feeling sick and just wanted to go home. It was getting late and we all needed to head to our respective homes. I cast a glance over at Mike, wondering what he would tell his parents, but his eyes were dark and clouded and gave nothing away. He looked back at me, his expression blank, as he left the tree house.

The next few days were strange ones. Stan's disappearance rocked our community and we were all asked by our parents if we knew what had happened to him. None of us came forward since the fear of being taken away was worse than anything we could imagine. Eventually, Mike's story that Stan was unhappy at home and that he had run away began to stick. Alex, meanwhile, had not been seen since our trip to the base. Three days later, my father came up to my room, where I was reading, and told me that Alex and his family had left town. When I pressed my dad for more, his cold glare told me that he knew a lot more than he was telling me but nothing more would be forthcoming, so I quit asking. I biked by his house the next day and saw it was all boarded up. When I looked through one of the back windows into the kitchen, I saw that the house looked like a storm had hit. The furniture was overturned and broken, but it was all there. There were broken dishes on the floor with food strewn all over. Looking in other windows showed the same thing. I found it odd that they would all leave and not take any of their stuff. None of my friends knew anything and, if our parents did, they never spoke of it.

After Alex's family left, we kind of went our separate ways. I stopped hanging out with the guys, finding other pursuits and a new circle of friends. DJ's family moved far away shortly after, his father having been transferred to a base on the West Coast. Jack seemed to become more and more withdrawn and started getting into trouble at school with increasing frequency. Less than a year later, he was shipped off to military school in the South.

Mike seemed the least affected. His grades improved in school, due in some part to sympathy from his teachers over his brother's disappearance. Less than a year later, he took up with Laurie and, while they were always seen together, she always seemed to have a sad, haunted look in her eyes.

The years went by and we passed from teens to adults. I took a job in Boston and moved south. Mike married Laurie and started a business that seemed to prosper, importing low cost goods from Japan. As for DJ or Jack, there was no news and, to be honest, I couldn't have cared less.

After that, the only thing that brought us together was death. Jack was the first to go, shot to death while committing a robbery. Mike let us know by way of a brief card like the one I got for DJ. Laurie followed next of cancer. Both times I attended the funerals and left for home immediately after, refusing any social contact with any of the old gang. We never found out what had happened with Alex, and suspected that he had died, long ago, from the bites he had gotten on the military base.

And that brings us back to today. I showed up at DJ's funeral, held in the local cemetery of the ugly little town where we had grown up, just as the services began and stood in the back, trying to be as inconspicuous as possible. DJ's wife stood next to the minister, sobbing and being consoled by two large, middle-aged dim-witted oafs I instantly took for their sons. I looked around at the mostly unfamiliar faces and did not see Mike. Just as I let out a small sigh of relief, I felt a hand on my shoulder and turned to see Mike, who was standing directly behind me. I hadn't seen him in years and he hadn't aged well. I remembered the tall, confident kid from my youth. What stood before me was a hunched over old man, mostly bald with bad leathery skin. He smiled and I saw that he now sported a pair of dentures clearly a size too big for his mouth. His eyes were the same, though. They still were hard and cold, the eyes of a very dangerous man. I acknowledged him by nodding hello and turned back to the service, feeling as if Mike were more intent on watching me than anything else.

After the service, I turned back to Mike. I decided that I might as well get the pleasantries done so I can go home.

Mike put his hand on my arm, and I found myself involuntarily recoiling at his touch. There were too many years and too much history behind us to change things now. "Hey, Mike," I said with a frown, "looks like we're all that's left of the old gang."

"Our turn will come soon enough, I suppose," he replied,

his pale features pinched and serious. "Eighty-three is a long road to travel, you know, especially the years we've had."

"How are you holding up?" I added, "I know you and DJ were close."

"Ah," Mike muttered with a dismissive wave of his hand, "I haven't seen him in ten years. His shrew of a wife would not allow us to have any contact. Said I'd be the death of him. I guess she never considered that the extra hundred and fifty pounds of fat which was slowly choking his heart might hasten his end."

"Wouldn't help," I agreed.

Mike put his arm over my shoulder and said in a low enough voice, "We need to talk. As the last two left, there are some things we need to discuss."

"I really need to be getting back, Mike."

"One hour is all I want. After all these years, it's not much to ask."

He was right, so I agreed. Mike led me to his truck and we drove in silence. I didn't need to ask where we were going. We both knew we would be going back to where it all had begun. Eventually, we came to the old military base and I felt the past come crashing back to me. "Now that we're here, Mike, care to tell me what was so important?" I asked, trying to keep the anger from my voice.

Mike smiled and pulled the truck to a stop alongside a gate in a chain link fence with razor sharp barbed wire all along the top. He climbed out of the truck, opened the gate, drove in and parked next to the stone wall which marked the perimeter of the base. He climbed out of the truck and pulled an aluminum ladder from the bed. "Give me a hand, will you?"

I nodded obligingly and helped him get the ladder from the truck and place it against the wall.

"Thanks," Mike muttered. "I'm too damn old for this, but I need to show you something." With that, he slowly scaled the ladder and came to rest at the top. "Come on up."

I looked up at him. "You've got to be kidding. No way am I going back up there."

"Get up here, you old fool," Mike growled. "I need to tell you things and, to be honest, it makes sense that it be done up here."

I decided I could handle Mike if things went south. He certainly had not aged well and, while I was no spring chicken, I was in pretty good shape for a man of my age. Better than Mike, anyhow. I climbed up the ladder and sat down next to Mike atop the wall. I was surprised at what I saw. Where there once had been a well-maintained park now stood an overgrown forest with several more trees than I remembered. This surrounded by grass that was over three feet high.

"What happened?" I asked Mike.

"Well, the government closed down the base in the early fifties. I waited until they put the land up for sale and bought it."

"Ever go in there?" I asked.

"I only went in once. The military wouldn't leave behind what they created here. Once I owned the place, I let it grow over and let nature take back what was stolen. I kept the stone fence around the property, though, and then had a chain link fence with barbed wire put up around that to ensure that no one ever sets foot on this property again."

"Why am I here, Mike?" I asked, trying to keep my tone neutral.

Mike sighed. "Remember the day our lives went to shit?" I nodded, giving Mike the look to continue. "Well, there's something you have to know." Mike whistled shrilly in three short bursts and pointed to the woods. A small figure came out of the woods, shambling unsteadily towards the wall. Even though it had been seventy years, I recognized Stan immediately. He looked as he had at thirteen, except for the fact that he was dead. His hair, which once was dark black, was now gray and dull, matted with dirt and grime and missing clumps of hair and scalp. His eyes were filmed over and looked sightless. His face was ashen gray and the entire right half of his face was missing, exposing the teeth in a smiling rictus of death. He was missing the lower half of his left arm and a huge part of his torso. He looked up at us and moaned, stretching his arms out as if he were reaching for us.

I gasped in horror. "How the Hell is Stan here, Mike? I thought the military cleaned house."

"They did," he replied, "but my brother was not found. I came back here right after our visit and managed to find Stan, get him tied up and then buried him near the wall. Stan was not part of their control group so the military had no reason to search for him when they rounded up the others. They never thought he might be buried in the woods as they had no reason to believe he had ever been here. After I bought the place, I dug him up and set him free. I didn't have the heart to put him down for good."

Mike stood and pointed down at his brother who looked up imploringly and moaned softly. "Remember that day on the wall, Stan? Do you?" Mike screamed.

"Sit down, you idiot," I hissed.

Mike turned to me. "You don't get it, do you? That day seventy years ago, when Stan died, it was my fault." Tears were streaming down his cheeks. They looked out of place on the dry and wrinkled skin which likely had never felt tears before this moment. "He was ahead of me on the wall when one of the dead grabbed my leg and started pulling me down. I panicked and grabbed Stan's shirt and yanked him back. His falling distracted the thing on my leg and allowed me to escape."

"Mike, why are you telling me this after all these years?"

"Don't you see," Mike yelled, his voice getting hoarse, "I saved my skin at the cost of his life. After a while, playing the grieving brother bit to the hilt, I even managed to get his girl. I could have pulled DJ down instead or even managed to get up without condemning my brother to an eternity of walking death, but I didn't. You see, I hated him for getting Laurie. I was better than him at everything. I always got what I wanted except for her. Seeing my brother so happy with Laurie was like he was sticking a knife in my gut. It drove me crazy. It should have been me. I hated his guts for that and that was why I ripped his sorry ass off the wall. I've carried this secret shame around with me for seventy years. I need to set the record straight seeing as we are the only two left and our time on this planet is winding down."

Without giving Mike a chance to react, I lunged forward and shoved him as hard as my body would allow. Mike's eyes went wide and his mouth opened as if to protest. His arms flailed and he made one futile attempt to grasp at something, anything, to stop his fall. Finding nothing to grab on to, Mike fell backwards off the wall into the waiting arms of his long dead brother. I turned away but still heard the screams and sounds of Mike being torn to shreds in my head long after I drove away.

Hours later, I sat in my hotel room getting gloriously drunk. Mike's death left me as the last survivor of our night of Hell. I went to my suitcase and removed the thin metal case and placed it gently on the bed. I took the key from my pocket, unlocked the case and picked up the Walther P38. I placed the barrel of the gun in my mouth and tasted the cold, metallic tang.

Mike wasn't the only one with a secret that he'd carried all these years. That day, at the base, the one thing I had never mentioned to anyone was what I had seen while helping Alex over the wall. I had seen Mike pull Stan off the wall and condemn him to death, yet I had never confronted him, nor did I tell anyone else. I was too scared. I was scared of Mike, of what my father would do, and what people would think of us. Even worse was that I was thinking of pushing Mike off the wall that day so many years ago. I had always hated him and saw my chance but froze, and Stan paid the ultimate price. My cowardice set a precedent that would be with me every day of my life. It led to a life of bad choices and loneliness, being apart from people, never taking a wife or family, never allowing myself to be loved. I did not deserve another's love, not after what I had allowed to be buried in the past. For Mike, his secret shame was guilt. Mine was cowardice. I know why he had brought me up to the wall. He wanted me to know his secret and hope for absolution.

I tightened the grip on the trigger and thought how lonely

life was, how my suffering would finally come to an end now that I finally had made things right. My hand trembled and slowly I pulled the gun from my mouth and placed it back in the case. I may have spent the last seventy years paying for my cowardice by keeping Mike's crime a secret, a crime I was just as guilty of as I had helped cover it up. But it wasn't enough. We had let an evil loose on the world and now, with my help, there are two of them, waiting and hungry. One day some unfortunate soul will uncover the legacy we've left to our tiny corner of the world. Hopefully by then, I'll be long dead. For now, though, I am still very much alive. Sometimes the biggest punishment one could have was not in death, but rather in living, and I still had plenty penance due.

My Thoughts are With You, My Beloved

My thoughts are with you, as always, my beloved.

I stand in the shadows of the train station, watching for you. It has been a long day and one where I have thought of you constantly. The platform is crowded with people milling about, waiting for their loved ones. I would so love to be there, waiting with the others for you, but today I wish it to be special. I want our reunion to be one we can both cherish. Nothing so mundane as picking you up from the train station. Today, things will be different.

I watch as the train pulls in and the people spill out after a hard day's work in the city. From their tired expressions, and slumped postures, one wonders why anyone would go through this on a daily basis. The daily grind, some call it. Life is too short, and far too precious to waste it toiling away needlessly.

Wait. I see you now, getting off the train. I am captivated by your beauty as you step on the platform, a bright light amongst the dreary sea of humanity. I watch you as I've watched you every day for endless weeks. I see you toss your head back, and smile, relishing the cool and crisp air that must feel so fresh and pure after being stuck on that crowded train for over an hour. You briskly walk off the platform, and I marvel at the way your lithe young body moves, so fluid, as if simple motion were your sonata or bird-song. To say I wasn't entranced would be a lie. But standing here and staring would do neither of us any good.

Even though the day is slowly waning, the dying embers of daylight seem to light up the chestnut highlights in your auburn hair, making it come alive as it cascades gently down to your slim shoulders. Today, almost as if you knew I'd be waiting, you chose to wear a striking designer outfit which simultaneously enhances your aura of professionalism, yet still allows your inner beauty to shine through and allow you to stand out amongst your peers. You never wear any make-up, I remember that well. Your distaste for it is something I always agreed with. Painted colors would only cheapen your visage which glows in beauty and kindness. No need to parade about like a painted courtesan when your inner goodness is the only enhancement you need.

I follow you home as I do every night, keeping to the shadows as always, in order not to startle you. The thought of making you uncomfortable would pain me greatly, so I choose to cherish you from afar. I watch as you confidently walk the suburban streets, secure in the safety your neighborhood has to offer. It is not a far walk, one I am rather intimately familiar with, yet the anxiety I feel as we approach your home becomes increasingly palpable.

You finally arrive at your house, a small but well-tended cottage at the end of a quiet cul-de-sac. I know that you live alone with only a small, chubby grey tabby named Misted Fluff to keep you company. I silently observe as you work the two locks and quickly let yourself in with only a cursory glance to ensure that no one else is around. I know I wasn't seen, as the neighbor's large weeping willow on their side lawn offers plenty of shade and is a great place where one can sit and watch undetected for hours, if one so desires.

After spending the last few weeks watching you from afar, I know that you are not romantically involved with anyone else. It has been so long since I've held you in my arms and breathed in the scent of your hair and felt the silky smoothness of your skin. I know it would destroy me to see you with another. Each night I whisper poetry to you through the glass of your bedroom window while you sleep, the gentle sonnets of Keats, Yates, Blake and even Wordsworth offering promises of unrequited love. I hope that your subconscious senses them and feels my presence nearby, with you, as it was always truly meant to be. I know that you share in our nightly rapture and that our connection goes deeper than mere words. Our souls are entwined, destined to be together for eternity.

I have said to myself each night for the last three weeks that I will stop hiding in the shadows and come forward, so that we can finally end this charade and be together. I know that you long for this, too. You want someone to bring passion and romance to a life which seems far too routine for one as special as you. And yet, each night I return to where I live, both alone and quite lonely, lost in the knowledge that tonight we could have been reunited once more. Living each day with a broken heart is no way to spend one's life and, yet, I feel that the time is not quite right for me to step forth from the shadows and bring us together again.

As I watch you go about your daily routines, I feel the stirrings of desire build once more within me. They are especially strong, as if giving me a sign that tonight should be the night. I nearly act upon my impulses, yet something holds me back.

I watch as you move from the kitchen and walk slowly to your bedroom. This is an odd turn of events, as it is much too early for you to go to sleep for the night. I need to find out more, so I quickly cross the street and glide around your home until I am safe in your yard, free from prying eyes. I peer once more through your bedroom window and feel my breath catch in my throat as I watch you undress, slowly and erotically taking off your designer ensemble. When you then peel off your undergarments to stand fully unclothed before your bedroom mirror, as if appraising your sheer perfection, I nearly call out. You need not look at yourself and wonder if your beauty is one of the ages when I would gladly be there, worshipping you at your feet attesting to that very fact.

My mouth is dry as I watch you slowly walk to your bathroom and turn on the hot water as you prepare your bath. While this has been a most pleasant change to our nightly rhythms, I wonder about this change of routine. Some small piece of me feels dread, yet I refuse to speculate on it. Better to let events unfold organically than worry needlessly.

I see you leaning over to test the water, gauging whether it is the right temperature to sit and soak. Your easy smile indicates that it is, and you slowly turn the faucet off and apply a lavender colored liquid to the water which you stir in with your hand. I stand there captivated as you step gingerly into the tub and slide slowly into the water's warm embrace.

After a time, I watch as you step from the tub and slowly towel-dry your soft skin which seems to shine after having been immersed in the steaming bath. I feel the stirrings of desire within me, emanating from deep within my very core. Tonight, I determine, as the thought appears unbidden from my subconscious mind. Tonight is the night that our love will be reunited. I watch as you begin applying lotion to your arms and legs, and I know that tonight is the night we will finally be together. I'm just about to leave my hiding spot when the doorbell rings. I see you quickly throw on a robe and rush out of your bedroom.

I can't see the front door from where I've been watching, so I quietly move around the house to have a clear view of who would dare show up and disturb your privacy. I feel a wave of anger rush through me and I have to force myself to push it back. Tonight is about being reunited with my beloved, and I do not want anything to darken this wonderful event.

From my vantage point, I can see a shiny red car in the driveway. Standing at the top of the stairs is a young man dressed in a nice, although unremarkable, suit standing tall and straight, yet looking decidedly uncomfortable. His light blonde hair is cut short and he is clean shaven. In his left hand he holds a bouquet of flowers while, with his right, he seeks to straighten his thin tie.

The door swings open and I see my beloved, her hair still damp and brushed straight back, standing there with her robe fastened chastely about her. Her face lights up and I feel something ache within me. Could this be jealousy? My beloved has never once entertained another. Surely this young man could not be a suitor for her affections. I grit my teeth and realize that I must know. She is mine and this…this invader into our lives will simply not be tolerated. He cannot come between me and my true love.

I watch with growing consternation as my love smiles and accepts the proffered flowers. She gently places a hand on his arm and leads him into her home. I watch with mixed emotions as the door closes behind them.

I slip silently around to the back of the house, making sure I once again stay in the shadows. Neighbors in suburbia are often wont to stare out their windows and observe the comings and goings of others in their neighborhoods. It would not do for an overly curious neighbor to spot me and alert the authorities. If I am detained, and my presence becomes known to my beloved and her neighbors, I fear I will never be able to come here again. The thought of never seeing my love again fills me with a feeling of icy dread.

The back door is well concealed from prying eyes, thanks in part to a large tree in the yard which obscures my presence from her neighbor to the left. The neighbor to the right does not have any windows facing her house, and her yard abuts the woods, so I feel that fate once more is paving the way for me to be reunited with my true love. I glide up the back stairs to the porch and try the door handle. It is locked, although I suspected it would be. My dear heart is nothing if not practical, and cautious, as well. After all, the night can bring many dangers, both seen and unseen and I'm glad that she had the temerity to ensure that means of entry into her home are locked to dissuade intruders.

Of course, I am not an intruder. I am her soul-mate and something as simple as this lock will not keep me from my destiny. I grit my teeth and twist the handle, slowly, yet with all my strength until I hear the tumblers snap open. It is a cheap screen door and one easily entered. I should know as I have done this more than a few times before.

Before entering, I peer into the kitchen to make sure that no one inside has heard me open the door. Each moment is an eternity, yet I wait in the shadows, still and unmoving until I feel that I may proceed inside.

There is no sign of my beloved or the young man as I make my way into the kitchen. It is brightly lit and sparkling in its near blinding whiteness. From the tiles on the floor, to the countertops and cabinets, to the stove and refrigerator, all is in white and brilliantly reflective of the overhead lights. I try and shield my eyes from the incandescent brilliance of the lights. I have spent far too long in the shadows and bright lights certainly feel most invasive. They do not have the softness of the shadows and are harsh and unwelcome. I would gladly take the cool, dark tendrils of shadows caressing me than the harsh, unforgiving glare of light. I would love to simply close it and return things to the natural order, yet I worry that, if I do, I will alert the young man, or even my beloved, to my presence. I am simply not ready. My reunion with my beloved will be on my terms, and no one else's.

I quietly walk through the kitchen, grateful that my soft-soled shoes do not make a sound on the cold, tile floor. Even though it is well-lit, I am impressed with the sense of order my beloved has kept the kitchen. Not a single plate, glass or utensil can be seen in the sink or the drying rack beside it. The table is clean and unencumbered, with only a basket of succulent fruits atop it, the scent both heady and aromatic and makes me realize it has been many hours since I last ate. Her kitchen looks unused but, of course, I know that to be untrue, as I've watched her spend countless hours here preparing her nightly dinners. I pass the refrigerator and see my reflection in the polished white enamel surface. It saddens me when I happen to cast a glance at my own reflection. I do not consider myself an attractive man. I wonder if my beloved will still look upon me with desire as I remember her doing so long ago.

As I pass from the brightly lit kitchen, I enter a hallway with the small, yet tastefully decorated living room to my right and the bedrooms and bathroom to the left. In the living room, the lights are off and the soft glow from several thick candles casts flickering and dancing shadows across the walls. The young man is seated on a chair with his back to me. He is listening to a record that spins languidly on the turntable. The noise hurts my ears, with the scratchiness of the needle on the vinyl and the awful blaring horns and string instruments that some people call music. I can see my beloved's cat, Mister Fluff, fast asleep on the center cushion of the couch.

The sound of the music is like a drill to my temple. I know I will need to be my best when I come forth to greet my beloved after so much time apart. I begin to see things through a haze of red. I no longer feel in control of myself and, at first, I try to tamp down the feelings of rage, then decide against it and act, instead, on impulse.

I move forward, silent but quickly and clamp my large hands about the young man's throat. He looks up in shock and tries to cry out in surprise, but I am far too strong. His eyes widen in panic and he begins to thrash about, clawing at my hands, desperately trying to find some purchase where he can hope to avert what he's suddenly realized is to be his fate. I merely squeeze harder, feeling the muscles in my forearms grow taut. It does not take long before the well-dressed young man ceases to resist and simply slumps forward. I squeeze for another minute, needing to make sure. I am filled with remorse for this poor man. He had no idea that the woman of his affections was not available to his or anyone else's advances. Feeling more charitable than I should to one who intended to take what is mine, I nevertheless lay him gently on the couch and fold his arms across his chest. He looks so peaceful lying there on the couch that I can almost believe he is merely sleeping.

The time is now, I decide, for me to reunite with my beloved. Feeling suddenly emboldened, I walk back to the hallway and towards her bedroom. I see her sitting there at the edge of the bed, still in her robe, gently toweling her hair. She does not notice as I stop in the doorway to stare at her. Her bedroom, like that of the living room, is draped in shadows, with the overhead light turned off and the gentle, flickering glow from several candles illuminating her personal space.

I cannot remember the last time I stood this close to her. I can smell the intoxicating scents of her clean skin, mixed with her perfume and the fragrance of the lotion she has applied to her body. She is softly humming a tune and, while I do not recognize it, I realize that it is the same one that is playing on the record player in the living room. It sounds so much better coming from her, the dulcet tones drawing me in.

I move closer until I am standing nearly beside my beloved. I watch in rapt fascination as she gently towels her hair dry. Unable to contain myself any longer, I move in behind her and gently take the towel from her and continue drying her hair. She reaches up and slowly caresses my large, scarred hands. She seems to pause and then quickly pulls her hands away and stands up. She turns and faces me, her eyes growing wide as she looks upon my face after all this time.

My beloved then does something I did not expect. She screams and then turns to run. Although I am a large man, I am surprisingly quick and grab her by the collar of her robe. I pull her back and she stumbles forward, falling naked on her bedroom floor. She turns around, looking for something to cover herself. Seeing nothing she can use, she scrambles to her feet and grabs a candle off the dresser and hurls it in my direction. For someone so soft and gentle, I am momentarily taken aback by the force of her throw. The candle hits me in the cheek and the flame striking my skin causes me a moment of pain. While I cry out, she turns and runs into her bathroom, screaming for someone named Ted, who I assume to be the well-dressed young man, to call the police.

Ted will not be calling anyone, I reason, yet I cannot risk that the noise my beloved is making will alert any of the neighbors. I must get her to calm down and allow us the chance to talk this out and reconcile whatever problems she may feel there are.

I knock on the bathroom door, gently calling to my love to open the door so we may talk. She keeps screaming, only she's getting louder. I am concerned that a neighbor might overhear. That simply will not do. I must speak with my love and find out why she pulls away from me.

The bathroom door is locked but, like the back door, it can be opened if one is truly of mind to open it. I turn and push on the door and, with enough effort, manage to force it open. I see my beloved at an open window above the tub, still unclothed and screaming out that she needs help. I cross the bathroom in three quick paces and grab her by her shoulders and turn her to face me. Her eyes are red-rimmed and she is crying. I pull her close to me, unembarrassed by the fact that she is undressed. I whisper in her ear that it will all be okay, and that I am here for her, now and forever. I press my lips to hers, gently probing forward with my tongue when her knee comes up hard, striking me between the legs. The pain is blinding and I feel myself doubling over in agony.

My vision goes red as I turn and grab her by the hair as she attempts to flee. Before I can stop myself, I slam her head down onto the edge of the tub. It happens so quickly, I can't stop myself. My beloved lies there at the foot of the tub, her bright red blood slowly pooling around her head like an angel's halo.

I don't hear the police come in, nor do I notice as they drag me away. All I can think of is my beloved, lying there so still and unmoving, lost to me forever.

Nurse Sanjay Patel rushed into room 348 with the crash cart. The Code Blue had sounded and he was the nearest nurse on duty. Code Blues were often touch-and-go and every lost second could mean the loss of the patient, so response time was critical. He saw Doctor Soong standing by the patient's bed, looking with concern at the Automatic External Defibrillator. She called

Sanjay over and said, "Please hurry. Patient Doe has suffered a massive coronary, and is showing no signs of a V fib."

Sanjay knew well enough what that meant. The patient was likely asystole, and in lay terms meant he was going to flatline. He tore open the patient's hospital johnny and applied gel to the AED paddles. He adjusted the charge and applied the first shock. The patient bucked, but there was no change to the heart rate. He still was showing on the AED as flatline. Sanjay tried two more times with the same result. "It's not working," he said to Doctor Soong.

"Give me the epi, Sanjay, and hurry."

Sanjay reached into the top drawer of the crash cart and handed the doctor the epinephrine syringe. She peeled off the plastic wrapper, pushed the first drop out and plunged the syringe into the patient's heart, injecting the contents.

Both Sanjay and Doctor Soong looked at the AED, but there was no change. She shook her head and said in a soft voice, "Please call it, Sanjay."

Sanjay read off the time of death and looked over at Doctor Soong. "Hell of a way to go, alone in the world with no one to mourn your passing."

Doctor Soong simply shook her head. "He was brought in over forty years ago. He had broken into a woman's house and viciously murdered the young woman and her boyfriend. By the time the police had responded to a neighbor's call, they found the young couple dead and the man in a clearly catatonic state. He's been here ever since. He hasn't moved or spoken or even shown a single sign that he's been in anything but a vegetative state in forty years."

"So why was the patient kept on life support all this time?"

Doctor Soong rubbed her temples. It had been a long night. She just wanted to finish her shift and go home. "I honestly don't know. Maybe the State felt it was like we'd be administering the death penalty if we did. Our job is to preserve life, Sanjay."

Sanjay walked out of the room with Doctor Soong. "Why don't you get some rest? I can wrap things up in here." He looked back at the still form of the patient. "I guess he's in a better place now."

"Not our place to pass judgment. That is for a higher power to decide. Our job is to try and save lives, no matter who the patient is."

My thoughts are with you, as always, my beloved.

I stand in the shadows of the train station, watching for you. It has been a long day and one where I have thought of you constantly. The platform is crowded with people milling about, waiting for their loved ones. I would so love to be there, waiting with the others for you, but today I wish it to be special. I want our reunion to be one we can both cherish. Nothing so mundane as picking you up from the train station. Today, things will be different.

Out of the Corner of His Eye

I opened the front door to find my buddy Mitch standing there. I was taken aback by his appearance. He stood there looking completely disheveled, hair a mess, unshaven, and looked as if he hadn't bathed in days. His eyes were wide open and glazed over, as if he were drunk. I wondered if there was a trace of madness there as well. Something was very wrong with my friend.

Mitch grabbed my collar and pushed me back into the apartment. "I'm scared, Gary," he screamed, his face close to mine. I could feel his spittle and smelled the sourness of his breath. "They're everywhere. No matter where I go, they're there."

"Mitch, calm down," I said, trying to be as soothing as possible. At six foot four, Mitch was a tank of a man and the last person you wanted to ever see get violent. "I'm not following you. Can you go back to the beginning?" I gestured to the couch. "Have a seat and let's talk, okay?"

Mitch paused for a second, almost as if weighing his options, and then sat down on the couch. "You wouldn't believe me. Even I don't believe it and I'm right in the middle of it."

"Mitch, you're my best friend. You can talk to me. I'm here for you."

Mitch looked around the room and wiped the perspiration from his brow. "All right, Gary. I'll go back to the beginning and tell you what happened. But understand this. Once you start down this road, there is no turning back. This is some seriously fucked up shit that I got involved in and because of that, I'm going to die. There are things we were not meant to know and sometimes we should just leave things alone. Are you sure you want to get involved?" Mitch paused to glance nervously at the front door and then continued, "I'm giving you a chance to steer clear of this, man. Tell me you don't want to get involved and I'll leave and never bother you again. Your life will depend on this."

I paused. Mitch was my best friend but something about his grim demeanor made me nervous. I walked to the kitchen and came back with two beers. I handed one to Mitch. "Okay, I've decided. I'm in. Tell me everything."

Mitch took the beer and drained it in one long swallow. His hands shook as he handed the empty back to me. "Got another?"

I got up and went back to the kitchen and came back with the rest of the case. I had a feeling that we were going to need them.

Mitch looked around the room again. I could tell he was terrified. He took a long pull from the bottle and wiped the back of his hand across his mouth. "It began about six days ago. No, let me change that. It began a bit over a week ago. My grandfather was in the hospital. He had leukemia and the doctors were giving him perhaps a day or two at best. They had moved him to hospice care to try and make him as comfortable as possible during his final hours. Well, it was pretty late and most of the family had gone downstairs to the coffee shop. I was alone with my grandfather sitting by his bed when the room began to feel cold. It was like the temperature dropped ten or fifteen degrees in a matter of minutes. Suddenly he sat up and grabbed my arm. He looked at me, his eyes wide and panic stricken. He screamed out that they were waiting and for me to not let them get any closer. I couldn't understand what he was saying. There wasn't anyone there. I tried telling him this but he wasn't listening and was clearly getting more and more agitated. I tried to get him to calm down, but he kept screaming that they were there to take him away and that he wanted me to help him. I didn't know what to do. His eyes then rolled back in his head and he fell back on the bed. He was dead and while I didn't want to admit it at the time, the moment he died, the room started to get warmer.

"Six days ago, I was back at work staying late trying to catch up on the work that had built up while I took my bereavement leave. I was trying to wrap up the brief I was working on when I swear that from the corner of my eye I saw someone moving just behind me on the peripheral edge of my vision. Now understand that this was a Tuesday evening around eleven. The office had been empty for hours. Even the cleaning crew had come and gone, so I knew that I was alone in there. Naturally I turned around and saw that there wasn't anyone there. I peered out my office door and looked both ways. The office was dark and empty. Like anyone would in such a situation, I called out asking if anyone was there. Of course there was no answer but for the life of me, I felt as if I was being watched. Have you ever had that feeling where you were sure you were alone and yet you felt as if someone was right there with you?"

I nodded. I've spent many a late night at the office and know that every sound the building makes is enough to make someone feel unsettled.

"Anyway, I walked around the office. First thing I did was check the front door. It was locked, of course. I also checked every cubicle and manager office and saw that I was indeed alone. But I know what I had seen. I was sure that there had been someone moving behind me. I just couldn't believe that my mind was playing tricks on me. Still, I felt foolish, so I returned to my office hoping to finish up and get home. Here I was, a grown man in his thirties and I was jumping at shadows.

"I sat back down and went back to the work on my brief. Not even ten minutes had passed when once again I saw movement out of the corner of my eye. I jumped up and looked around but no one was there. Unless the person could simply blend in with the shadows, I was alone in the office. I kept telling myself that, yet I felt a cold tightness around my heart because even though I couldn't see anyone, I felt that someone was indeed there with me."

Mitch paused and finished his beer in two more gulps. He opened his third and slouched back against the back of the couch.

"Did you ever consider," I asked, trying to be as sympathetic as possible since Mitch was clearly under a lot of strain, "that maybe all you saw were shadows shifting in the low light."

"Yeah, Gary, I did."

I saw the anger beginning to build in Mitch. I also saw something else I had never seen before from my friend and that was fear. Mitch who would never back down from anything was truly afraid.

"Anyway," Mitch continued, "I couldn't work after that. I packed up my laptop and paperwork and headed home. The next day I went to work at the client's office to review some paperwork. They had me set up in their conference room, which I need to add was very well lit. In fact, the entire conference room had three glass walls which allowed people to look over the office. The back wall was floor to ceiling windows which gave you a great view of downtown Manchester."

Mitch paused again and took three more swallows of beer. "As I was saying, the conference room was very brightly lit. There were no shadows in any part of the room. I was glad for this because I was still shaken from the night before. So, I was pretty calm and going about my work when it seemed as if someone moved by me in the conference room. Someone had moved on the periphery of my vision moving around the shadows. There was no denying it that time. I jumped up and looked around. Again there wasn't anyone there. The conference room was empty and the door leading out to the main office was closed. Whatever was there had moved by too quickly for my mind to get a real visual lock on it. I asked the receptionist whose desk was directly across from the conference room just who had come by to see me as I was too lost in my work to notice. She looked at me as if I had two heads and replied that I had been alone in the room all morning. I asked if she was sure and she replied that anyone would have to get by her to go to the conference room and that she had been at her desk all morning.

"That was enough for me. I packed my things and made an excuse to the client that an urgent matter had suddenly come up. At that point, all I wanted to do was get home."

Mitch reached for another beer. As he drank, he looked around my apartment as if he were expecting someone to come out of the shadows and take him away into the darkness.

I asked Mitch if he wanted me to order a pizza. I was definitely hungry and the beers were giving me a decent buzz. I had to admit, Mitch's story had captured my interest. I always enjoyed a good ghost story and I suspected there was a lot more to the tale. Mitch agreed to the pizza so I called and placed the order. "So what happened next?" I finally asked. I sat back down and opened another beer while I waited for Mitch to continue.

"After the incident at my client's, I headed straight home. I turned on all the lights in the den and made myself comfortable in front of the television. I couldn't focus on any show because just as I started to relax, I would see movement off to the side which would cause me to get up and look for the source. Even though I could sense someone there with me, I couldn't clearly see who was there. It was as if I could get a glimpse, but nothing more. This went on for the rest of the day. I finally took a sleeping pill to knock me out so I could get some rest.

"The next day things got worse. I began to see movement on the periphery of my vision with a greater frequency. I began to get a better sense of who they were. They appeared to be dressed all in black with long black trench coats and black fedora hats. I still couldn't make out any features, but I got a sense that their skin was a neutral shade of grey. And while it seemed as if their very essence was getting clearer, my sense of discomfort was growing as well. They seemed to be here watching me. They also seemed to be waiting for something. As to what their purpose was, at the time, I still did not know."

The doorbell rang and I nearly jumped out of my seat. It seemed as if Mitch' story was getting to me. I don't know why I looked over my shoulder as I went to get the door, but I was suddenly feeling very paranoid as if I were being watched as well. I opened the door a crack and to my relief noted that it was only the pizza delivery guy. I paid for the order and brought the pizza and paper plates back to the living room and set it on the coffee table. Mitch was looking pretty pale and I asked him if he was okay. He simply nodded and reached for a slice of pizza.

After we ate, Mitch continued. "By the fourth day I was so shaken, I called in sick to work. I just couldn't face being around people. I wasn't sure if I was hallucinating or seeing something else. Either way, my nerves were shot and I wanted to spend some time online to see if anyone else ever had these symptoms. You see, by this point, I was able to see the people in my peripheral vision with much greater clarity. I saw their faces, or at least what passed for their faces. You see, their skin was indeed a pale grey, but they had no other features. They did not have eyes, a nose, a mouth or even ears. Their heads were simply smooth and featureless under their black hats. The odd thing was, they kept looking at me and while I still did not know what they wanted, it was clear that they were waiting for something and it involved me.

"Trying to ignore the presence of the others I went online. I googled everything I could think of relating to the grey men in black who appeared to me but no one else. I spent most of the day going from one website to another and felt that the search was truly a waste of time. I was about ready to give up for the day when I hit upon a link that looked promising. It was a blog written by some teenage kid a year ago who talked about seeing the Grey Men. He provided links to online libraries and other websites which gave documented accounts of sightings of these men going back as far as recorded history would allow.

"The similarities between each documented case were quite frightening. In each instance, a person had reported having either visions or hallucinations of movement in the shadows from the periphery of their vision. And while they tried to get others to believe what they saw, no one else did as they were the only ones who had the visions. With each case, the individual mentioned that they saw the shadowy figures clearer and clearer with each passing day until they finally reached the seventh day."

Mitch helped himself to some more pizza and another beer. I was pretty drunk by this time and had already started nursing the beer I had. I had work the next day and I knew that it was not going to be a good one at this point. "So what happened after seven days," I finally asked, getting impatient at my friend's extended silence.

Mitch looked at me. His eyes were red and already slightly glazed over. He glanced over his shoulder and continued. "Well, in each case, people claimed to have seen the Grey Men for a full week, starting as nothing but vague shadows but gradually evolving into clear figures with no faces dressed all in black. As with me, no matter how hard they tried, they could never see the Grey Men head on. It was always off to the side, just out of reach. And like me, each person's visions were personal. No one ever had anyone else see what they saw. So that led to the seventh and final day." Mitch turned quickly and his vision seemed to linger in a spot near the corner of the room. I followed his line of vision but didn't see anything.

"Did you see something?"

Mitch nodded. "They're here. I can't escape them, Gary. They're everywhere. It's already too late, you see. Tomorrow makes the seventh and final day. Are you sure you don't see anyone against the wall?"

I shook my head. "Something is different, isn't it?"

Mitch looked at me. "They are slowly moving out of the periphery. I can almost see them head on. Want to know what I see?" I didn't want to. I swear to God I wish I never answered my door tonight because while I couldn't see anyone, Mitch's story was getting to me. I actually felt as if there was someone in the room with us. "Yes," I replied, my voice low and raspy.

"Very well," he continued. His voice was low and somber, "I see three men in the room with us. At least I assume that they are men. They are walking around the room but seem focused on me. They move as if they were images in stop motion photography. As if they were still frames shifting slightly with each successive image. As I said before, they are all dressed from head to toe in black. Their clothing is unique in that there are no lines or seams or any distinguishing designs. It simply is black and seems almost fluid as if it is part of the men rather than clothing. The darkness is so deep it almost appears as if their forms are nothing more than outlines of nothingness where one could get lost in the dark void of their bodies. They all look to be the same height, perhaps six feet or maybe a bit less. At first I assumed they all wore black gloves but now I see that their hands are nothing more than extensions of their coats. The most horrific thing is their faces. As I said, while they have no features, their grey skin seems to be liquid and seems to flow into the darkness that makes their hats and coats. While they move and appear to be following me, there is nothing to indicate life in any of their faces. Just before, the three I saw all turned to face each other and it looked as if they were speaking to each other, although they did not make a sound. Then they all turned in unison and seemed to point at me, I knew then and there that whatever they were, they were sentient."

"That's horrible," I said while hugging myself to suppress the chill. "What do you think they want?"

"There's more, Gary," Mitch said as he stood up. He began pacing back and forth. "You see, on the seventh day, everyone who had seen the Grey Men died. In each case, the death was horrible and violent."

"Surely you don't believe this to be true. It's clearly nothing more than an urban myth that someone blogged about."

"Listen to me," Mitch screamed, "it's all real."

"How can you be sure," I protested.

"The kid's blog had all kinds of personal information online including his school. It didn't take much searching to find out where he lived and who he was. You see, I looked online for the local papers from his hometown for deaths of a fifteen year old kid around the time of his last blog entry. Sure enough, the Akron Beacon Journal had an online piece a year ago about Jimmy Barnes who was tragically killed by a commuter train as he crossed the tracks. Apparently the train hit him and then dragged him for a full quarter mile as the conductor tried in vain to stop the train. There wasn't even enough left of the kid to even have an open casket.

"That doesn't prove anything, Mitch. It could simply be a coincidence."

"Let me finish. The article also interviewed some of his classmates. What was most disturbing was how Jimmy's best friend claimed that Jimmy had been acting very strangely the week before he was killed and even claimed that Jimmy was worried about some guys in black suits who had been following him."

"That's a hell of a ghost story," I said to Mitch. "What are you going to do?"

Mitch stood and slowly walked to the front door. "I had better be going. Thanks, Gary, for being such a good friend."

"Are you okay to drive?" I asked.

"Does it really matter," he replied sadly. "They are here with me, Gary. It's only a matter of time now."

"Wait," I cried out as he tried to leave. "Who are they? Why do some people see them and not others? Was there anything on the website?"

Mitch sighed. "They're death. We are not supposed to see them until it's our time to die. Sometimes a person sees them by accident. The best way to describe it is like peeling back the curtain to see the workings of the universe. The Grey Men gather the dead. Where they take them I don't know. No one who ever witnessed the Grey Men lived long enough to confirm this, but it seems to make the most sense. There are things we are not meant to see or know. I got a glimpse of what lies beyond and now they are coming to collect. I guess there are things we simply are not meant to know."

Mitch then turned, whispered that he was sorry and left without another word. I stood there alone in my apartment and no matter how much I put up the heat could not shake the chill that ran down my spine.

Mitch is dead. The whole idea of him dying seems like a bad dream, but it happened. I would say I was shocked, but somehow I knew that when he left my apartment that would be the last time I would ever see him again. His sister called me the day it happened. It seems he was on his way to visit his grandmother at the nursing home in Concord when he lost control of his car on route 93. He plowed into a flatbed truck in front of him doing at least 70 miles per hour. The bed of the truck sheared off the roof of his Lexus and the top of Mitch's head as well. He was killed instantly.

Mitch's funeral was the next day. I paid my respects to his family and watched as they lowered his coffin into the ground. I was numb as it hit me that I'd never see my best friend again.

Just as I was getting set to leave I felt a chill and swore I was being watched. I turned around but there was no one behind me. I turned back to the service and then, out of the corner of my eye, saw some movement in the shadows of my peripheral vision. My mouth went dry as I realized that thanks to Mitch's tale, the fabric of reality had been exposed for me as well and that one could never really get the genie back in the bottle. I wondered how I would spend the next seven days and whether I would tell anyone.

The Kids in Black and White

June 4, 1980.

Lake Bodom was still and eerily silent. The water had a perfect unblemished crystalline surface which reflected the azure sky above and masked the dark depths which lay hidden below. Nothing stirred by the water's edge. It was as if time stood still on the shores of the lake, waiting for someone to venture forth and breathe life back into the earth. Until that time, everything remained a frozen portrait keeping a lonely vigil, silently waiting.

The beat up BMW sped along Route 1, the tires whispering softly on the asphalt. Eric looked out the window, enjoying the scenery. In two years at the University of Helsinki, he had never left the city. This camping trip in Espoo would be his first foray out of what he had slowly grown to consider his adopted home. The Finns were a cold and distant people on the surface, but as Eric had gotten to know them better, he found their bleak exterior masked a warm and generous interior.

Driving the car was Eric's best friend at the University, Antti Laitinen. Eric sat in the passenger seat next to him. Sitting in the back were Antti's sister, Riikka, her friend Katya and a quiet, surly guy in his thirties named Nils that had made no effort to respond to anyone when they tried to engage him in conversation.

The trip to Espoo was Antti's idea and, even though Antti was his closest friend at school, the idea of spending a night in a tent did not exactly thrill Eric. It was only when Antti told him that his sister Riikka and her friend Katya would be coming that Eric had agreed to go. Riikka was a gorgeous sixteen year-old and, though Eric was eighteen, the sight of Riikka made him weak in the knees. While she did flirt with him, that was the extent of their relationship. Eric hoped that this overnight camping trip might take their relationship to the next level.

Riikka was five foot four with ample curves. Her platinum blonde hair fell lazily about her shoulders, the bangs hanging down over her ice- blue eyes. She had a pert little nose which was dusted with a few freckles and a full, sensual mouth. Her high cheekbones rounded out the perfect Nordic look. While she did like Eric, with his all-American looks and awkward charm, she wanted him to be more direct and assertive and make the first move by actually asking her out. She knew that, when he did, she would make it worth his while.

Katya, on the other hand, was the complete opposite of Riikka. She was taller and thinner, with few curves. Her hair was jet black and cut short, in a pixie-like Pat Benatar look. Her complexion was pale as were her grey eyes. Her family had moved to Helsinki from Moscow ten years earlier and, while the other kids had avoided the brash and sometimes abrasive Russian girl, Riikka had been drawn to her and the two quickly became fast friends. Riikka knew that her brother was sleeping with Katya and, while the thought did make her cringe, she knew her brother really cared for Katya and that neither would willingly hurt the other.

After Antti and the girls had gone to pick up Eric, they had driven to the train station in downtown Helsinki. Antti was being purposefully vague and had refused to answer everyone's inquiries as to who they were waiting for. He told them he would explain everything in due time. They were surprised when a scruffy man in his thirties came over to Antti and then silently climbed into the back seat, only curtly introducing himself as Nils. He looked as if he were homeless; in addition to being dirty and unwashed, he had a stale, acrid odor about him. Eric had pressed Antti about why Nils was joining them on their camping trip, but he remained unusually stoic. Eric glanced back at

Riikka and saw that she was also clearly uncomfortable with the older man accompanying them.

The car drove into Espoo and soon Antti pulled off the main road and started down a dirt path that was well hidden. The path was rough and uneven and caused the BMW to bounce and jostle as it drove forward.

"Slow down, Antti," Eric said, "the road is a mess. If we break an axle, we'll be walking home."

Antti frowned and dropped down a gear. The car slowed and the ride seemed a bit more bearable. They kept on the dirt road for over an hour, going deeper into the woods. Eventually, Antti stopped the car, got out and opened an old wooden gate that was mostly hidden by the deep brush. He got back in and drove through the gate. He grinned and looked around at his passengers. "We're almost there." He continued down the over-grown path and glanced at the man sitting in the back seat. "I'll bet this brings back a lot of memories."

The man grit his teeth and replied, "I've been thinking and this is a really bad idea. I don't care what you're paying. Take me back. I want no part of this."

"Tough luck, friend," Antti replied, "I'm not stopping and, even if I did, there isn't anywhere for me to turn around."

"Then stop the car. I'll find my own way back to the main road."

"No!" Antti shouted. "I paid you four thousand markka and went to a lot of trouble for you to come along this weekend. If you want out, then I want my money back now. So unless you have it on you, I'm not stopping."

The man muttered a curse and sat there scowling. Katya look nervously at Riikka. She didn't like where things were going. She clutched her purse tightly and tried to make herself as small as possible. Everyone rode in silence for another five minutes before Antti pulled the car into a clearance and killed the engine.

"We're here, folks," Antti exclaimed, his mood suddenly brighter. "Let's get our camp set up."

Antti popped the trunk and he and Eric unloaded their bags. Nils was the last one out of the car. Instead of helping the others set up, he walked to the edge of the clearing and sat down with his back to a tree. He lit a Saimaa cigarette and inhaled deeply before exhaling. He seemed resigned to his circumstances.

"Hold it," Riikka called out. "Antti, before we do anything, I want some answers. Where are we? And who is this guy you brought along?"

Antti sighed. He put down the cooler he was carrying and called over to his sister. He motioned for Eric and Katya to join them and handed out Karhu beers. Once everyone had a beer and was sitting, he began. "Okay, here's the deal. Twenty years ago, to the day, a horrific crime was committed." He pointed to the trees behind him. "Do you see those trees?" Everyone nodded. "Good. Well, right behind them is Lake Bodom."

"What?" Riikka screamed. Her face had gone deathly pale. "Please tell me that you're kidding."

"What's going on?" Eric asked nervously.

Antti continued. "Twenty years ago, two guys and two girls were viciously attacked here at Lake Bodom. They were savagely beaten. Three died and one survived. The survivor kept a low profile, trying to escape the notoriety of the murders. As lone survivor, he was considered the prime suspect by many people. He was eventually acquitted, but no one was ever formally charged and, to this day, it remains one of the country's most infamous slayings."

"Thanks for the history lesson, Antti," Eric replied. "So why are we here and who is he?" he asked, while pointing to the stranger.

"Come on, Eric. We're here to camp out, tell scary stories and get good and drunk." He opened his backpack and pulled out a video camera. "We're also here to film a twentieth anniversary documentary of the Lake Bodom murders for a film course I'm taking. As for my new friend, I'm surprised none of you has guessed. Nils here is the only one to survive the Lake Bodom massacre. He was living in Kemi under an assumed name. I spent a small fortune tracking him down"

"Why, Antti?" Katya pleaded. "What do you hope to accomplish? Now that I know where we are, I refuse to stay. There's a reason that no one camps here anymore. The lake is haunted."

Antti laughed. "Seriously, Katya? There's no such thing as ghosts. This documentary with the elusive survivor of the Lake Bodom murders will guarantee me a top grade. I'm hoping that I can use it as a springboard for a film career."

"I don't care," Katya pleaded. "You know how this stuff gets to me."

"Relax," Antti said as he put his arms around her, "I'm here to protect you. Trust me. I wouldn't be here if it weren't safe."

The group grabbed their packs and walked the short distance through the woods to the shore. The sun was slowly starting to set and cast a rich orange-yellow palette over the smooth silvery surface of the lake.

Eric, Antti and the girls quickly set about getting the tents up. By the time they were done, it was early evening and the azure sky was giving way to a navy-black mixed with reds and purples.

Antti sat down on a large rock and motioned for Nils to sit on the rock across from him. He picked up the camera and focused on Nils, making sure to get the lake in the background. "I'm sitting here with Nils Gustafsson, the only survivor of the Lake Bodom massacre which took place twenty years ago today. Behind us, still as the grave and not giving up her secrets, is Lake Bodom. Nils, let's start with your – wait…Who are they?"

Nils turned to look behind him. "Who are you talking about?"

Antti put down the camera and looked over in the direction of the lake. There was no one there. The lake was still and silent as always. He was sure he had seen three teenagers standing there by the water's edge. The teenagers had been still and unmoving and seemed to be cast in black and white. "No one, I guess. Maybe it was an afterimage from the camera. Let's do this a bit later, okay?"

Nils shrugged and walked away. He lit another cigarette and sat down by the fire.

Antti put the camera down and went off in search of his friends. He approached his sister, Katya and Eric who were busy putting the girls' bags into the second tent.

"Have you guys seen anyone else around?" Antti asked.

Riikka saw, with concern, the look of worry on her brother's face. "What happened, Antti?"

Antti considered not telling them what he'd seen, but decided it best to tell the truth. "I started filming the opening scene for my documentary with Nils when I thought I saw some kids standing in the background. When I looked again, they were gone. I just want to make sure you didn't see anyone else here."

"Where did you see the kids?" Eric asked.

"I saw them by the lake. I must have been mistaken since no one comes out here. The lake has a bad reputation."

"We didn't see anyone else." Katya added. "Are you feeling okay, Antti?"

"I don't know," Antti sighed. "Let me find Nils and continue my documentary."

He found Nils sitting by the BMW. He looked up at Antti with a haunted, defeated look. "I don't want to be here. There are too many memories of the past. I just want to go home," he said softly. "It's too dark to walk through these woods, and you have the only car."

Eric walked over and sat down next to Nils. "What's going on?"

Nils sighed. "I remember the day that they came out of the woods and killed them. Their screams have echoed in my head every day since."

"Whose screams?" Eric asked.

"My three friends, Seppo, Anja and Maili, who were killed here twenty years ago. They were savagely murdered and I was unable to do anything to save them." Nils stood and seemed tense as if he were readying himself for fight or flight.

"You suffered a traumatic event here," Eric said gently. "Of course the memories will haunt you. They would haunt anyone."

Nils face grew red. He pointed a finger accusingly at Eric. "You weren't there. After my friends were killed, my life went to Hell. My friends and family shunned me as if being in my presence would somehow taint them."

Antti grimaced. "I likely didn't see anyone, Nils. It was probably a trick of the setting sun reflecting off the lake. Come on. Let's head back to the campsite. We'll get a fire going and cook up some *makkara*. I've also got plenty of Karhu so we'll pass a quiet night and, in the morning, we can resume filming. Probably have better light anyways."

"Forget it," Nils hissed. "I'll stay by the car."

"Suit yourself, Nils," Antti replied. "If you choose to join us, we'll be at our campsite." He turned and walked back to the campsite, followed by Eric.

"Think he will come?" Eric asked when out of earshot.

Antti smiled. "We have the fire, and food and beer. He'll come when he gets too cold or too hungry."

They returned to the campsite and quickly dug a fire pit. They searched the immediate area and soon had enough wood to build a fire that would last the night. True to his word, Antti had a roaring fire going. They cooked the *makkara* on sticks and ate them with mustard. Before too long, Nils joined them and sat silently by the fire. Antti grinned at Eric and then handed a cooked *makkara* on a stick to Nils who nodded his thanks and then ate it greedily.

After a few hours, and several beers, the five of them were quite tired. The fire had gotten smaller as most of the wood had already burnt down. Katya excused herself, saying that she wanted to get some sleep. She looked over anxiously at Antti, but Riikka stepped in and replied that she had a good idea and that she would join her.

"We'll see you boys in the morning," Riikka said, and looked over and gave a long, lingering look at Eric.

"I think she likes you, Eric," Antti said.

"Are you okay with that?"

Antti smiled and patted Eric on the back, "Sure. I know you're a good guy. You'll treat her right. I think the girls have the right idea. Let's hit the sack. Tomorrow's another day."

Antti and Eric started for the tent. Eric looked over at Nils who sat there staring at the lake. "Are you coming to sleep, Nils?"

Nils looked up and nodded and followed them into the tent.

Katya awoke in the middle of the night with a dull throbbing in her bladder. She had to pee and knew that she should have gone before bed, but she couldn't bear going with everyone there. She was a private person, and considered herself to be quite shy, even if she knew she projected an entirely different persona to others. She looked at her watch and saw that it was already four in the morning. She couldn't wait until it got light out. She put on her jeans and quietly slipped out of the tent. She worked her way around the fire to the edge of the woods and proceeded to do her business. She quickly finished and, as she stood, she got the feeling that someone was watching her.

Katya looked towards the lake and saw a girl about her age standing there by the water's edge. The girl stood perfectly still, and was completely devoid of any color, making her a stark contrast to the rich hues of the lake and surroundings. Katya took a tentative step forward, trying to work her way around the fire to the relative safety of the tent. She glanced over at the girl and saw she hadn't moved. She then took a second step and then a third, moving slowly closer to the fire. She looked over at the girl and, to her horror, noticed that the girl was not only in black and white, but was also flat like a photograph, having height and width, but no depth whatsoever.

Suddenly, the girl by the lake spun around and fixed her gaze on Katya. She opened her mouth to an impossible length, pointed at Katya and emitted a loud and mournful wail. She tried to move but found herself frozen in place as the girl seemed to glide across the sand towards her. Katya saw, with creeping horror, that the girl had no eyes; in their place were empty black voids, like her mouth. The girl moved quickly across the sand, yet left no footprints. Katya was able to emit one brief scream before the girl passed into her and made everything go black.

Antti snapped awake. *Was that a scream?* He looked around the tent and saw that Eric and Nils were both fast asleep. He glanced at his watch and noted that it was four-thirty. Too early to get up, but he may as well empty the bladder and check on the girls. He was feeling guilty about lying to everyone about what he had seen, but he needed this documentary. He wasn't doing well in the class and it was tearing him apart that he wasn't succeeding. He was used to everything coming easily to him. This film would turn things around.

Antti climbed out of the tent and walked to the tree line. He was about to relieve himself when he saw someone standing by the water's edge. He walked around the dying embers of the fire and saw that it was Katya. She stood there, with her back to him. His breath seemed to catch as he realized that she stood there completely naked, with the moonlight casting bluish grey highlights on her flawless alabaster skin.

He started walking towards the lake. Maybe she was waiting for him. He couldn't take his eyes off her small, yet inviting, body. As he got closer, he decided to call out to her. "Katya are you okay? It's Antti."

Katya stood there, still as a statue. Antti grew a bit concerned. Was she sleepwalking? He called to her again. "Katya is everything alright?"

She still did not respond.

Antti reached the water's edge and put his hand on Katya's shoulder, and quickly pulled it back. She was as cold as ice. He turned her around and felt his bladder loosen as he saw her face. Hey eyes were gone, and only shadows could be seen in their place. Even worse was the twisted, elongated shape of her mouth, which seemed to stretch her face to twice the length that it normally was. Her skin was bluish-white and mottled with tendrils of grey and black.

"Oh God!" he gasped as he turned to run. She clamped a cold hand on his shoulder and held him with a vise-like grip.

She started to moan, a long and haunting wail. From the water's edge rose the image of a boy about Antti's age. He looked like Katya did, with only darkness where the eyes should be and a long and impossibly twisted facial expression. The boy looked like a photograph come to life. He was in black and white and had no depth. He glided over the water's surface, his feet pointing downward inches above the water, toward Antti.

Antti started screaming for help. The boy glided over to Antti and seemed to be absorbed into his body. The last thought Antti had before the world went dark was that the film was not worth it and that he should have dropped the damn class.

Eric was awakened by Antti's screams. He sat up, slightly disoriented and took a moment to gather his surroundings and clear his head. He noticed right away that Antti was missing. He saw Nils next to him tossing and turning in his sleep. Eric shook him forcefully.

"What is it?" Nils grumbled.

"I heard a scream and Antti is missing," Eric said. "Come on, get dressed."

Nils grumbled and shook his head. "I've got a bad feeling about this. I knew that I should have stayed home."

"Just shut up and get dressed," Eric growled, "and let's wake the girls and find Antti."

They crawled out of their tent and saw that Riikka was already out of her tent and looking around with a worried expression on her face. Eric ran over to her.

"Riikka," Eric cried out. "Antti is missing. We heard a scream and were coming to make sure you and Katya were okay."

"I also heard a scream," Riikka said, her eyes filling with tears. "I got up and saw that Katya wasn't in our tent, either."

A low and mournful howling broke the silence. They looked down toward the water and saw Katya and Antti standing there naked and unmoving in the moonlight.

"What the Hell!" Eric cried. "Here we are all worried and they slip away for a late night swim. I'm going back to bed."

"Wait," Riikka cried out. "Please, Eric. Something's wrong. Look at them. Do they look like a couple slipping away to be together?"

Eric looked as best he could. They were a good distance away, with the smoke from the fire between them. He had to admit, Riikka had a point. Something didn't seem right. "I don't know, Riikka. Maybe they will feel we're intruding."

"Look at them!" she screamed. "I've known Katya for years. She may be attracted to Antti and she might be going all the way with him, but she is still pretty bashful. Even at gym class, I've seen her cover herself shyly after taking a shower. Why would she stand there so immodestly?"

Eric put his arms around Riikka. "I'm sorry. You're right. Why aren't they moving? It's like they're in a fugue state or something. I'm going over."

"Don't do it."

Riikka and Eric turned to see Nils standing there behind them. He had been so quiet they had forgotten that he was there.

Eric looked back to where Antti and Katya stood. They still hadn't moved. Under the bright moonlight, their bodies looked like bluish-white marble. He found the coldness of it very unsettling. He turned back to Nils and grabbed him by the collar. "What happened here, Nils?"

Nils looked at the two teens standing by the lake. "Let's leave. I'll tell you everything along the way."

Riikka looked at Eric. "That's my brother and best friend standing there. I can't just leave them."

"It's no longer them," Nils said grimly. "And if we don't go now, we're likely to join them."

"Tell us what's going on. We're not leaving until you do. You can either tell us what you know and we drive out together, or you take your chances in the dark on foot," Eric growled.

"Fine," Nils replied. "Twenty years ago, I was here at this very spot. We were two couples, Seppo, me and our girlfriends Anja and Maili. We came here to swim, drink, smoke and make out. It was supposed to be a simple weekend having fun.

"Sometime around four in the morning, Seppo and his girlfriend decided to go for a late swim. They stripped down and ran to the cold water. My girl asked me if I wanted to join them, but I couldn't swim and, instead of telling her the truth, made some excuse about being too drunk. She looked disappointed but sat down next to me without saying another word. Well, we sat there by the fire having our beers and talking about meaningless stuff when these four guys came out of the woods. They were clearly drunk and as surprised to see us as we were them. Well, one of them grabbed Anja and tore at her blouse. I stood up to stop him and the other guys beat me senseless. When I came to, my friends were all dead. Nils paused to wipe his eyes. "I'm sorry. It's been years since I spoke about that night to anyone."

Eric glanced nervously at the still forms of his friends. They stood there silent and unmoving. "Okay, so what happened?"

"I must have been hurt worse than I initially thought because I was found unconscious by the lake with a whole slew of injuries. The ruined bodies of my friends were found by the water's edge. I eventually healed from my injuries, but the scars remained. I then did my best to disappear. Twenty years later and folks still want to know what happened here at Lake Bodom. I just want to put it behind me and try and live my life. But I never could because, for years, people kept seeing my friends' ghosts here at the lake. Eventually, people stopped coming here because it got the reputation of being haunted. People say that, at night, the spirits will rise out of the water and join with anyone foolish enough to be here. Then, before dawn, they will march into the lake, taking with them the hapless souls they have possessed. As you can see, your friends now belong to the restless spirits of my dead friends, and they are beyond our help."

Riikka looked at Eric. "I believe him. I don't want to leave them, but I don't want to end up like that, either." She took his hand. "Please, Eric. Let's go. We'll get the police and come back."

Eric nodded. "Let me get Antti's car keys. He has them in the tent."

"Please hurry."

Eric crawled into his tent and rifled through Antti's jacket until he found the car keys. He heard Riikka scream so he rushed out of the tent. He saw what she was staring at and nearly froze himself. Antti and Katya were walking toward their campsite in complete unison as if controlled by a single mind.

Eric grabbed Riikka by the arm and pulled her toward the BMW. Nils followed quickly behind them. They got in and Eric tried to start the car only to find that the engine was dead and wouldn't turn over.

Eric tried again and again and finally punched the dash in frustration. "It's dead," he said, "We're going to have to run for it."

They hurried out of the car and found Antti and Katya standing there. The possessed teens grabbed Riikka and started dragging her back toward the lake. At the water's edge, a teenage girl in black and white rose silently from the water.

"My God," Nils exclaimed, "that's Anja!"

"Snap out of it, Nils," Eric screamed, "we need to save Riikka."

"Leave her. She's as good as dead." Nils turned and ran into the woods, leaving Eric at the campsite.

"Damn him," Eric cursed and ran after Antti and Katya to try and help Riikka.

Anja's spirit rose up until she appeared to be standing on the water and then she glided out to the beach. She kept gliding over the sand, rapidly approaching Antti and Katya.

Eric reached his former friends and tried to grab Riikka who was thrashing wildly in an attempt to escape. They both turned as one, moaning loudly with their distorted mouths. The thing that once was Antti grabbed Eric and threw him back toward the campsite where he crashed into a tent.

Anja's spirit reached the pair and, even though Riikka was fighting to escape, glided easily into her body. Riikka stopped fighting and stood up slowly. She tore the clothes from her body and howled as her eyes dissolved into hollow pockets of nothingness. Her features elongated and soon she was moaning along with what once was her brother and best friend. As one, they turned and returned to the water's edge where they stood immobile.

Nils ran until he felt his lungs burning. Memories of this night twenty years ago flashed back and he forced them from his mind. He had told the kids a great story, but it wasn't the truth. He had come here with his friend and their girlfriends only to find that his best friend and his girl were cheating on him. After that, all he remembered were the screams and the blood. So much blood, he thought it would never wash away. Thankfully, there was Lake Bodom whose cold waters would forever hide his guilt.

Yet, they were all here now. He had seen Anja enter Riikka's body. He was sure that it was Seppo's spirit in Antti's body and Maili in Katya's. They were here for him. The past never forgets or forgives its secrets.

Nils stopped running, a painful stitch in his side. He looked around and saw that he was back at the campsite. *How is that even possible?* He saw Eric lying unconscious on top of a broken tent. *Screw him.* He turned to leave when he felt a cold hand on his shoulder. Riikka stood there, her eyes hollow voids and her face impossibly long. Her skin was a bluish white with tendrils of grey and black. She moaned and was soon joined by Antti and Katya. They all grabbed Nils and started dragging him toward the lake. He screamed and thrashed about but was unable to break free from their icy grip.

Eric stirred and heard Nils screaming. He looked down to the beach and saw the figures of Antti, Riikka and Katya dragging Nils into the water. They disappeared beneath the surface and soon all was still. Eric wept silently and started the long walk out of the woods. The first rays of light began to appear over the horizon and, while the air was pleasant and warm, he felt a soul-numbing chill. He knew the secret of Lake Bodom and would take it to his grave. He'd book the first available flight to the United States and would never return to Finland. He couldn't chance staying. Even now, in the daylight, he felt the pull of the lake drawing him back. He knew if he ever returned, Riikka, Antti and Katya would be there waiting. A piece of him would always exist in Lake Bodom and that was enough.

Lake Bodom stood still and was silent once again. The water's perfect unblemished crystalline surface reflected the sun shining bright above and masked the dark depths which lay hidden below. Nothing stirred by the water's edge. It was as if time once more stood still on the shores of the lake, as if it were waiting for something. Until that time, everything remained a frozen portrait keeping a lonely vigil, silently waiting for the dark depths to reveal her secrets one more time.

Of Lights and Shadows

I awoke with a splitting headache as the light filtered through a thin slash in the blinds. Swirls of dust motes seemed to come alive in the razor line of light.

I stood on trembling legs, feeling little sensation as my bare feet touched the cold floor. I looked over to the bed and the remains of my wife, who lay there as she had last night after I ripped her to shreds and eaten her flesh.

I still had the coppery after taste of her succulent flesh and licked my cracked, dry lips in an almost futile effort to give me a sensation of feeling.

Suddenly, a burning need wracked my body in spasms and flooded my vision in red. I hungered and needed to eat once more. I looked back to the remains of my wife and turned away with disgust. The cold flesh and congealed scraps of meat that were left held no interest.

The last three days had been a blinding collage of television and radio reports issuing warnings that the dead had risen. Sickness was spreading through our little seacoast town like wildfire and I wasn't opening the door for anyone.

We were safe, we had food and we would wait it out.

Locking the house may prevent physical entry, but an airborne virus would not be denied. I must have somehow gotten infected because last night was when the first stirrings of need hit me.

I awoke with a start. I thought I just needed to use the bathroom, but that wasn't it. In the bathroom mirror I looked at my reflection and noted the grayish pallor to my skin and the yellow rims around my eyes. My mouth was dry and I rubbed my swollen throat as I struggled to make my glands salivate.

I suddenly doubled over in pain. My insides felt like they were being turned inside-out and lanced with sharp knives. The agony spilled over to my head and my vision seemed to go red as the world took on a crimson hue. I bent forward and dry heaved, my thin frame wracked by convulsions.

I staggered back to bed, to my wife. The moment I touched her was like a shot of electricity through my body. Before I knew it, I leaned close to her, so close that I could smell her and, before I could stop myself, tore her throat apart with my teeth. She barely had a moment to scream as the blood poured out from her ruined throat. I lost control then, tearing her apart and swallowing pieces of her flesh without even chewing and then drinking in the spicy hot blood until the need passed.

The need was upon me again. I staggered from the bedroom, the world awash in shimmering hues of red and stumbled into my daughter's room where she lay sleeping peacefully in her crib. I thought of how the neighbors used to tell me what a sweet little girl she was. As I hungrily reached for her, I hoped that they were right.

Grey

The man was almost upon us before I noticed him. I was lying on the beach, reading the latest Laymon novel, trying to see the print on the page in the blinding white glare from the overhead sun. My brother was sitting in the chair next to me, completely engrossed in a Follett offering. Our wives had left to go shopping hours ago and, although it killed me to admit it, I was starting to worry. It wasn't like my wife to be gone for hours without letting me know where she was. It just wasn't her style.

So there I was, engrossed in my novel, ruminating about my wife's whereabouts, when I happened to notice this guy steadily approaching us. Although at the time it didn't register, it was odd to see a man walking down the beach toward us wearing a navy pinstripe three piece suit, navy shirt and matching tie, and polished dress shoes. It certainly wasn't beachwear by any stretch of the imagination. Also, there was something about the way he moved that didn't seem right to me. He moved with an almost mechanical gait, not quite a glide, and not quite a shamble.

Feeling perplexed, I took a closer look at the guy. He glared at my brother and me, and I almost fell back off the chair. His skin was grey and hanging from his face in tatters, as if he were trying to escape from the confines of his own hide. His eyes were rheumy and red-rimmed and seemed unfocused and glazed over. He moved purposefully toward us, making a beeline for my brother. His lumbering, shambling stride seemed to intensify the closer he got. As he approached, he raised his arms as if reaching for us.

"Bryan," I called out, "move, damn it!"

Bryan looked up and seemed to freeze. His mouth opened wide, as if to say something, or to scream, as he watched the man advance toward him. With blinding speed, the man grabbed my brother by the throat with one hand and placed the other hand on his forehead. Bryan didn't even have a chance to scream as the man and my brother became enveloped in electrical charges, spitting off him in bristling sparks.

I watched in horror as my brother seemed to shrink and wither before my eyes as the man drained him of his life essence. His skin seemed to lose its color and pull in tighter to his face. His eyes rolled upward and he threw his head back to scream, except the only sound that came out was one that sounded like air escaping. When the man was done, he pulled his hand from my brother, glanced over at me, and walked away down the beach. He acted as if I were invisible.

I ran over to my brother and came face to face with the desiccated corpse that was once a living, breathing person. His skin was mottled and grayish and tight against his face. His mouth hung open, jaw slack. His eyes were shriveled and grey and seemed to be lost in the depths of the sockets, and the pupils had rolled back in his skull. Fighting repulsion, I brought a finger to his neck to check for a pulse. Through the cold, papery feel of the skin, I felt nothing nor, I suppose, did I expect to.

I grabbed my cell and tried my wife. The phone rang several times and finally transferred me to voice mail. I cursed and hung up. Ever since I had bought her the damn phone, I always got voice mail. I even remember telling her that I could be lying dead in a ditch with an urgent need to connect and would still get her voice mail. I tried my brother's wife and got a message that her number was currently unavailable. As a last resort, I tried 911 and, to my surprise, got a busy signal. I needed to find the police, or someone. I didn't want to leave my brother there, but he was dead, and the thing that killed him was still walking around, doing Lord knows what to whom.

I dressed quickly and ran up to the street. The road was empty. Not a car moving in either direction. The street stretched out as far as I could see. The beach was to my left and not a soul was to be seen. To my right was the strip with restaurants, shops and clubs and, normally, where it would be packed with the throngs of humanity, was now still and desolate like a painting of a town, still and devoid of life. I've been to Lauderdale several times in my younger days, and never have seen the strip so utterly deserted. I glanced down at my wristwatch and realized that it had stopped hours ago.

I walked the streets for hours, checking stores, restaurants and bars, anywhere that people congregate. Most places were empty. Eventually, I found a bar where there was a woman of indeterminate age, in the same dried up condition as my brother. Her skin was cold, dry, and papery and flaked to a fine powder with my touch. Her mouth hung open, her tongue black and leathery and lolling from the side of her mouth, the teeth yellowed and chipped.

I was in a state of panic. Where the Hell was everyone? After three hours of walking the streets of Ft. Lauderdale, I'd only come across one other person, and she was long dead. She looked as if she had been hiding behind the counter in an upscale restaurant bar on the beach strip. Apparently, hiding didn't help as something had found her and finished her off.

I was just about to head back out to the street when I heard a scream. A man and a woman were hurrying down the street with several people who were in the same state of decay as the man who had killed my brother shambling after them. I wanted to call out, but there were too many of them to risk detection. Those people were on their own and, as much as I wanted to help, I knew that getting killed wouldn't help them any more than if I minded my own business. Besides, I had my own shit to protect.

Over the next few days, I learned a few things. All clocks had stopped at the same time, exactly 10:27 AM. The same could be said for all other electrical appliances. The city was powerless and deserted. After a day or so, food was getting scarce. Dried goods were still available, but in dwindling quantities, and anything fresh or frozen had long since begun to go bad in the moist heat of a Florida summer. Careful excursions out from my hiding place did not find any other survivors. What I did see were dozens, maybe hundreds, of the walking dead, obviously driven by need or hunger. I didn't wish to get close enough to find out which and whether I would satisfy those needs. I had some food available but, surprisingly, found that I wasn't all that hungry.

After a couple of weeks of my using the restaurant as a base, a young woman broke in. Her hair was filthy and matted to her skull. Her clothing was ripped in places, and she was bleeding from a deep wound raked across her chest.

She saw me and her eyes got wide. "Who are you?"

I emerged from the shadows and heard her gasp as she saw me clearly for the first time. "I've been hiding," I rasped, my throat parched. "My name is Andrew, and you're the first person I've spoken to in over two weeks."

"I've been moving around, avoiding contact with everyone." She extended her hand which I shook. "I'm Teresa, by the way."

"Do you know what's going on?" I asked. I found it hard to speak. My tongue seemed to be glued to the roof of my mouth and, though there was no running water in the restaurant, there was bottled water yet, no matter how much I drank, it could not quench my growing thirst.

Teresa nodded. "It's like something out of a horror movie. Something happened to our world. My husband…" she paused, "my late husband was a scientist. He thought it may have been a magnetic shift. But, of course, that was speculation. Whatever it was changed some people into the walking dead, existing only to feed off the living. One of them caught my husband and drained him down to a husk."

I sat back down. The last few weeks of virtually no physical activity and barely any food was taking its toll. I felt tired and my joints ached. "Look," I suggested, "it's late. Stay here tonight and tomorrow we can look for others. What do you say?"

Teresa nodded her agreement, so I helped her get a couch ready. I went back to my makeshift cot in the back of the restaurant and sat down. I was exhausted, worn out and hungry. Perhaps a decent sleep would do me good.

I awoke feeling much better. No aches or pains. I stood and went to get Teresa. I tried to call her name, but no sound came out. I had an intense thirst and could barely open my mouth. I grabbed a bottle of water, took a deep swallow, only to spit it out. It tasted foul and rancid. I looked at it closely. The water seemed to have a grayish tint to it. Come to think of it, so did everything else in the room. Passing a mirror on my way to where Teresa slept, I caught a glance at my appearance. My hair hung down, dirty and greasy, and seemed to be turning grey to white. Although I am only thirty-seven, it didn't bother me. The skin on my face and hands was all grey and was beginning to flake. I opened my mouth and noticed that any residual color had leeched from my tongue and gums. It was like looking at a partially exposed negative. I thought that this should be upsetting but, instead, I felt quite calm, as if things now made sense.

I found Teresa still asleep on the couch. I went to wake her but found myself drawn to her instead. She seemed to glow or radiate like a beacon, drawing me closer and, almost without thinking, I placed my hand on her forehead. The sensation was electric. I felt alive again as the energy that was Teresa started flowing into me. She opened her eyes and saw me and felt what was happening, yet didn't scream. She smiled, as if in relief of it all being over. The next minute or so was a blur as I fed off her essence and didn't stop until I had drained her of her entire life force. I left her there, a dry, withered corpse. I felt rejuvenated, and more alive than I ever had in life. This feeling was electric and I knew I needed more, and would do what it took to get it.

I heard the voices now, in my head. The voices were all around me. I walked out of the restaurant and stood at the entrance. A little ways down the boardwalk stood a large group of other recent dead. They turned as one and approached me. The one at the front of the group regarded me for a moment and then nodded to me in recognition. I walked over to them and, as a group, we headed off in search of food.

The DRC

It had been a long and exhausting trip. After an eight hour flight aboard Delta to Amsterdam, followed by a three hour layover, Jerry and Allan had boarded the KLM flight to Johannesburg for the final twelve hour leg of their journey. Feeling tired and completely jet-lagged, they passed through customs control and the infrared medical screen. After collecting their bags, they exited the terminal and stepped out into the warm South African air. Jerry breathed in deeply, letting the humid, near-tropical air fill his lungs. It felt denser than the air back home in New England, almost primal.

Welcome to the cradle of civilization, Jerry mused.

The trip was far from over. They had hired a local to take them, via private plane, from Johannesburg to a small, remote airfield into the heart of the DRC. From there, they would travel by car until the roads ran out and, following that, on foot. The route in the Congo was what worried Jerry most of all. The drive alone would be several hours, but the trip on foot could be well over a day in perhaps one of the deadliest jungles on earth. Jerry and Allan had both told their wives that they were going to South Africa for a conference. They knew that neither of their spouses would have approved their going across the world on a treasure hunt.

Their true destination lay deep in the heart of the Congolese jungle in the central part of the Democratic Republic of the Congo. When Jerry's grandfather had given him the map to the hidden African temple while on his deathbed, Jerry was certainly skeptical. Still, his grandfather had been quite lucid and swore that the map was legitimate. He had paid a huge sum for it and, for one reason or another he never had managed to find his way over to the Dark Continent. With his life coming to an end, he wanted to at least die with the knowledge that someone in his family would benefit from the treasure.

Outside the terminal, they met Hans Volker. The man who greeted them was tall, thin and wiry. He had short cropped blonde hair and piercing blue eyes. His craggy face was lean and unshaven and he looked more like a mercenary than a guide. When he spoke, his accent was thick, and sounded almost Australian.

Afrikaans, Jerry thought.

After introductions were made, Volker led the way to his car. He drove them a few miles away to a small airfield where he had a small Cessna 172 Skyhawk parked.

"You got the money, yeah?" Volker asked after they parked the car.

Allan watched Jerry count out twenty thousand Rand. He handed it over to Volker. "Here's half. The rest I give you on the way back."

Volker's eyes narrowed. "That wasn't the arrangement."

Jerry smiled. "Call it insurance that you'll still be around for the ride back."

Volker snatched the money out of Jerry's hands and walked over to the plane. "Let's go then, bra."

Volker climbed aboard the Cessna followed by Jerry and Allan. They sat in the row behind the pilot's chair and watched with idle curiosity as Volker started up the plane and slowly turned it onto the dry and cracked asphalt which served as the runway.

Allan leaned forward. "Excuse me. But how are we going to just fly into the DRC? We don't have Visas and no one checked our passports."

"Listen, the *slapgats* in the Congo don't care about your passport. When we land, I give the bloke at the airfield a thousand Rand and a carton of smokes and he waves us in, yeah? Officially, we've never left Johannesburg." Volker adjusted a dial and pushed a lever forward. The plane started accelerating. "Just sit back and enjoy the ride."

The plane took off without incident. Both Allan and Jerry looked out at the African landscape with curiosity. Neither of them had ever been this far from home before and, now, here they were on the adventure of their lives halfway across the world. Jerry was rather surprised to note that South Africa was actually quite developed and was somewhat reminiscent of Europe in the way the cities were laid out. It wasn't until they were crossing over into the Democratic Republic of the Congo that things were more the way Jerry had always envisaged Africa to be.

Volker, for his part, was silent. He occasionally sipped from a bottle of water or chewed on a piece of biltong, but made no effort to engage the two men in conversation. After a few hours, Volker landed the plane on what looked to be an open field with a small shack at the end. He guided the plane and brought it to a stop by the side of the shack.

A large, stocky black man wearing military fatigues and mirrored sunglasses came out of the shack. Jerry looked on in horror when he saw that the man was carrying a Kalashnikov AK 47.

Volker turned back to the two men. "Stay here, yeah? I'll bribe the *Kaffir* and we can then be on our way." He pulled a small Tokarev pistol from a knapsack and slipped it in his waistband. To hide the gun, he pulled his tee shirt over his pants. He then counted out ten hundred Rand notes and took a carton of Princeton cigarettes. He stepped out of the plane and met the man.

Jerry and Allan watched the two men engage in a very animated conversation. At times, it seemed as if the men were getting nowhere when, suddenly, the large black man broke into a wide grin and shook Volker's hand. Volker handed over the money and cigarettes and the black man gave him a set of keys in return.

"What was that all about?" Allan asked as they were driving away from the airfield.

Volker grinned. "He said that it wasn't enough to be a fair bribe. I promised him more on our return."

"That wasn't part of the deal," Jerry said.

"Relax. We'll make sure to return late in the night when he's likely at home. I have no intention of giving him another Rand."

The three men drove for a few hours, following the river as they went. They passed fewer and fewer signs of civilization and seemed to be getting deeper into the Congolese jungle. The air was heavy and humid and redolent with the smell of vegetation. Their road became nothing more than a pair of rutted dirt tracks which Volker expertly managed.

Volker pulled the car to a stop. Jerry, who had been lightly dozing, looked up. "What's going on?"

"End of the road. We go on foot from here, yeah?"

Jerry and Allan grabbed their packs and followed Volker into the jungle. They walked for hours through the dense brush. Volker frequently had to use his machete to hack their way through. The mid-day sun was beating down on them, making the mid-nineties temperature seem much hotter, especially with the humidity being as high as it was. Jerry was soaked with perspiration and he kept reaching for his canteen. A quick glance over at Allan showed he wasn't faring much better. Only Volker seemed unfazed, whistling an unfamiliar tune as he effortlessly led the way.

Volker stopped and looked back at the two men who were clearly struggling. "You okay, boys?"

"How much further is the temple?"

Volker studied the map and then checked his compass. His took a moment to light a cigarette. "Assuming the map is more or less to scale and everything I've seen here indicates that it is, perhaps another three or four hours."

Allan looked defeated. "Are you sure?"

"Pretty much. We're heading into the heart of the Congolese jungle. It's not like we're heading out to the pub. You boys need a break?"

Both Jerry and Allan nodded wearily. Volker took the time to smoke and check the surrounding area. He started back toward the men when he suddenly broke into a run, grasping his machete as he went. He rushed over to Allan and swung the blade down less than a foot above his head. The men stared in horror as Volker sheared the head off a huge, emerald- colored snake which was suspended above Allan.

Allan jumped back as he got hit with the sprayed blood from the decapitated snake.

Volker grinned and wiped his machete on his trouser leg. "Anaconda. I'd say it measured over fifteen feet. If I'd been a moment slower, it would have dropped down on you and coiled itself about your body. If that had happened, there is a good chance you'd be a goner."

Allan looked at the thick, coiled form that hung limply from the branch above where he'd been sitting, the blood dripping from the ragged stump where its head had once been. "Thanks, Volker. I really hate snakes."

"It's nothing. Come on, guys, daylight is wasting."

Jerry and Allan picked up their packs and trudged after Volker.

The three men walked laboriously through the jungle. The heat and oppressive humidity left them all drenched in perspiration. At times, the insects were so dense they couldn't see more than a foot in front of them. In addition to being bitten more times than they could count, Jerry was sure he had swallowed dozens of the filthy things.

They watched the sun slowly disappearing beyond the horizon. The sky at dusk was filled with bright reds and purples and the encroaching darkness made shadows appear in every corner of the jungle.

"Volker," Jerry complained, "How much further?"

Volker stared at the map. "From my estimate, we should be almost there. Come on, boys."

They pressed on, the jungle growing darker by the minute. Volker pulled out three flashlights from his pack and handed one to each man. The lights cast a welcoming path through the darkened jungle. Volker stopped and shone his light upwards. It illuminated the horrible snake-like visage on a stone carving. Its large obsidian eyes seemed to be staring at them.

"Jesus!" Allan cried out, taking a step back. "What the Hell is that?"

Smiling, Volker pointed his flashlight at the map. The end of the map showed the drawing of a snake next to an 'x'. "I'd say that we're here. According to the map, this is where we find the temple."

"So what's with the snake?"

That statue is symbolic to the cult of the python, although it typically was reserved for the Dahomey, who lived quite a bit to the north of here. Let's camp here tonight and, in the morning, we find our way into the temple and get rich, yeah?"

Jerry looked around. "I don't see a temple here, but I'll trust you. You've gotten us this far."

Morning dawned and the sun cast a welcome light over the jungle. Jerry was the first up and he looked at his copy of the map. Sure enough, the drawing of the snake, while crude, was clearly meant to represent the statue. Next to the drawing of the snake was written:

Kyk binne te vind wat jy soek

Jerry had had the phrase translated when he was given the map. He knew it was Afrikaans and meant 'Look within to find what you seek'. Look within what? Walking over to the statue, he looked up at the face of the snake. It was hideous in appearance and, no matter where Jerry stood the snake seemed to be watching him.

He walked around to the back of the statue and noted what looked like grooves in its back leading all the way up to a fist-sized opening in the back of the statue's head. Wrapping his arms around the stone, he slowly made his way upward. The stone was rough and scaly, and bitterly cold to the touch.

Jerry kept climbing until he reached the top. He looked into the opening at the back of the statue's head but could not see anything through the darkness. He was about to put his hand in when he heard a scream from below.

"Wait!"

Looking down, Jerry saw Volker racing over.

"Why didn't you wake me?"

"What for? I was only checking out the statue."

Volker tossed Jerry his knife. "Jam that in the hole, will ya? It's a lot better than using your hand, yeah?"

Jerry grasped the hilt of the knife and plunged it deep into the hole. He felt it wedge onto something soft, so he pulled back the knife. Attached was a small, greenish snake. It writhed and twisted, hissing furiously. Jerry was about to pull the little snake off the knife when Volker called out, "Let it drop. I'll take it off. These little beasties are very poisonous."

Jerry dropped the knife and Volker stomped the snake to death. He pulled the knife free of the ruined snake and wiped it clean on his pants. He tossed Jerry a flashlight.

"Here, take a look inside."

Jerry shone the light into the hole. "There's a lever in here." He reached his hand into the hole, grabbed the lever and pulled. At the base of the statue, a portion of the ground fell away, leaving a gaping hole into the darkness below.

Jerry climbed down and joined Volker at the opening.

"Good job. You've found the opening to the temple. Go wake your friend. Let's go see what's inside."

While Jerry went to wake Allan, Volker took a length of rope from his pack and tied it around the statue's base. He looked around and found a suitable piece of wood on the ground which he set alight and then dropped down the hole. Watching the light fall lazily into the darkness, Volker counted to himself the time it took for the makeshift torch to hit bottom.

Allan and Jerry joined Volker at the opening. Volker pointed to the torch burning below. "The drop to the temple's floor looks to be about twenty-five feet or so. Unless you boys are experienced climbers, I'd suggest tying the rope around you and lowering you down. Then you untie it and I lower the other guy. Lastly, I climb down and then we explore. That work for you?"

The two men agreed and Volker carefully lowered them down to the temple and followed by easily climbing down after them. All three men shone their flashlights; the beams of light showed the motes of dust swirling in the air, disturbed for the first time in decades. They were in a small room with well-polished stone walls. There was a thick layer of dust on the floor and the air, while cool, was clearly stale and had a sharp and bitter smell to it. The room itself was empty except for a large stone altar near the far wall.

Jerry walked over to the altar, kicking up more of the dust as he walked. The altar was also covered in a thick coating of dust which Jerry wiped away with his hand. He saw that it was made of the same polished stone as the walls and had intricate carvings of serpents on its side. He wiped his hand on his jeans, noticing that the dust felt almost damp and that there seemed to be a sticky residue left on his hand. Between the altar and the wall was a hidden set of stairs which descended further into the earth. Jerry called the other two men over and showed them what he had found.

"I reckon that if they went to this much effort to build such a large underground temple free of prying eyes," Volker began.

"….they had something worth hiding," Allan added, his voice rising in excitement. "Come on. Let's go."

Jerry led the way, holding his light ahead of him to try and maximize the visibility in the darkened temple. Volker went next, followed by Allan. At the bottom, the stairs opened up into a large room with stone benches lined up before a stone pulpit. Passageways led off in the back to the right and left

"Do we split up or go together?" Allan asked.

Jerry smiled. "This isn't a bad horror film, Allan. We'll go together."

They decided to take the passageway on the left. It was wide enough that the three men could walk abreast of each other. They kept their flashlights trained ahead, giving them a good ten feet of light. The carpeting of dust was thicker in the passage and, with each step, caused more of it to be disturbed, making the air even more clogged with airborne dust particles. Jerry began coughing. He had to stop and hack a thick wad of phlegm onto the dusty floor.

"Are you okay?" Allan asked.

Jerry nodded and coughed some more. "I think the dust is getting to me. I've always had asthma, but this is pretty bad. I feel like I have some fluid in my lungs and that it's getting hard to breathe."

"Want to leave and go outside? Volker and I can search the rest of this place."

Jerry shook his head and forced a weak smile. "I'll be fine. I'll just stop for a moment and then catch up."

"Okay," Allan said, only half convinced "You don't have to be a hero. I'm glad to do this for you." He turned and caught up to Volker.

Jerry, meanwhile, looked at his right hand. It was completely red and had small boils erupting all over the palm. Jerry clenched his fist and felt a burning pain shoot up his arm. Raised lines beneath his skin made their way slowly up his arm. Jerry had wanted to tell Allan that something was wrong, but he didn't know what it was and he didn't want to worry his friend. Instead, he found himself feeling more out of sorts as they moved deeper into the temple. He grit his teeth and sprinted to catch up to the others.

The passageway turned to the right and came to an end at a thick wooden door. Volker tried the handle and the door swung easily inward. They shone their lights into the room and froze, utterly speechless. The room was filled with hundreds of desiccated corpses. Most were dressed in rags and all were bound at the arms and legs with old rope or vines. Like everything, they were covered with a thick carpeting of dust.

Jerry made a motion to go into the room, but Volker grabbed him by the shoulder and pulled him back. "You don't want to be going in there. They were tied up for a reason, yeah?"

Jerry looked at Volker and forced a smile. "Thanks. Not sure where my head is today."

"Guys," Allan cried out, "do you see this?" He shone his light on one of the corpses. "That one looks alive."

The men all stared as one of the corpses seemed to shudder. It looked as if it were trying to sit up.

"Got to be some trick of the light," Volker replied. "These guys have been here since before we were born. Nothing could survive for that long." He grabbed the handle and pulled the door shut. "Let's keep this one closed, okay?"

He turned and headed back the way he had come. Allan followed and then Jerry, who kept glancing anxiously behind him, as if expecting something to come bursting out of the room.

They came back to the intersection and followed the passageway on the right. It seemed to mirror the passageway on the left. They followed the corridor as it turned left and came upon a large wooden door. Volker once again tried the handle and, with minimal effort, pushed the door open.

All three men shone their lights into the room and were shocked by its contents.

There was a stone table in the center of the room. On top of it was the largest gemstone any of them had ever seen. It looked like a diamond, but it was a deep cobalt blue. The gem was multi-faceted, easily three feet across, and polished to a mirror-like shine. Unlike the floor, it was completely free of the thick carpeting of dust seen in the rest of the temple.

The walls were lined with shelves and, on each shelf, were several large bowls filled with diamonds, emeralds, rubies, opals and several other stones the men could not identify. Unlike the massive gem on the table, the shelves and stones were also covered in a thick layer of dust. It was a king's ransom in precious stones and was theirs for the taking.

Jerry quietly slipped into the room.

He walked over to the diamond on the table. It seemed to twinkle, even with the dim light in the room from the flashlights.

He put his palm out to one of the gem's facets and felt a surge of energy rush through his body. He threw his head back and emitted a loud scream which built in volume and crescendo.

Allan and Volker ran over to Jerry.

"What's wrong with your boy?"

"I don't know, but it started when he touched the gem stone."

Volker grabbed Jerry by the arm and tried to pull his hand free of the stone. It wouldn't budge.

"C'mon, bra. Help me out here, yeah?"

Allan came over and also grabbed Jerry's arm. The two men pulled but could not pry Jerry from the stone. Suddenly, Jerry stopped his screams and he turned to face the others. His eyes were entirely white and tears of blood streamed down from both eyes. He issued what sounded like a cross between a growl and a roar and backhanded Volker in the jaw, sending him crashing back into one of the shelves, which cracked under the force of his impact, and spilled the dozens of bowls of gems on him as he fell limply to the ground.

Allan took a tentative step backwards. "Jerry? Come on, man. It's me."

Jerry pulled his hand from the gemstone and turned to face his friend. The blood was now pouring freely from his eyes and nose. He looked like he was struggling to speak, but the only sounds he made were low gurgling growls. He took a steady step towards Allan, then another. He slowly raised his arms and growled.

Suddenly, Jerry lunged at Allan, knocking him to the ground. He sat on his chest and put his hand to his face, trying to force his mouth open. Allan took a swing and solidly connected with Jerry's jaw. Jerry shook off the punch as if he didn't even feel it. Allan had been a high school football star and he considered himself to be pretty strong, but could not dislodge Jerry who was several inches shorter and a good forty pounds lighter.

Jerry managed to get Allan's mouth open. He leaned forward so that their noses were nearly touching.

"Get off me," Allan screamed. He saw Jerry's mouth fill with tiny, milky-white writhing worm-like things. One wriggled free of the teeming mass and dropped from Jerry's mouth. Allan fought against Jerry's vise-like grip and managed to turn his head an inch. He felt the worm-like thing land wetly on his cheek. He screamed as it slowly slithered up his face, leaving a burned furrow in his flesh. It then burrowed into his eye and he felt it crawling around behind his eye and into his brain. Jerry leaned forward and the full writhing mass of the creatures fell from Jerry's mouth to land on Allan's face.

Volker got weakly to his feet and ran over to where Jerry had Allan pinned down. Something was wrong with Jerry and, if he didn't get there quickly, Allan would be done for. He took his flashlight and, using it as a club, swung and connected solidly with the side of Jerry's head. Jerry fell off Allan and Volker watched in horror as Allan swiped the mass of worm-like creatures from his face and then stamped them into a milky-white pulpy mess.

Jerry slowly got up and moved awkwardly toward Allan and Volker.

"We need to get out of here!" Allan screamed.

Volker watched Jerry approach. He licked his lips as he looked at the mess of gems scattered across the ground.

"We can't just leave. There's a fortune in gems here."

"You can have them. I'm getting out of here." Allan turned and bolted down the passageway toward the way out.

Volker ran into the room, easily dodging Jerry. He picked up dozens of gems, shoving the emeralds, rubies, diamonds and others into his pockets. Wiping the sticky layer of dust from his hands, he turned to find Jerry standing directly behind him.

"Back off, man," Volker said with a snarl. "I will go through you if I have to."

Jerry cocked his head and leaned forward, as if staring at Volker. His eyes were solid white and, though they still bled, most of it had already dried to a light copper on his face. Small, worm-like creatures could be seen moving beneath the skin of his face.

Volker pulled out his Tokarev pistol and aimed it at Jerry. "I mean it, Jerry. I don't want to hurt you. I like you well enough, but not enough that I won't shoot you if I have to."

Jerry spit a wet mass at Volker, striking him in the face. Several of the milky-white worm-like creatures worked their way across Volker's face. Some started burrowing where they landed, getting in deep under the skin. Others crawled up his nostrils or into his mouth. Volker swiped at the things, but knew he was too late. They were inside him.

"*Fok jy!*" he screamed and fired the Tokarev. He hit Jerry squarely in the forehead and his head burst, sending blood, brains and thousands of the worm-like creatures all over the wall behind him. Jerry collapsed without making another sound.

Volker grabbed some more gems and, with his pockets filled, headed down the passageway after Allan. He raced up the stairs and saw Allan scrambling up the rope and cresting the entranceway to the temple. He looked on in horror as Allan began pulling up the rope.

"Wait!" Volker screamed. "I'm right here. Lower the rope."

Allan looked down at Volker. "I heard the gunshot, Volker. You killed Jerry."

Volker pleaded. "He was *besmet*. He was infected. Whatever it was that was in him took what made him your friend and changed him. Please, Allan. I didn't have any other choice."

"You did!" Allan screamed. "You didn't have to go back for the gems. We could have gotten out and gotten help for him."

"He was too far gone for help." Volker called out. He waited but no answer came. He looked around the room but knew that there was no way he could ever make the thirty foot climb out of the temple without a rope. He suddenly felt a sharp, stabbing pain in his head. It felt like someone was drilling inside his brain. His eyes welled with tears. He would never see his friends or family again. Wiping his eyes with his hands, he saw that his tears were alive with dozens of the small worm-like things. They were inside him and multiplying. He realized that, even if he got out, he could never go home again. He looked at his Tokarev, a gift from a supervisor from his time in the South Africa Secret Service. He wondered if he would be able to make the right choice.

Allan ran through the jungle. He was about a mile from the temple when he heard the gunshot. He didn't know where it had come from, but it made him acutely aware of his surroundings. He was alone in a dense and dangerous jungle without weapons, food or water.

Allan felt a sharp pain in his head, with building pressure behind his eyes. His throat was dry and burned all the way into his lungs. He stopped and made his way to the river he'd been following. He cupped his hand in the water and took a sip, knowing full well that it was likely laden with bacteria. Allan took a second sip and then doubled over and vomited. He watched with horror as hundreds of the worm-like creatures crawled free of his bile, heading off into the jungle.

He staggered forward, following the river. He knew that villages and towns were often built near water. If he could find people, perhaps he might find help. He walked blindly for what seemed like days without stopping to eat or sleep. He didn't even notice when he voided his bladder.

Eventually, the jungle thinned out and he saw signs of settlement ahead. He coughed and tried to remember why he was going there. His head hurt and he found that he couldn't even remember his own name. He took another step and collapsed face down in the river. The worm-like creatures burst free from his body and spread out by the thousands.

Within a week, no one was left alive in the village.

A month after that, every settlement up to Kinshasa was under quarantine, with over fifty thousand reported cases. The government sent in the military to contain the threat.

They were not successful.

Timepiece

The cold wind buffeted against the windows, making them rattle in their frames. Even though the attic was perfectly insulated, Linda shivered and hugged herself, trying to stave off the chill from the brisk fall New England winds outside.

Linda looked over at her husband Sam and smiled. Sam was hard at work going through her mother's things, oblivious to the violent gusts of wind that were raging outside. That was one of the things she liked about him. He was steady and reliable, predictable to a fault, and she wouldn't have it any other way. In appearance, Sam was just average. He stood at perhaps five foot ten, a slim frame that seemed to be showing a bit of thickness around the middle, and calm and gentle features. His brown hair was showing hints of grey and his brown eyes twinkled with intelligence. Of course, these were always well hidden behind the tortoise shell frames that he favored. Still, he was safe. He didn't cheat and he never raised a hand to her. If anything, he treated her like a queen. All in all, Linda felt she had found a real keeper.

Being in her mother's house made the painful memories come flooding back to her. She had always known that she was attractive and, from an early age, had begun getting lingering glances from men both young and old. She was tall and slim, with raven black hair and green eyes, a pale, almost fragile looking complexion and full red lips. *A timeless beauty*, one nice young man at the local church had once said to her mother, and that seemed an apt description. Still, Linda kept far away from men. She never dated and had actively avoided social situations well into in her thirties. She had intimacy issues and, only recently, with a good therapist and Sam's gentle strength had she been able to trust again. She knew her mother was at the core of this dilemma and, when she had moved out at fifteen, she hadn't looked back. Her last words to her mother were in anger and now, well over twenty years past, she still bore the scars from their numerous heated exchanges.

She had tried to let go of the anger, but the minute she had walked through the door into her childhood home, all her mother's betrayals came flooding back from the dark vault of her mind, a hidden place she had kept locked for fear of losing her very sanity.

When she had gotten word of her mother's passing, she was not surprised that she had felt a sense of relief. What surprised her was she also felt a profound sense of loss, as well. Her mother was a monster and, while she was considered a pillar of the community, she had a secret life which far too often dragged her daughter down to its depraved depths.

She held back a tear, hoping Sam wouldn't notice. She did not feel that she could explain it, even to Sam. In fact, it took her mother's death from cancer which had brought her back to the sleepy little Maine community where she had spent her mostly miserable childhood.

Now, with Sam's help, she had the unpleasant task of going through her mother's things, determining which could be sold, and which needed to be thrown out before the home could be put up for sale. Linda's mother had a ton of debt, mostly on large credit card balances, so even with the sale of the home, there wouldn't be that much left. Hardly seemed fair, Linda thought, especially after Jimmy.

"Son of a bitch," Sam blurted out and stuck the fingers of his right hand into his mouth.

"What is it, honey?" Linda asked. Sam never cursed so, for him to swear, something must be wrong.

Sam held up his hand, a thin trickle of blood welling up on his fingertip.

"What happened?" Linda asked.

"I seemed to have cut myself," Sam replied, as he lifted up

a small crystal clock to show his wife, "on this."

Linda suppressed a scream, but still managed to drop the pile of books she had in her hands, causing them to clatter loudly on the wooden attic floor.

It can't be here, Linda thought, *because I know I buried it years ago.*

"It's really a beautiful clock," Sam remarked, turning it over in his hands. The backing was solid crystal, molded like a small triangle. The clock face, made of a darker crystal, was built into the triangle base. The whole thing was set before a small mirror and framed in a thin gold band. "This must be worth quite a bit," Sam added, but frowned slightly and began rubbing the top with his finger. "It seems the top is stained with something, like rust. It's coming off a bit when I rub it with my hands so, maybe when we get home, I can clean this piece properly.

Linda wanted to scream that it wasn't rust as the memories came flooding back.

Her father had died when she was six, the victim of a head-on collision with an eighteen wheeler late one night near Portland. The trucker had been driving under the influence and was sentenced to ten years at the Maine State prison in Thomaston. Linda's father got a pine box. But, then, nobody said life was fair. Years passed and Linda's mother met Jimmy, whom she had married after less than a year of dating. Linda never liked him, and often told her mother so, but her pleas fell on deaf ears as her mother repeatedly pointed out how few eligible men wanted a woman in her thirties with a ten year old in tow, and that they were lucky to have Jimmy.

Linda knew that luck had nothing to do with it. Jimmy was a parasite. His idea of a hard day's work was bellying up to the bar from noon to close. He lived off a meagre inheritance and considered himself to be of society. Linda saw through his bluster and saw him as he truly was. Even worse was that he was also a predator. She saw it in his eyes and feral grin. Linda often felt that he always seemed to be leering at her as if she were nothing more than a piece of meat.

Within six months after her mother's marriage, Jimmy's true nature began to reveal itself. His drinking increased and he became verbally abusive toward Linda and her mother. Had this been the extent of it, Linda felt she could have survived. But then, one night when she was eleven, Jimmy came into her bedroom stinking of beer. Linda awoke with Jimmy's rough hand clasped firmly over her mouth, his face inches from hers, whispering in his alcohol-sodden breath that if she made a sound, or told anyone, that he would not only kill her, but her mother as well. What followed next was the most painful and humiliating experience of Linda's young life. When it was over, she lay on the blood soaked sheets and sobbed herself to sleep.

The next morning, Linda took her stained sheets outside and disposed of them with the trash. She tried to forget what had happened but, in her mind, she relived it again and again. She imagined feeling his rough hands on her and his breath, stinking of meat and beer on the back of her neck. Her mother asked if she was feeling okay at breakfast, and Linda said she was just tired as she glanced over at Jimmy, his ice blue eyes cold and threatening.

"I'm sure she's just having a tough time at school, isn't that right, Linda sweetheart?"

Linda had forced a smile. "I guess, Jimmy." She had to fight to keep the tears from falling.

Later that night, Jimmy came home with a small package for Linda. Inside was a small crystal clock, perhaps a foot high. Even though she didn't want anything from him, she had to keep up appearances and grudgingly accepted the gift. Jimmy went on and on about how the crystal clock had been in his family for generations and was supposed to be a good luck piece. Linda shuddered, not wanting anything from him, but one nervous glance his way convinced her to keep quiet. The way he stared at her with his ice blue eyes made her feel like he could see right through her as if she stood there naked and vulnerable.

"You like it, Linda?"

"Yes, Jimmy. It's beautiful."

Jimmy smiled. "Who loves ya, baby?"

"You do, Jimmy."

Things settled down after that. Jimmy's gift seemed as if it was his way of apology, and the incident from the night before was not repeated. Months passed and life became a tense routine. Jimmy slowly got surlier and surlier as his inheritance got used up and money grew tight. His inability to find work became a glaring point of contention between her mother and him. After a particularly bad day, Jimmy came home and sat at the kitchen table, not saying a word. Linda watched her mother put a dinner plate down in front of Jimmy as well as a cold Budweiser. He drank it down in two long swallows and then grunted for another while he shoveled food into his mouth.

Linda watched her mother bring Jimmy beer after beer. He began slurring his words and making lewd comments to Linda. Wanting no part of it, she got up from her seat and headed to her room.

Jimmy came to her room around midnight that night. Linda had been reading in bed, fully awake, and tried to run. With surprising agility, Jimmy grabbed her by the arm and threw her forcibly to the bed. He climbed on top of her and ripped her tee-shirt open. Linda screamed in terror and fought to cover herself while trying to dislodge her drunken step-father. He flipped her over and grabbed her pajama bottoms, pulling them and her panties down to her ankles.

Linda pleaded with him to stop and screamed for her mother. Jimmy wasted no time in pulling down his own trousers and pulled himself on top of Linda. She felt his breath on the back of her neck as he held her arms down, preparing to violate her.

Linda screamed and thrashed and pleaded with Jimmy to stop. Linda's mother rushed into the room and saw her husband on top of her daughter. Something finally must have snapped because she grabbed the clock that Jimmy had given Linda and slammed it down on top of his head, driving the top point a full inch into his skull. Jimmy shuddered and lay still, dead on the bed with his pants down around his ankles and blood pooling around his head.

The police eventually ruled it self-defense, but life was never the same. It was a small town and word of what had happened quickly spread. Linda knew that her mother was a private person and having their dirty laundry aired for the world to see surely broke her spirit. Linda's mother took to heavy drinking and regularly blamed her daughter for her being alone.

No man will ever have me now, and it's all your fault, you bitch, was a common enough utterance at the house. It was as if her mother had decided to fill Jimmy's absence with alcohol. In addition to verbal abuse, her mother began to physically abuse her daughter as well. There were many days where Linda had to go to school with bruises which drew questions from her teachers. Linda was quick with a cover story and no one ever pressed the issue. Eventually, the drinking got worse, and her mother began to bring men home during the day to help pay for their basic needs.

It was clear that Linda was not wanted and viewed as nothing more than a burden to her mother. It became so bad that Linda's mother eventually left her, at the age of fifteen, with child services complaining that she couldn't afford to keep her. Linda was so glad to be away from the daily torment that she happily went into the system, where she bounced around for the next three years with four foster families, never allowing her to get close to anyone.

"Linda, did you hear me?"

Linda looked at Sam who stared at her with concern. "I'm sorry. I was just woolgathering. There are a lot of memories being back here. Not all of them good ones."

Sam hugged his wife. "I understand. Come on, we've boxed up enough. Let's call it a day."

"I agree." Linda smiled. "Feel like grabbing a bite out?"

Sam nodded.

They returned to the old house at nine thirty, after a great dinner at a small Italian restaurant in town. Everything was homemade and their dinner had been delicious. They finished off two bottles of Chianti and were in good spirits when they pulled into the driveway.

Linda felt the air shift as they walked through the door, and her good spirits evaporated. "Do we have to stay here?"

Sam sighed. "It's only for two nights. We'll have the place boxed up and you can decide what we keep and what we donate."

Linda felt a sense of unease being in the house, but didn't want Sam to think her foolish. It would only be two days, she told herself.

They took the spare bedroom and prepared for bed. Sam leaned in, his hands gently stroking her hip, but she pushed him away. "I'm sorry, Sam," Linda said softly, "but not here. Not in this house, okay?"

Sam sighed and rolled over and was soon fast asleep.

Despite having downed several glasses of wine, Linda found it hard to sleep. She kept rehashing the fights with her mother and how she had been made to feel like nothing for years. After an hour of tossing and turning, she realized she had to go to the bathroom.

Not wanting to wake Sam, Linda quietly climbed out of bed and padded down the hall to the bathroom. The house was cold and she hugged herself as she walked. She sat on the cold toilet and felt relief as she drained her bladder. She turned to flush and thought she saw movement in the hallway behind her.

"Sam?" she called out. Linda peered down the hallway and did not see anyone. She heard footsteps heading downstairs. The old floorboards creaked with each step she took and Linda silently cursed the fact that she was making so much noise.

Why am I so worried, she thought? *It's probably Sam going downstairs for a drink of water.*

Linda quickly descended to the ground floor and saw that there was a light on in the kitchen. She felt a flood of relief. It had to be Sam. She walked into the kitchen and saw that there was a glass on the table half-filled with water and that one of the chairs around the table was pulled back, but there wasn't anyone around.

"Sam? Are you here?"

No answer.

Linda checked the front door and made sure that it was locked. She then checked the back door and the ground floor windows. Each was locked and the house was secure. She was about to head upstairs when she saw the light go off in the kitchen. She ran upstairs and climbed into bed next to Sam. She pulled the blanket up to her neck and lay awake the rest of the night.

Come morning, with the light of the new day, Linda decided against telling Sam about the prior night. He was too level-headed to ever see things that weren't there and she didn't want him to think that the house was having any kind of effect on her.

They climbed up to the attic and found that all the boxes they had packed the previous day had been emptied out over the floor.

"What the Hell?" Linda yelled.

Sam looked around the attic. "We packed these yesterday." He kneeled by one of the boxes and pointed to the ripped tape. "See, the tape was clearly ripped off the box. Who could have done this?"

"I thought I saw someone in the house last night after we had gone to bed," Linda said. "I heard a noise downstairs but, when I got there, the lights were on but the place was empty." She looked around the attic and softly added, "Maybe there was someone in the house, after all."

"It doesn't look like anything was stolen," Sam added. "So, who would want to come in and vandalize things?"

Linda shrugged. "Kids, perhaps? There's no reason for this. Mom wasn't my favorite person, but I don't think there was anyone angry enough at her from town to do this. Let's just clean this up."

They spent the next three hours packing up what they had done the previous day. By noon, they were both hot, sweaty, tired and in low spirits. Sam suggested they break for lunch, and Linda readily agreed.

They went downstairs and heated up the leftovers from the prior night's dinner. They ate in comfortable silence when Sam noticed the crystal clock on the counter next to the stove. "Linda? Did you move the clock down here? I thought I had packed it."

Linda frowned. "No, Sam. I saw you pack it yesterday."

"Then how can it be here in the kitchen?

"I honestly don't know." Linda got up, walked over to the clock and was about to pick it up when she stopped and took a quick step back. "Sam, could you come here please?"

Sam joined his wife by the clock. "What's wrong?"

Linda pointed at the clock. "Look at the minute hand."

Sam stared at the clock. "I'm sorry, but I don't see anything."

"Just keep looking!" Linda screamed. "There. Do you see it?"

Sam looked at the clock in horror and turned to his wife. "Did the hand just move backwards?

Linda nodded. She was feeling sick. The clock was a reminder of Jimmy, and now someone was using it to mess with her. *Who could be doing it and why?* "Throw it out, Sam. Please."

Sam grabbed the clock, dumped it in a bag and took it out to the garbage cans they had behind the house. He came back in to find his wife sitting at the table sobbing.

"Honey, what's going on?"

Linda looked up at her husband. She had kept her secret shame bottled up her entire life. She hadn't told anyone, even Sam. She motioned for him to sit and, when he did, she told him everything. It was as if she had opened the floodgates of her soul and once she started, she could not stop. When she was done, she looked to Sam who had sat there quietly the entire time.

"I'm so sorry, Linda. You should have told me. Come on, let's just leave, okay? We'll pay someone to do this." Linda nodded and hugged her husband.

They returned home and Sam told Linda that he'd handle all the details. Linda thanked him and set about preparing for work the next day. She was a financial planner who worked in the city and needed to get up early. Sam was a software engineer and worked mainly from home. Having Sam handle the details was a godsend and Linda was once again reminded of how lucky she was to have had found a man like Sam.

Linda came home from work after a long day and was looking forward to one of Sam's wonderful home cooked meals. He had a great touch in the kitchen and loved to cook, for which Linda was eternally grateful. She had never acquired basic skills in the kitchen and, had she not met Sam, she would have continued on her steady diet of take-out. She walked through the front door and found all the lights out.

"Sam?" she called. She wondered if he had gone out. Usually he called or at least texted, but she hadn't heard anything. She turned on the hall light and walked into the kitchen which was also dark. She turned on the kitchen lights and saw that the oven was cold to the touch and nothing was on the stove. *That's odd,* she thought, *Sam always has dinner ready, even if he has plans for the night.*

Linda walked into the den and saw that it, too, was empty. She felt a moment of panic. Could something have happened to him? She climbed the stairs to the upper level. "Sam, are you home?" she called out. Again there was no reply. The upstairs was dark, as well. She checked the bedrooms and found all were empty. She walked to Sam's office and noticed a thin sliver of light under the door.

Linda tried the door and found it locked. "Sam, are you in there?"

"Go away, Linda. I'm working."

"Is everything okay?"

"I'm fine. I'm just really busy and have some deadlines to meet."

"I'm going to pick up a pizza, Sam. Would you like some?" She waited for a response and, when none came, she stormed down the stairs and left the house. She ended up getting a large pie, just in case Sam wanted some. She ate dinner alone and watched television, hoping that Sam would decide to come down and join her. At eleven, she went upstairs to bed.

She awoke next morning and saw that Sam's side of the bed was undisturbed. *Did he really stay in his office all night?* Linda got ready for work and headed to the door of Sam's office.

"Sam, I'm leaving. When I get home, I think we should talk." Sam didn't answer and Linda left for the office.

She spent a rough day, not being able to focus on her work. In the years she had spent with Sam, he had never been so abrupt with her as he had the previous night. She hoped it was just stress and deadlines. Either way, she fully expected to discuss it at home after work.

Linda got home that night and found that, once again, the house was dark. She made a beeline for Sam's office and found that, once again, the door was locked.

"Sam, open the door!" she demanded.

"I'm working. I told you not to disturb me."

"Damn it, Sam. What the Hell is wrong with you? Can you open the door so we can talk?"

"I said go away."

Linda pounded on the door. "I'm not leaving until you open the door."

She heard movement and the door swung open. Sam looked disheveled, with a two- day growth of stubble and unkempt hair. He was wearing the same clothes that he had been wearing since they had left her mother's house.

"There," he said dryly, "I opened the fucking door. Can I go back to work?"

"What's going on, Sam? We're a partnership. We don't keep secrets from each other. Something is clearly wrong. You don't act like this."

He exhaled sharply. "Nothing is wrong. I have a lot of work and little time in which to do it. Standing here arguing with you is time taken away from my work." He stepped back and slammed the door, leaving Linda standing there in shock.

Fuck him, she thought. *Men are such children.* She went downstairs and heated up the leftover pizza from the night before. She wondered if he had even eaten since he had locked himself in his office. She found that she was so upset, she didn't even care. Linda tried watching television, but she couldn't focus. She was too distraught. She ended up going to bed early.

Linda was awakened by Sam climbing on top of her and pulling off her tee-shirt. He then grabbed her panties and yanked them down. She tried to push him off, wanting nothing to do with him sexually after his poor behavior the last two days. With a strong grip, he held her face down on the bed, his hand on the back of her neck. He forcibly entered her and thrust until done, oblivious to her sobbing into the pillow. Sam then climbed off her and silently left the bedroom. Linda listened to his footsteps walk down the hall and the door of his office slam shut.

The bastard, she thought.

The next day, Linda left in the morning but did not drive to the office. She drove around the corner, instead, and walked back to the house. She slipped in through the back door and quietly made her way up the stairs and headed for the bedroom. She stood under the fire alarm, took a lighter and held the flame close to the alarm. Within minutes, the fire alarm went off, the wailing filling the house. Linda waited in the bedroom and kept watch on the office door at the end of the hall.

Ten minutes later, as expected, the doorbell rang. The town was small enough that if there ever was a fire, the response would be quick. The office door opened and Sam shambled downstairs to answer. Linda took the opportunity to hurry down the hall to Sam's open office. She stepped inside and froze.

There were dozens of pictures of her taped to the walls from when she was a pre-teen. In most of the pictures, she was sleeping. In some, she wore pajamas; others, she was fully undressed. What caught her eye, though, placed in a position of reverence atop the bureau, was the crystal clock.

"I guess the cat's out of the bag, eh Linda?"

Linda turned around to see Sam standing there. He looked as if he hadn't slept or eaten in a week. His hair was greasy and messy. He reeked of alcohol and swayed slightly, leaning against the doorframe to keep him steady.

Linda rushed him and managed to run down the hall and lock herself in the bedroom. Sam came running after and kicked the door open. She froze when she saw him clutching the crystal clock in his right hand. He slowly advanced toward her.

"Please, Sam. Whatever is wrong, we can work this out together."

He leaned in close. "Who loves ya, baby?" His ice blue eyes twinkled with anticipation. As he swung the crystal clock, the last thing she thought before everything went dark was how she always believed that Sam's eyes were brown.

The Congregation

Baruch atah, Adonai, m'chayeih hakol (hameitim)
Blessed are You, God, who gives life to all
(revives the dead)
- from the weekday t'filah, prayer Siddur

Cantor Steven Katz slowly stepped up to the podium, the ark for the Torah closed tightly behind him. He clutched the neck of his classic Martin acoustic guitar, fingers naturally loose over the strings as he surveyed his congregation. It was the smallest congregation yet, although the recent virus that was sweeping through the country was surely the cause of such a low turnout. People who were sick stayed home and, sadly, so did many who feared getting sick by being exposed to those who were infected. Plus, there was the danger to consider. Families either tried to flee to somewhere safe or stay put in their homes, hoping for the government to come in and bring order back to things. Still, it was the Shabbat and, even in these trying times, there was a need to bring together what was left of the congregation and give prayer to God.

Katz took a handkerchief from his pocket and wiped the perspiration from his forehead. It was cloyingly hot in the stuffy hall, although he should be grateful that it wasn't worse. The month of May had been seasonally cool so far, for which he was thankful. Power had been out for the last two weeks and there seemed little hope of it being restored. Between the long lines at the supermarket, the rationing of groceries, and the uncertainties at the gas station, running their pumps on emergency generators, life had become far more difficult. Many people had stopped going to work, with survival for themselves and their families taking top priority.

The members of the congregation looked up at the Cantor expectantly. Rabbi Glickstein hadn't shown up in over a week, and Katz assumed that he had either fled, gone into hiding, or had come down with the virus and was beyond God's help. With the phones down and the power out, the only means of communication was the old fashioned way – you needed to actually visit in person. Of course, people were afraid and rightly so. The number of sick was rapidly escalating and no one seemed to know what was causing the increase. All people knew was that once infected, you eventually came down with the virus. Hoping to try and slow the spread of infection, the CDC had warned people to wear surgical masks and gloves and avoid as much human contact as possible. That was two weeks ago, before the power went out. Now, all people had to go on was idle speculation, and they were afraid.

As long as the Rabbi was unavailable, Katz assumed double duties. He conducted the service and maintained his responsibilities as Cantor. The good members of the congregation who still came to service seeking solace and comfort in these times of need looked to the Rabbi and, by default, the Cantor to be their spiritual leader. People came to synagogue so they could be closer to God when they prayed. It helped them forget that the life they once knew was slowly spiraling down the drain.

Cantor Katz tapped the microphone, more out of habit than anything else. He looked at the lit candles on the podium and around the hall and the scared and expectant faces and it saddened him that things had gotten so bad so quickly. Still, it was his job to bring the word of God to his congregation and to bring joy to the people through songs of prayer.

"My friends," Cantor Katz began, "Rabbi Glickstein will not be here again today, so I will be conducting the morning services." He looked out over the congregation, noting friends and neighbors. Many of the congregation had been coming to Temple Emmanuel for many years and Cantor Katz knew them on a personal basis. "Please open your *Siddur* to page 23."

Cantor Katz began reading in Hebrew and paused when it required a response from the congregation. He spoke for another five minutes, then asked the congregation to turn to page 51, to the hymn *Aleinu*. He plucked a few notes, and then began strumming his guitar in earnest. Cantor Katz had a rich Bel Canto baritone and it reverberated through the hall as he began to sing. The congregation joined in and soon the room filled with the rich melodies of the tune. Cantor Katz felt his eyes well up with tears as the congregation sang with all their hearts, their voices filled with their inner strength. They were a people who had had an eternity of suffering and yet they had refused to give up. No matter what trials they faced, he knew that his people would overcome.

The song ended and he strummed a few more notes, choosing an upbeat ending, a joyous chord to lead the congregation into his hastily prepared sermon.

"Friends," the Cantor began, "our numbers grow smaller with each passing day. The virus has ravaged not only our community, but the entire country as well. Conservative estimates project that perhaps five, maybe ten, percent will find themselves immune to the virus. Unfortunately, that means ninety to ninety-five percent of people will get sick. According to the CDC, all of them will die and then turn. It's a horrible thing to contemplate, but we must face facts and be strong for the survival of our people. It's through times like these that the Lord does test us and see if we are worthy. My friends, looking out at all of you, I can say that we are."

There were murmurs from the congregation. Katz's words were strong and carried in the great hall. He put his guitar down, leaning it gently against the podium. He turned to face the Ark. No matter how many times he opened the Ark and read from the *Torah*, he always got a chill. Reading directly from the *Torah*, the holiest of books always made him feel closer to God. It had been like that since the age of thirteen when he had read from the *Torah* on his bar mitzvah in an ancient synagogue in Haifa.

He swore he heard angels singing with him that day. Here it was, nearly thirty years later, and he still felt closer to God when he read the holy passages.

Cantor Katz opened the left side of the Ark, then the right. He reached in and gently lifted the Torah. He pulled the cover off and reverently placed it on the podium. He put on his reading glasses and began singing the selected text. When done, he covered the *Torah* once more and returned it to its place in the Ark. He then closed both sides and silently returned to the podium.

"God is with us on this day," Cantor Katz began, "as he is on every other day. Our faith must be stronger than ever when we face rough times like these."

The door to the hall suddenly burst open, revealing a man in the doorway. His hair was in complete disarray, looking filthy and knotted. His clothes were torn, covered in grime and hung on his now gaunt form. His face was ashen grey and covered with a thin sheen of perspiration. What stood out, though, were his eyes. They were bloodshot and rheumy, but also filmy, and looked as if his vision had faded.

Cantor Katz stared at the man and, even with the dramatic change in his appearance, he could easily tell that it was Rabbi Glickstein.

"David," Katz called out, hoping that his old friend hadn't turned, "are you okay?"

Rabbi Glickstein began a slow and awkward walk toward the Cantor at the podium. He moved slowly and stiffly and Katz took an involuntary step back. Glickstein was clearly infected.

Harry Miller, a member of the congregation, reached out from his seat and patted Glickstein on the shoulder. Glickstein turned and lunged at the man with a savage ferocity. He slammed him into his seat then leaned forward and bit into the man's neck, tearing a huge chunk out of his throat. Blood sprayed all over the people around them. They started to scream and scrambled over the pews trying to get as far away from the Rabbi as possible. Edna Hirsch was sitting next to Harry Miller and, as she turned to get away, she tripped over a small boy, causing them both to fall hard.

Cantor Katz grabbed the microphone stand and swung it down hard on Rabbi Glickstein's head. The Rabbi stopped tearing the flesh from Harry Miller's neck, looked up at Katz with red- rimmed eyes and snarled. Blood and tissue were smeared over the Rabbi's face as he leaped at Katz. The Cantor swung the microphone stand as hard as he could and connected squarely with Glickstein's chin, sending him flying backwards into the pews.

Having a moment to catch his breath, he saw that people were still rushing out of the hall and into the lobby. Katz grabbed his guitar, more from sheer habit than anything else, and followed his congregation. He kept a watchful glance at Glickstein who was slowly getting back to his feet.

Cantor Katz ran into the lobby and saw the congregation standing there looking outside through the glass double doors. One of the men, Charlie Rosen, was taking the *tallit* and using them to tie the doors shut. Katz nearly froze when he saw why. Outside the glass doors were several dozen of the infected, each one recently turned. He knew that the situation was bad, but the military had still been in control when he had left for synagogue that morning.

"People," Cantor Katz called out, "we can't stay here. The infected are at our door and we are drawing their attention. Come on. Let's go back to the sanctuary. We can barricade the doors there if things get out of hand."

There was a murmur of assent and the congregation slowly followed the cantor back to the hall. Katz was about to go back in when he remembered that Rabbi Glickstein was still in there. He stopped and held up his hand, indicating that they should all stop.

"The Rabbi should still be in there," Katz said, his voice barely above a whisper. "We will need to address this." He pointed to Charlie Rosen, Neil Smith, and Fred Kleiner and motioned for them to come over.

With the men assembled, Katz laid out his plan. The men nodded in unison and, although grim and horrified, their families' lives were far more important. The men slowly crept into the hall and tried to use the pews as cover to keep their location a secret from Rabbi Glickstein. They needn't have worried as he was still bent over Harry Miller, scooping sections of his entrails and shoving them down his throat.

The Cantor grabbed a folding chair from the back and motioned for the other men to do the same. They then crept up on the Rabbi and Katz lifted the chair high and sent it crashing down on the Rabbi's skull. He was followed by each of the men. Katz was about to make a second swing with the chair, but saw that the Rabbi's skull was caved in and that he was no longer moving.

The Cantor grabbed the Rabbi by the collar and pulled him out toward the lobby. He indicated that one of the other men do the same for Harry Miller's body. The other two men then ushered the rest of the congregation back to the great hall.

While people were getting settled, Katz ran down to the kitchen and found two loaves of *challah* which were still edible. He grabbed the bread and a gallon jar of water and hurried back to join the congregation.

Everyone was inside the hall and either seated or milling about. Several small pockets of conversation were in progress. Cantor Katz caught snippets of each and saw that they were all along the same lines, either about survival, family or concern over what to do next. He closed and locked the door near the Ark and one of the two double doors leading to the lobby.

"Everyone, please gather round," the Cantor called out. People stopped what they were doing and looked up expectantly. He was the de facto leader of their small group which, at quick count, numbered close to twenty. "I brought some challah and some water. We will need to wait it out and I'd like to start by offering something to eat and drink to the children who are here with us."

"What do you mean by 'wait it out'?" Edna Hirsch asked.

Cantor Katz tried to appear as calm as possible for the sake of the children. "We need to wait here and hope that the turned lose interest and leave. If they don't see us, and we're reasonably quiet, there is a good chance that they will forget that we are here and wander elsewhere."

"And what if they don't just wander off?" Adam Berlin added.

"I honestly don't know. Let's cross that bridge when we come to it."

"The army will restore order," Charlie Rosen's wife, Sheila said. "They wouldn't just abandon us."

"I think that ship has sailed, dear," Charlie answered his wife and put his arm around her shoulder. "I trust Cantor Katz. Let's see if the turned lose interest and simply walk away."

The Cantor smiled. These were good people who were up-standing members of their community. Most of them were very active at the synagogue and Katz had built a relationship over the years with all the families. "Okay, let's get the children some challah and some water and we can then tell stories and sing songs to help pass the time."

The mothers helped get the children some food and Katz noticed that, even though they were clearly terrified, they kept a brave face for their kids and tried to make their situation seem fun.

The fathers took turns watching the open door to the lobby for any more surprises and occasionally peered out at the crowd of turned outside. They noticed that, as the day grew, more and more of the turned found their way to the outside of the syna-gogue. Many of them were clawing at the glass in an attempt to get in.

By nightfall, the congregation was starting to get restless. Looking outside, the number of turned had increased to well over a hundred and more seemed to be coming every minute. Many of the children were crying and were asking to go home. Their parents did what they could to comfort their kids, but were feeling the stress of the situation themselves. Katz had passed around one of the challahs to the parents and, before long, both loaves were gone. It was nowhere near enough food for twenty people and if they were going to be stuck there for an extended period of time, things would get ugly pretty quickly.

Fred Kleiner and his wife Sophie came over to where the Cantor was sitting. "It doesn't look good, Steven. I know that you've been the glue holding this congregation together over the last month, but things are falling apart."

Cantor Katz looked at his old friend Fred and his wife, two people he'd known for many years. "What do you want me to say, Fred? You want me to say that everything will be fine? I can do that. You want me to put on a brave face for the kids? Sure, I got that. If you want the truth, I think we're in a lot of trouble. We have no food and no way out. I had hoped that the turned would lose interest and leave. There were too many of them for us to leave before. Now, it's even worse. If you have any suggestions, I'd sure like to hear them."

"No one blames you, Steven," Sophie said softly. "I think what Fred is trying to say, in his own roundabout way, is we are thinking of leaving"

"Leaving? How would you get away?"

Fred sighed. "We don't expect to. There are too many of them outside. We can't get past them. There's no food here. At least when we do step outside, it will be quick."

"No. I can't condone your own suicide, and I can't allow you to leave. There's no guarantee that the turned will not get in when you try to leave. Your actions could condemn all of us to a painful death."

"Damn it, Steve," Fred hissed, "we're all already dead. This is it, the endgame. If there are this many of the turned outside, it means that the military has either been overrun or has pulled out. We've all been left to die."

"Choosing when the others die is not up to you, Fred," Katz growled. "My job is to keep them safe as long as I can."

"I checked, Steven," Sophie added. "There are only a few around the back door. We can easily get out, and ensure that none of the turned gets in.

150

"I won't allow it." The Cantor looked defeated. "I'm sorry, but I have to consider the other families' welfare too."

Fred and Sophie got up and walked away without another word. They sat down next to the Weiss's and whispered something to them, looking back at Cantor Katz. He felt terrible for having to refuse his old friends, but he was an eternal optimist. He still held out hope for a positive outcome to their dilemma.

The Cantor stood up and left the hall. He wandered down the corridor to the back of the synagogue. He stepped into the library and looked out the windows. A dozen or so of the turned were milling about. Further down, he walked past the kitchen and small hall and saw several dozen of the turned clawing and hammering at the back door. They noticed Katz and seemed to get worked up, scratching and pounding at the back door with a renewed ferocity. Katz frowned. If the Kleiners tried to get out from the back, it was a given that several of the turned would get in.

Katz made his way back to the great hall. He stopped in the lobby just outside the door and saw that there were now perhaps two hundred or more of the turned out front. Their constant pressure on the front glass was taking its toll as the glass was beginning to crack in several places. He knew it was only a matter of time. With a heavy heart, he walked back to the great hall and closed the doors.

Cantor Katz looked around the room and was surprised to see everyone looking at him expectantly.

"Is everything okay?" Janet Cohen asked.

Canto Katz shook his head. "Everyone," he began, "I looked outside from windows at both the front and back of the synagogue. The news is not good. We have hordes of the turned around the windows and the rear entrance. If we try to get out that way, I can guarantee that many of us will not make it. Even if we were to get by the dozens of turned in the back, we have no idea what the streets are like around here. If you've seen the front, you know that there are hundreds of them outside, pushing at the glass doors. From the condition of the cracks in the glass, it's only a matter of time before the glass gives way and they get in. So, we need to make a decision as a group as to what we do next."

"Can we stay here?" Sheila Rosen asked.

"That is an option," the Cantor replied. "Please understand that, sooner or later, they will break through the glass on the front doors. Can we barricade ourselves in here? I think so, but we have no food and very little water."

"So what are the other options?"

"We try to make a run for the cars. Of the twenty of us, there is a good chance that many of us won't make it. That said, if we wait any longer, we may not have the option to leave."

"I say we leave," Fred Kleiner said. "You heard the Cantor. If we wait any longer, we might not get another chance."

"We have kids here," Ellie Smith added. "We're staying."

Everyone had an opinion and it seemed as if neither side would sway the other. Cantor Katz finally put his hands up to get the congregation's attention.

"I've listened to all of you, and I'm going to throw out a suggestion. It might not be perfect, but it's the best we have right now." Katz walked up the three stairs and stood before the Ark. "I won't leave as long as a single member of my congregation stays. Since The Smith, Rosen and Cohen families all wish to stay, that is twelve people whom I have sworn to watch over and guide, that means I'll be staying. That said, the Kleiners, Hirschs, Berlins and Kathy Miller all want to go. They will make a break for it by going out the back window, where there are the lowest number of the turned, and run for their cars. Those who make it will send help for those of us who have stayed behind. I will go to the back door and try to draw the attention of the turned away from the window. Anyone have any questions?"

Everyone seemed to be lost in their thoughts. Those who were leaving hugged those who were staying and promised to send help as soon as they could. Cantor Katz walked with the seven members of the congregation who had opted to leave and showed them the back window in the library. A dozen of the turned were seen nearby.

"Okay, everyone," Katz said, "Wait until you hear me yell. That will attract the turned and get their attention. When you see them moving toward the back door, make a break for the cars."

The Cantor hurried to the back door and was shocked to see the number of turned had more than doubled since he last had looked. He started to pound on the door and scream as loud as he could. He found that the turned seemed to sense his presence and were whipped up into a violent frenzy. They slammed their hands down on the door with more force than Katz had seen earlier. They leaned in, pushing their faces directly to the glass. Katz recognized some of the turned as members of his congregation. They looked unnatural, with- red rimmed eyes, sallow skin and slack jaws. Many of them had dried, smeared blood all over their faces.

The turned clawed and scratched at the door while Katz made as much noise as possible. He saw the Kleiners run past, heading for the parking lot. They were closely followed by the Berlins, Kathy Miller, and the Hirsch's who were bringing up the rear.

The Cantor watched as the Kleiners reached their car. Before they could get the door open, they were swarmed by dozens of the turned who came from the woods at the side of the parking lot. The turned tore the Kleiners to shreds while Katz looked on with horror. He ran to the library and screamed out the window to warn the others. Many of the turned who were at the back ran to join the attack. They joined the other turned who cut off the Berlins and Kathy Miller. The Berlins fought as hard as they could before they were eventually pulled down and pulled apart. Kathy Miller just fell to her knees and was lost under dozens of the turned.

The Hirsch's had been further back and turned around, deciding to make their way back to the synagogue. They ran for the library window, with dozens of the turned right behind them. Edna Hirsch reached the window and, as she climbed through, saw her husband pulled back. She screamed as three of the turned tore into him, ripping huge chunks from his legs, chest and arms. Edna screamed for her husband and started to climb back out when Cantor Katz grabbed her by the ankles and pulled her back into the library.

"It's too late!" he screamed as he slammed the window down.

Edna Hirsch curled up in the corner sobbing as the turned violently slammed their hands against the window. Katz tied to help her get to her feet but she refused to move.

"Edna, please," he said as gently as he could, the pounding on the glass getting more frenetic. "We need to go back to the hall. The turned will get through any minute."

"I don't care, Steven," she sobbed, "what's the point?"

Cantor Katz gritted his teeth and grabbed Edna by her arm. "Listen to me. Your husband would not want you to lie down and give up. We need to go now."

Edna wiped her eyes and slowly got to her feet. She nodded, but refused to meet the Cantor's eyes. As he led her out of the library, he saw the turned shatter the window. It was only minutes before they would be overrun.

Katz rushed Edna Hirsch back to the hall and saw the look of concern on everyone's faces. "Shut the doors!" he screamed. When no one reacted, he rushed to the door and slammed it shut. He grabbed the edge of one of the pews and began dragging it toward the door. "A little help, people," he called out.

Charlie Rosen and Neil Smith ran over and the three of them quickly pulled the pew in front of the door. They ran back to get another and stacked that one on top of the first.

"What's happening?" Janet Cohen asked. "What happened to the other families?"

"They didn't make it," the Cantor said grimly. "And the turned have gotten in."

The mothers went over to comfort their children who were clearly petrified.

"Is there anything we can do?" Neil Smith asked. "We can't just sit here and wait to die."

Cantor Katz was about to respond when they heard a loud crash from outside the door, followed by a chorus of wails and moans. "Dear God," he said, "they've gotten through the front door."

Within moments, a furious pounding was heard at the doors to the hall. There were clearly hundreds of the turned outside the door as the incessant pounding was starting to cause the thick wooden doors to buckle and crack. The children started to scream and several were crying. Their parents comforted them the best they could as the noise at the doors grew louder.

The Cantor looked at the last thirteen members of his congregation and knew that they would not survive the night. He wiped away a tear, feeling a profound sense of loss for the lives that were already taken and those who held on so tenuously to hope. He climbed the steps to the Ark and picked up his guitar and turned to his congregation.

"Can I have everyone's attention, please?" he had to yell out to be heard over the hammering at the doors. Everyone turned, their eyes wide with shock when they saw their Cantor standing there with his guitar.

Cantor Katz strummed a few chords and, then, with a rich and soulful voice started singing *Yistabach*. After a few lines, others from the congregation joined in. It wasn't long until the entire remaining Temple Emmanuel congregation was singing. When the song was over, there wasn't a dry eye in the hall.

Cantor Katz noticed something else. The pounding at the door had stopped. He looked around and slowly started to walk to the doors. It was so quiet, like the calm before the storm. He reached the door and, just as he was about to put his ear to the door, the noise outside resumed.

He picked up his guitar and played a few chords. The hammering at the door did not abate. Suddenly, it all made sense. He started playing *Y'did Nefesh* and sang with all his heart and, once again, heard that the noise outside the door had stopped.

Motioning to his congregation to join him at the door, Cantor Katz stopped playing. "Do you see?" he told those assembled around him. "The word of God is given through song and prayer. As long as we sing our hymns, we can get out. Come on, help me move the pews. I'll then start singing and we can walk to our cars in safety."

The growls outside the doors from the turned started up again. Their clawing and pounding at the doors was growing more frantic. The wood cracked in several places. No one from the congregation moved.

Sheila Rosen looked imploringly at the Cantor. "If you're wrong," she said, her voice trailing off.

"I know," he sighed. "But if we stay here, we meet the same fate. God has always told us that He helps those who help themselves. You have to trust me."

Without another word, Neil Smith and Charlie Rosen rushed to the door and pulled back the pews. They returned to their families and waited for the Cantor to lead them once more in song.

Cantor Katz started singing *Shiru Lashem*, and indicated for Charlie to open the door. Outside, in the lobby, the turned stood there, swaying slightly to the music, but otherwise unmoving and not making any overt moves in their direction.

The congregation started singing and followed the Cantor as he walked out of the great hall and into the lobby. Families clustered together and they made their way quickly to the front door. They kept singing as they walked outside and through the parking lot, weaving their way through the hundreds of the turned.

They made their way to the cars and the Cohens, Rosens and Smiths all ushered their families in. The Smiths helped Edna Hirsch in with them.

"Please come with us," Janet Cohen begged the singing Cantor, "We have lots of room in the SUV for you."

Cantor Katz smiled, but sadly shook his head. "My place is here. God be with you."

With tears in her eyes, Janet Cohen rolled up her window.

They drove slowly out of the parking lot, maneuvering around the turned. The Cohens were followed by the other two cars.

Once alone, Katz started singing *Aleinu*, one of his favorite songs ever since he had been a child. He sang with all his heart as he walked back into the temple. He walked back to the great hall and sat before the Ark. He finished singing and gently put down his guitar. He was one with his God and felt at peace with the world. He closed his eyes and heard the turned starting to stir. He smiled and embraced his destiny full of hope.

Heart's Desire

"Please let me see your face once more again"
– Dreamtale, *Heart's Desire*

He stands at the edge of the woods, his heart pounding in his chest with anticipation. The moonlight casts a pale yellow hue, clearly reflected off the sheen of perspiration on his forehead. His right hand firmly clutches a large axe which is covered in dried blood all over the blade and down the shaft. In his left hand, he holds a large burlap sack which contains five freshly severed heads, black candles, a two-pound bag of salt and various other sundries required for the ritual. It also contains an ancient tome, the pages yellowed and stiff with age.

The book...

The man remembers it all, as if it had happened yesterday. It had all started with Callie. He first had seen her in his class on developmental psychology at Southern New Hampshire University. He had noticed her the moment she walked in. Time seemed to slow down as he watched her, her movements a mixture of innocence and raw unbridled sexuality. She was slim with shoulder length wavy brown hair that moved as if caressed by a gentle breeze. She had big green eyes, a small, pert nose, and rich full lips. Her skin was pale, almost alabaster, with a faint touch of pink, lending her an air of gentle fragility. When he thought of her, he knew that she was the epitome of perfection.

He found that he could not focus on the lecture and knew he had to speak to her after class. After class ended, he found her and, in his own awkward way, managed to ask her out; to his surprise, she accepted. Their first date was dinner at a local bistro followed by a few too many drinks. Each of them agreed that it was the best date either of them had ever had. One date led to another and, for the next six months, they were inseparable, hitting every restaurant and watering hole in town. It seemed as if the party would never end.

And then things went to Hell.

One night, after a great meal at a new restaurant in Boston's North End, they made their way to Faneuil Hall for drinks at the Black Rose. The band was one of the best they'd seen in a long while and, before they knew it, it was closing time.

They drove home and made it back to Hudson, New Hampshire without incident. A mile from home, the car came to a stop on Route 111.

"Shit." The man punched the dashboard and cursed again.

Callie put a hand on his shoulder. Her touch always managed to calm him when he seemed about to fly into a raging fit of anger. "What's wrong?"

He gripped the wheel and took a few minutes before answering. "We're out of gas. Son of a bitch! How could I have forgotten to fill up?"

Callie gently took his arm. "It's okay. We can walk. It's not that far."

He slammed his fist into the dash once more. "I'm not leaving the car."

"Please, honey. I just want to go home. Besides," she said with a small grin, "I have to pee and there are no places open at this hour."

"Then you go. I'm not leaving my car here."

"Kirk, please just come with me."

"Damn it, Callie. I'm not leaving my new car by the side of the road here. God knows what will happen to it."

Callie got out of the car without another word and slammed the door as hard as she could. Without a backward glance, she started walking.

Kirk watched her walk away. Even mad as Hell, he couldn't take his eyes off her ass as she walked. He was about to go after her when he saw a car come barreling down the road toward him. The car was going well above the speed limit and swerved slightly, scraping against the side of his car.

The car sped on, weaving as it drove. Kirk got out of his car and saw Callie far ahead down the road, clearly lost in her thoughts. He called out to her, and started running in her direction, screaming her name as he ran.

Callie turned in time for the car to slam into her, flipping her like a rag doll, first onto the hood, then against the windshield, before she fell off to the side of the road. The driver swerved after impact, then straightened his vehicle and drove off, leaving Callie lying in a crumpled heap by the side of the road.

Kirk burst into a run, but it was too late.

Ten minutes later, a couple coming home from Logan airport found Kirk lying across Callie's body sobbing uncontrollably. The police officer ruled it a hit and run and put out an alert for the car and driver. He told Kirk that the impact of the car's hitting Callie would have caused considerable damage to the vehicle and that all body shops within a hundred mile radius would be notified to keep an eye out for the car. He swore that they would get the prick. Kirk nodded, but it was small consolation. They wouldn't get Callie back, no matter what they did.

Kirk withdrew into himself. He dropped out of school, cut ties with all friends and family, and then spent the next year wandering around the country, stopping briefly in various towns to hold down odd jobs which would allow him to survive. Try as he might, he could not overcome the guilt of Callie's passing. He started to drink heavily to numb the pain, but nothing worked. Thoughts of suicide were his constant companion.

One day, nearly two years after Callie's death, Kirk found himself in Los Angeles. He had been living on the streets and was turning tricks on Sunset Boulevard to earn enough to keep him drunk. It was early morning and he was restless, so he began to wander the streets. Down a small side road, he saw an old occult bookstore and, though he hadn't read a book in two years, he had once been an avid reader. The sky was getting dark and Kirk felt the first cold drops of rain hit his skin. He had nothing else to do and wanted to keep dry, so he decided to go in, hoping that the shopkeeper wouldn't throw him out the moment he laid eyes on him.

Kirk walked in and passed a counter where an old man looked at him suspiciously. The air was thick with dust and he noticed that it seemed to be clinging to him like a second skin. Kirk nodded at the man and began to browse the shelves, making it look like he was a potential customer. The shopkeeper followed Kirk to the back of the store. He noticed that the shopkeeper was much older than he initially appeared, with sallow leathery skin. The man's hair was wispy and thin, snow white in color and fell loosely about his shoulders. His greyish eyes twinkled and seemed to be evaluating Kirk.

"Can I help you?" he asked, his voice soft and dry, and barely above a whisper. The shopkeeper smiled, exposing small, but oddly elongated, yellowed teeth.

"Uh, no thank you," Kirk replied. "I'm just browsing."

The shopkeeper kept smiling. "We all browse until we find what we need."

"And what do I need?"

"Why, your heart's desire of course."

Kirk paused. "And what do you know of my heart's desire, old man?"

The shopkeeper laughed. It was a cold laugh, devoid of any mirth. "That, my friend, is where you are wrong." He touched Kirk's arm and Kirk felt a jolt from the touch.

"Maybe I should just leave."

The old man tightened his grip on Kirk's arm. His long nails dug into the skin, drawing blood. "Two years ago, your world changed as your heart's desire was taken from you. You've been lost ever since."

Kirk pulled back, but the shopkeeper held him firm. "Let me go. How the Hell do you even know this?"

"It's written on you like a book." The old man paused.

"What if I told you that I can get you your heart's desire?'

Kirk stopped struggling. "How can you do this? What I desire is unattainable."

The old man's eyes blazed. "That is where you are wrong. Everything can be had, for a price."

Kirk had a bad feeling about this entire exchange. He wanted to leave, but felt rooted in place, as if his will were no longer his own. "What do I have to do?" he asked hesitatingly.

The old shopkeeper relaxed his grip on Kirk's arm and seemed to glide past him through a narrow path between two bookshelves which were overflowing with old, musty tomes. He beckoned for Kirk to follow him past the bookshelves into a dusty, darkened alcove. There, built into the walls were shelves with ancient, leather-bound books covered in a thick coating of dust.

The shopkeeper scanned the titles inscribed on the spines, many of which were not in any language Kirk recognized. He soon stopped at one book, pulled it slowly from the shelf and blew the dust from the cover. He handed the book to Kirk with a big smile. "This is the one you want. Here, in these pages, you will find the means to your heart's desire.

Kirk looked over the book. Aside from a few runes inscribed on the book's spine, the book was pretty plain and unremarkable. It seemed to grow warmer in his hands, as if handling it brought it to life. He ran his fingertips over the cover. The material was a pale brown and felt soft to the touch.

Gently opening the old book, Kirk thankfully saw that the inside was set in type, although he did not recognize the language. There were numerous illustrations in the book which seemed to graphically represent what was in the text. The old man seemed to sense Kirk's consternation.

"It's written in ancient Sumerian," the shopkeeper said as if in response to a question Kirk never asked.

"How is this supposed to help me?" Kirk asked. "How will this book bring me my heart's desire?"

"In those pages," the shopkeeper said slowly, "is the means to be reunited with one's long lost love, no matter what the circumstances."

Kirk felt a chill go down his spine. He looked at the old man and, for a split second, saw something pass behind the shopkeeper's eyes. He couldn't be sure whether it was understanding or malevolence.

He was shocked to hear himself ask, "What do I have to do?"

The old shopkeeper extended a gnarled hand and quickly snatched the book back. He flipped it open and smiled. "Your love's passing left its mark. I can see the dark stain on your soul."

Kirk didn't know what to say. The shopkeeper clearly knew about Callie, yet he was also rambling about stains on his soul. For some reason, though, the last two years came crashing back. "I loved her, old man. And then she died. There is nothing you or anyone can do."

The shopkeeper glared at Kirk. "You are wrong," he said while tapping a long, bony finger on the page in the book. "If you read the text while following these steps, your heart's desire will come back to you."

"How can I follow the steps when I can't read the language? You said Sumerian, right?"

The old man threw his head back and laughed. "Just follow the illustrations, Kirk. Read the words as written while doing the accompanying illustration. That is all you need to do."

Kirk paused. He didn't remember telling the old man his name. His head was telling him to get out while he still had a chance, but his heart would not allow it. For a chance to see Callie again, no matter how remote, he'd fight the hounds of Hell. "What do you want for the book?"

"A small price for what it will bring you." His eyes twinkled and he smiled widely. "I want the pinky finger on your left hand."

"Are you fucking crazy, old man?" Kirk shouted while taking a step back. "That is not going to happen."

"Then," the old man growled, his genteel nature replaced

by something darker and more menacing, "you do not get the book. You do not get your heart's desire. All you get is a lifetime of wondering *what if*. Go on, get out."

Kirk stood there for a moment, shocked at the sudden turn of events. He turned to leave, the old shopkeeper's mocking laughter at his back. Something snapped then. Kirk turned and lunged at the shopkeeper, sending him crashing into one of the bookshelves, throwing up a cloud of dust and causing the old man and a pile of books to go crashing to the floor. Kirk reached over and grabbed the old leather-bound book from the shopkeeper's gnarled hands.

"Fuck you, old man." Kirk turned and walked away, leaving the old man sprawled in the corner.

"You must pay the price!" the shopkeeper screamed. "A sacrifice must be made. Those are the rules." He got to his feet and threw himself at Kirk with a speed and ferocity that belied his age.

Kirk reacted, more so from instinct than anything else, by swinging the heavy book, striking the shopkeeper firmly on the side of his head. The old man fell back and hit his head on the edge of the bookshelf with a sickening crunch. He crumpled without making a sound. A thin trickle of blood pooled beneath his head, and spread out onto the dusty floor.

Kirk panicked. He hadn't meant to hurt the old man. All he wanted was the book. No one would believe a homeless drifter like him didn't kill the shopkeeper as part of a robbery. He ran to the front of the store and opened the ancient cash register. He was surprised to find several hundred in small bills. Grabbing the money as fast as he could, Kirk ran out of the shop, the old book cradled under his arm.

The streets were empty, and Kirk said a silent prayer as he tried to put as much distance between himself and the store. It was still raining outside and the cold drops of rain felt cleansing as they washed the dust from the bookstore off his skin.

Kirk found his way to the train station and purchased a ticket to Massachusetts with the money that he had stolen from the old man's shop. There were no direct routes, so Kirk had to settle for going to Chicago then, after a layover, taking another train to Boston. Still, it beat hitch-hiking.

He found a seat on the train and opened the book to the page the old man had shown him. As he read through the ritual, memorizing the words, he found himself involuntarily tracing some of the runes with his fingertips. The pages seemed to warm to his touch and Kirk felt himself become drowsy. He nodded off and, in his dream, saw the old shopkeeper rise from where he lay. The blood was dried on the side of his head. He turned and seemed to look directly at Kirk, his eyes blazing with fury. Then he threw his head back and roared with laughter. Kirk awoke abruptly.

The rest of the train ride was uneventful. In Boston, at the South Station terminal, he boarded a bus heading north and, an hour and a half later he arrived in Salem, NH. He managed to hitch a ride into town and found a motel where he booked a room and proceeded to shower and make himself appear more presentable. Next, he called Enterprise and rented a car for the week. He then drove to the Home Depot on Route 28 and made the purchases that he would need. He smiled. Things were falling into place. Only one set of items remained.

Night came and Kirk drove to Whippersnappers, a local bar in Londonderry. He parked in the lot and waited for two women to walk out of the bar. He got out of his car, clutching the newly purchased axe behind his back.

"Excuse me, do you have a light?" Kirk asked as he gave his most charming smile.

One of the women, a young blonde with short cropped hair and black lipstick, looked at him with suspicion while the other, a slightly stocky redhead mumbled something as she fished through her purse. Kirk turned and swung the axe, driving it deep into the blonde's neck. She tried to scream, but it only came out as a wet sounding gurgle. The redhead looked up just as Kirk wrenched the axe free and plunged the blade deep into her chest. Her eyes went wide as she fought to breathe and then fell to the ground reaching for Kirk.

He knew that he did not have the luxury of time. Someone could leave the bar at any moment. Kirk pulled the axe from the redhead's chest and hacked her head off in two strokes. It took four swings to sever the blonde's head from her shoulders. He threw both heads into the burlap sack he had bought earlier and hurriedly got in his car.

That's two, he thought.

Next stop was back to Salem. He made his way to Maggie May's pub and parked in a dark corner of the lot. Before too long, a slim, young woman in her early twenties with long dark hair came out of the pub. Kirk decided to try the same approach that he had used in Londonderry.

"Excuse me, miss, do you have a light?"

"Fuck you, asshole," the woman said and kept walking. Kirk turned and swung the axe, burying it deep in her back. He pushed her to the ground and put his foot on her back to pull the axe out. It only took a single swing to decapitate the woman. He threw her head into the burlap sack and dragged the body, with blood still pulsing from the neck, around the side of the bar.

Kirk wiped the axe on her dress and walked around the front of the building in time to see a short, heavyset girl and a tall, gangly man leave the bar. Kirk walked up to the couple and swung the axe with all his strength, burying the blade deep in the man's side. The short woman started to scream and turned to run back in the direction of the bar. He grabbed the axe and chased the woman down. He swung as he ran and sliced across the back of her thigh. She fell forward and landed hard.

She turned, her eyes darting for a means of escape. Kirk was on her before she could make a move.

"Please," the girl cried out, "I'm only sixteen. Don't kill me."

Kirk paused and lowered the axe. The woman breathed a sigh of relief. It was short lived as Kirk raised the axe and, with a snarl, swung it with all his might, burying it deep into her neck.

He pulled the axe free and, with another good swing, got his fourth head.

Smiling, Kirk saw that he was almost there. Only one more and he could complete the ritual. He walked over to where the skinny man lay on his side, whimpering as he tried to keep his intestines from spilling out onto the pavement.

The man stared at Kirk in horror, his eyes wide.

"Nothing personal," Kirk whispered, "but I need five heads. You're number five."

The man looked away, his eyes slowly glazing over. He was dead before Kirk even raised the axe.

Kirk threw the last head into his burlap sack and hurried to his car. He popped the trunk and threw in the sack. He drove north on route 28 for a few miles into Windham. The road narrowed to two lanes and the woods grew thicker on each side of the road. He found a small townhouse development and pulled in. At the back were the woods where he would conduct the ritual.

Kirk stood at the edge of the woods, his heart pounding with anticipation. He gripped the axe tightly in his left hand, and his right clutched at the burlap sack. The moonlight cast a pale glow, giving the woods an almost preternatural appearance. The air was still and a bit cool, and Kirk shivered as his perspiration began to cool on his skin.

With a quick glance back to where he had parked the car, Kirk strode into the woods. He was surprised that this close to town there would be green space as dense as this, but he wasn't going to look a gift horse in the mouth. He walked deeper into the woods until he came upon a well-worn trail. He followed the trail for a while, marveling at the peace and stillness around him. After some time, he came upon a small clearing. He discovered the remnants of a fire pit and, directly behind it, an old shack.

The shack was of gray, rotted wood which bent and bowed from age and exposure to the elements. A small window and door were in the front, both of which had been sealed shut with boards hammered over the opening.

Kirk walked up to the old shack and put his hand to the wood. It felt cool and dry to the touch. The air smelled clean, with a subtle hint of old vegetation beneath the surface. He took the axe and began prying the wood from the door. The wood was old and broke easily. Kirk casually tossed the boards aside. He soon had all the wood removed and stepped cautiously into the shack. Inside, the air was thick and moist and had a heavy, cloying smell of rotten weeds and ripe earth. It was also noticeably warmer than outside. The shack itself was made up of one room bereft of any furniture or anything else which might have indicated that anyone had ever lived there. There was a thick, greenish-black growth on the walls and this was thickest in the corners. As foul as the place was, Kirk felt drawn to it. He knew the ritual had to be done here.

Kirk emptied the burlap sack onto the floor. He took out a bag of salt and poured a thick circle on the dusty wooden floor. He removed a sharp knife and cut deeply into his right palm. The pain was excruciating, but he made sure to cut all the way across the palm. He let the blood well up in his palm, then stepped inside the circle of salt and drew a pentagram with the blood. In each point, he let a few drops fall and then placed one of the heads he had harvested earlier in the evening on top of the blood. He then took a thick, glossy black candle, lit the bottom until the wax got soft, and placed it on top of a head. He repeated this step for each of the severed heads from the sack.

Kirk began to feel faint from the loss of blood, his hand already feeling numb. He tore a strip of fabric from his shirt and bound his wound as best as he could. He pulled off his shirt and then jabbed the knife into his finger tip. He then used the blood to draw a pentagram on his chest. He peeled off the rest of his clothes and placed them aside, outside the circle of salt. Kirk picked up the book and a pack of matches and gently stepped back into the circle, careful not to disturb any of the salt. He sat down "Indian style" in the center of the pentagram.

Taking the matchbook, Kirk reached over and lit each of the candles, casting their soft, flickering lights around the room of the shack. Kirk opened the book to where the old shopkeeper had shown him and began to recite the words of the ritual. Words he now knew by heart. As he read, the wind began to gust outside the shack. With each word spoken, the wind blew harder, howling fiercely and trying to drown out his words. The old wooden door blew shut, slamming hard into the frame and nearly caused Kirk to pause. At this point, he wasn't sure if he were still chanting or whether the words were being ripped from him. As his voice grew louder and higher in pitch, the cacophony outside the shack increased as well. When he finished, the wind stopped and the air was still once more. He sat there for a moment, panting from exertion, his labored breathing being the only sound in the shack.

Kirk looked around. Was this it? He was sure that he had read the words correctly and followed the ritual faithfully. He was about to stand when he heard footsteps outside the shack. The slow, heavy footsteps came to a stop outside the old wooden door. Kirk stood, naked and bathed in perspiration, and faced the door, waiting.

He felt that someone was standing there outside, and he suddenly became very self-conscious of his nakedness. "Is anyone there?" he called out, trying to sound braver than he felt. "I have a gun, and will use it if I have to."

The door was slowly pulled back and a blast of cold air filled the shack, extinguishing all the candles, plunging the room into complete darkness. A shape stood there in the doorway, hidden by shadows. Only the moon provided ambient light, revealing the outline of a person. Kirk saw that it seemed to be a woman. She stepped through the threshold, her bare feet padding on the dusty floor, and slowly walked towards him.

"Callie?" Kirk called, his feelings of fear mixed with that of desire.

The figure shambled a bit closer, then stood at the edge of the circle. Kirk grabbed the matches and lit one of the candles.

The light cast a warm glow in the utter darkness and he saw her at last. It was Callie and she had come home to him.

She stood there, completely naked, her skin a pale alabaster with areas that seemed to be greyish-green and purplish, with black splotches all over. A thick Y-shaped incision had been made from her belly to her chest and was now sewn over. A yellow, viscous fluid leaked in spots from the incision. Several of her ribs protruded through the skin. Her right arm hung limply by her side and her left twitched as she reached forward to caress Kirk's chest.

Kirk tried to move but was petrified with fear. Her body was banged up and broken from her accident, but her face was the worst. The entire left side of her face was caved in where she had struck the pavement after being hit. There was no skin remaining on the left side from the forehead down to her chin, giving her features that of a grinning corpse. The right side was not much better. Her right eye was clouded over and what remained of her mouth was pulled back into greyish black lips. Her hair was filthy and hung down in greasy knots, plastered to what was left of her skull.

Callie slowly stepped over the circle and stood facing Kirk, their bodies just barely touching. With her good arm, she pulled him in close. He felt her skin, cold and clammy, press against his. She licked his neck and kissed his cheek. When her cold, decayed lips touched his, he found himself kissing her back. He knew, as he slipped into the warm embrace of madness, that he now had his heart's desire, and she would be there to love him forevermore.

Her Time of the Month

It was early Tuesday morning when the receptionist walked into the conference room and called me out of our weekly management meeting. I excused myself to see what was so important. She told me that my wife had called and said that it was urgent that I call her back immediately. I wasn't surprised. I suppose that I had left my cell phone in my office on purpose because she always called me like this when it was her time of the month. Let me just say that, while I do love my wife, when it's her time of the month, living with her becomes an unbearable Hell.

I walked to my office and grabbed my cell phone. I knew what to expect. Every month was the same, almost as if scripted. I suppose we really are all actors in our own lives. I hit her number on the speed dial and waited for her to pick up. First ring, as expected.

"You called?" I asked, feigning innocence.

"It's coming," she said matter-of-factly. "I feel it. Could you stop and get me a few things on the way home?"

I sighed. "Sure. Is there anything in particular you'd like me to get?"

"You know damn well what I need," she snapped, her voice starting to rise. "I ask for the same things every month. If you're too damn stupid to remember what I need, I'll get them myself."

"I'm sorry," I replied, trying to keep my voice soft and neutral. When her time of the month was imminent, the littlest thing sent her into the worst rage. I've been on the receiving end of her anger. It was something I've learned to avoid at all costs.

"You'd better be," she snapped, "and don't be late." Thank God for cell phones. At least she couldn't slam down the receiver on a cell.

I stood up and walked to my office window. I had a scenic view of the company parking lot. The back of my shirt was soaked through with perspiration. I hadn't realized until just then how much I actually was afraid of her. I stared out at the parking lot and the woods beyond and relished the tranquility. I had purposely chosen a low profile accounting position in a small, non-descript company that was never going to advance more than it currently had. I also made sure that the office was over fifty miles from home so I always had an excuse to head right home and never get to know anyone on a social level. It was simpler that way because it made it easier to cut ties if need be. The thought of any of my colleagues seeing my wife and her aberrant behavior during her time of the month was enough for me to maintain that sense of aloofness at work.

Instead, we always chose to live somewhere far off the beaten path and keep our interactions with others to a minimum. On those rare occasions where others have met my wife, they always told me afterwards how positively charming she was. I smiled because, if they only knew the truth, they might think differently. They saw the best of her. I usually got the other end of the spectrum.

As was often the case, after I got the call from my wife, the day seemed to drag. I suppose part of it was attributable to the anxiety of going home and facing her. I worried that whatever I got for her to help her through this stressful time would not be sufficient. There were times I considered leaving her, just getting in my car and driving far, far away but, in the end, I know I couldn't. I had made a vow to her and I always honor the vows I take in life.

Every time I heard the phone ring in the office, I'd jump. I kept checking my cell phone every ten minutes to ensure that I didn't miss one of her calls. Even then, she still called me six more times that day. With each call, she grew more hostile and I could tell her mood was rapidly spiraling out of control. Some months were worse than others, and this one was shaping up to be a very bad one, based on all indications. I looked at my watch and saw that it was already four o'clock. Almost time to leave.

It's hard to believe that I had met her only six and a half years ago. I had been vacationing with some friends, backpacking our way through Europe. We were in Paris at the time and, while my two friends were sleeping off their hangovers at the youth hostel, I decided to walk the streets and absorb some of the culture the city had to offer.

It was a cold and windy day for September and I was walking down the right bank of the Seine on my way to the Louvre when I passed a young woman chasing her hat which was being blown away by the gusting wind. Not to sound callous, but normally I would have minded my own business and simply walked away. There was something about this woman that made me chase after her hat and retrieve it for her. She thanked me and told me that she was from Balzac and was spending the summer in Paris to study at the Louvre.

I asked her if she would like some company and, much to my surprise, she leaned in and kissed me softly on the cheek. She was fairly tall, standing about five foot seven with an incredible figure. She had a heart shaped face and full, red lips. Her eyes were dark and her skin was slightly dusky. Her jet black hair fell lazily to her shoulders and perfectly framed her face. She told me that she was an artist and hoped that her time at the Louvre would help define her style. She smiled coyly and told me that she'd like to paint my portrait. I hoped that was code for something else and eagerly followed her to the museum where we spent hours looking at paintings and discussing artists and artistic techniques. We stayed in the Louvre until closing and, as we walked out, she asked me if I would like to come back to her hotel. I readily agreed.

Back at her hotel, she showed me some of the recent paintings that she had done since she had arrived in Paris. I certainly wasn't any authority on art, but I clearly recognized that she had talent. Her brilliant use of reds created some of the most strikingly visual pieces of art I had ever seen.

She then told me that she wanted to paint my portrait. I

agreed, she handed me a sheet and asked me to disrobe. She actually looked away, but I could swear that she was blushing. She told me to wrap the sheet around myself and directed me to a stool in the corner of the room. She dimmed the lights and lit several candles and covered them with colored glass. This bathed the room in a flickering array of colors unlike any I had ever seen. I watched her as she began to paint. The flickering colors seemed to give her a feral appearance. When she smiled, her teeth appeared impossibly white. The flickering lights cast shadows over her features, obscuring her eyes. The effect was surreal and quite mesmerizing. I couldn't take my eyes off her.

Before too long, she indicated that she was finished. She called me over to look at her painting. I had seen some of the other paintings in her hotel so I knew she was talented but, even then, I was not expecting the masterpiece that she had just finished. It was positively brilliant. She had not only captured my essence but the figure on the canvas seemed to be alive and I swear that you could almost see it breathing. The depth of the image made me believe that the painted version would stand up and walk off the canvas. It was that good.

"Do you approve?" she asked demurely.

I replied that it was perhaps the greatest work of art I had ever seen. She promised to give it to me when it fully dried.

I realized that I didn't even know her name and, when I asked her, she laughed and realized that she didn't know mine, either.

We ended up spending the next two weeks together. My friends were not happy at being ditched for some girl, but I simply didn't care. We went to museums and art galleries and spent many hours exploring the City of Light. When it was time for me to return to the States, I asked her to join me. She quickly accepted and promised to join me in a few weeks after she settled her affairs back home.

We were married within a few weeks of her arrival in Boston and, by then, I was completely smitten. She was not only a great beauty, and an incredibly talented artist, but she was a sparkling conversationalist and a sensational lover. Those first few weeks, we were insanely happy. Then, things started to go wrong…

The drive home from the office was quite stressful and took longer than usual because my wife had very particular needs when her time of the month came. Because of those needs, I often had to go far out of my way to get her what she wanted. I decided to head west on the Mass Pike and look for a quiet town. An hour later, just north of Route 495, I found the perfect place to stop and pick up what she needed.

In retrospect, it's amazing that I've put up with her demands for over six years. I still remember the first time that I saw her during her time of the month. It was just after we were first married and I was so shocked, I almost left her. I actually did leave for two days but returned home when I realized that I was miserable without her. I suppose that no matter how bad things got during her time of the month, the other days more than made up for it. I knew then, as I do now, that I'd never leave her and would stick by her through the roughest times.

I found a CVS pharmacy on the outskirts of town. They had everything that I needed, for which I was grateful. Nothing is worse than going from pharmacy to pharmacy trying to find a missing item. With my purchases in hand, I returned to the car. I drove a grey Toyota Camry because it was a car that always blended in wherever I went. I chose it specifically for that purpose.

I sat in the car in the pharmacy's parking lot and lit a cigarette. I normally don't smoke but, around her time of the month, I tend to get very nervous. It probably isn't doing a thing for my nerves, but I suppose the routine does help me stay calm. I started the car and drove through the small town, enjoying how quiet the streets were. Before too long, I knew I was lost. I keep telling myself to invest in a GPS and, I suppose, sooner or later I will. For now, though, hindsight is twenty-twenty and I had to make do without one.

I soon came across a young boy walking alone down a quiet tree-lined street. I could not believe that any sane parent would let their child out alone at this time of day. I don't care how safe a neighborhood is, there are crazies everywhere.

Pulling the car up alongside the boy, I rolled down the window and motioned him over. He shrugged and walked over to the car. I told him that I was lost and asked how to get back to the highway. He turned slightly and pointed down the road to start giving me directions. He never saw the cloth or the half empty bottle on the seat next to it. The rest was easy.

I arrived home a bit over an hour later. The house was dark and silent. I drove into the garage and quickly shut the door before I opened the trunk. I then carried the boy to the basement and placed him down on the stone floor. I looked over and saw my wife crouching in the shadows in the corner of the room.

"Get out," she hissed in a low and menacing snarl.

I didn't need to be told twice. I ran back up the stairs and locked the heavy steel door. I sat down with my back to the door and held my head in my hands, wondering how I could keep doing this. I stayed there until sundown. Minutes later, I heard the boy scream and a growl that still terrifies me.

I grabbed a beer and stepped out onto the porch and looked up wistfully at the clear night sky. The moon was full and bright. It was a beautiful fall evening. I tried to block out the sounds I heard from the basement, horrible screams and rending noises that could even be heard on the porch. Thank God our nearest neighbor is over a mile away. We sure do need our privacy, especially on days like this. I hate doing what I have to do every time it's her time of the month, but I really have no other alternative. What can I say, I love my wife.

The Puppeteer

John Aronson was a puppeteer, and a damn good one. A relic of a bygone age, he was aggressively plying a trade that few people still found interesting. In the past, he had been on network television - CBS no less- with a weekly children's show. Now he was lucky if he could eke out a meager living performing at Church functions, children's birthday parties or performances at local town fairs. Still, he somehow managed to pay the rent and put food on203 the table.

Aronson was tired of the constant searching for gigs and wished he could simply retire. Of course, back in the day, network television did not pay royalties and he never had thought about putting anything aside for a rainy day. With virtually no savings, Aronson figured that he would carry around his chest of puppets until the day he dropped. At seventy-six, he understood that day was coming a lot sooner than he'd like.

It was a grey and rainy Saturday and Aronson was up early. He had a children's party at the home of a well-to-do family in town. A good performance and he could line up enough engagements to cover his costs for a year. He wanted to make sure that everything went exactly as planned. He loaded up his rusted 1979 Ford Econoline van and decided to do one last check to ensure he had all his props before he drove to the McMaster estate where the party was being held. The plan for today's show was that he'd stick with an old stand-by, the continuing adventures of Rudolfo the puppet. Rudolfo, who was a knight, would set out to do battle with the evil dragon and save the princess. The king would then make Rudolfo a prince and he and the princess would live happily ever after. He was amazed that, after so many years, kids still loved the same routines. It gave him pleasure that after fifty years of putting on puppet shows he could still make children smile.

There were other puppets in his repertoire, but he always found that he was drawn back to Rudolfo. It made sense because Rudolfo was the first puppet he had ever created and, on some level, he was like the child he never had. When he had public appearances, it was Rudolfo that the children requested to see and, to this day, he still got stopped in the street by people who remembered watching his show when they were children.

Aronson finished his last minute walk-through of his apartment when he heard a loud knocking on the door. He wondered who could possibly be looking for him this early. He lived a pretty solitary life, never having married and had no family or real friends to speak of. He opened the door and looked at the peculiar little man who stood there.

"Good morning, Mister Aronson," the stranger said in a high, nasally voice. He stood at no more than five feet tall and wore a black felt overcoat. On his head was a black bowler hat, also made of felt. He had large round glasses which made his small, beady eyes look even smaller. The glasses rested on a large, bulbous nose that made Aronson immediately think of the late Jimmy Durante. His mouth was thin and pale and seemed to curl into an imperceptible grin. He stood with a slightly stooped posture and leaned against a jet black walking stick with a silver wolf's head at the top.

"Can I help you?" Aronson asked, taking in the little man's bizarre appearance.

The stranger smiled and his face seemed to fill with his smile, as he showed large and yellow stained teeth. "Actually, Mister Aronson, I'm here to help you. May I come in?"

Aronson was not one to allow strangers into his house. He regarded the man with the same apprehension that he afforded anyone he did not know. "What do you want mister..."

"Jones," the small man said affably and extended his hand. Aronson shook it and was surprised by the stranger's cold, clammy grip. "The reason I'm here has to do with your craft of puppetry. I have an offer which I think will interest you."

Aronson stepped back to allow Jones to enter his apartment and to have a seat on one of the threadbare chairs in the sitting room. Aronson sat on the adjacent chair and looked expectantly at Jones who sat there in silence, a big grin on his features. "I'm sorry, but I don't have much time, Mister Jones. What would you like to discuss with me?"

Jones sat up stiffly and made an exaggerated show of straightening his jacket's lapels. "How would you like to become wealthy beyond your wildest dreams?"

Aronson chuckled softly. "Of course I would, but I know that will never happen."

"I can make that happen. All I wish is to become a…silent partner in your business. I will provide the clients and be of help behind the scenes and you will find work that pays more money than you have ever seen." Jones gave his best smile and Aronson couldn't help feeling that Jones was eying him like a piece of meat.

"You wish to be my partner?" Aronson asked. "Mister Jones, I am an old has-been barely eking out a meager living performing, at best, a few puppet shows a week. If not for social security, I'd likely be living on the streets. I have nothing to offer you."

"I beg to differ, Mister Aronson," Jones said. He leaned forward in his chair, never taking his eyes off Aronson. "My employer seems to think that your work is quite good and would like to arrange a partnership. He opened his briefcase and took out four stacks of bills wrapped in paper currency straps. He handed them to Aronson. "Here you go, as a sign of good faith."

Aronson counted the money and looked at the little man in disbelief. "There's twenty thousand dollars here. That's a lot of money for good faith."

Jones managed a twisted grin. "We wouldn't come here with this offer if we did not believe in your abilities."

"Can I think about it?" Aronson asked, all the while thinking about all his debt that could finally be paid off.

Jones stood up, brushed his coat once and extended his hand which Aronson reluctantly shook. "Of course you can. Go and do your show. I will come back next week and you can let me know your decision. In the interim, please keep the money with you. We wish for you to know that we are quite serious in our desire to partner with a man of your obvious talents."

Aronson nodded and watched as Jones left without another word. He walked to the window and looked outside, but didn't see Jones anywhere. He swore he didn't hear a car start. He put the money in a kitchen drawer and headed out to the McMaster mansion for his show. No matter how much energy he put into the show, or the fact that he performed his tried and true best routines, the children seemed disinterested. He saw that some of them were busy playing on little electronic devices. The few who were paying attention were quiet and barely even engaged in the storyline. After he was done, Aronson packed up his gear and collected his check. He sensed that the McMasters were regretting hiring him for their child's party. Even worse, not a single parent approached him about potentially performing at their own child's party. He wondered if it was time he retired. He drove home, climbed into bed and curled up to sleep.

The week passed in a blur. Aronson forgot about Jones's visit and the money remained untouched in his drawer.

Exactly a week after his visit, Jones showed up at Aronson's door. Aronson let him in and Jones went straight to the seat he had perched on during his previous visit and sat right down. Aronson shut the front door and joined Jones in the sitting room.

Jones was wearing the same black felt overcoat and bowler hat. He flashed Aronson a wide grin and asked, "Have you made a decision?"

"Before I agree to your offer, Mister Jones," Aronson replied, taking a moment to collect his thoughts, "what will I have to do?"

"All we ask," Jones said, "is that since we will provide the clients and these are shows that we've arranged, you utilize our puppets and follow the scripts we give you."

Aronson frowned and got up. He walked to the kitchen and got a glass of water. Something was very wrong with this whole arrangement. Who in their right mind would care what an aging puppet master had to offer, let alone offer him huge sums of money. He should get the twenty thousand from the kitchen, return it to Jones, and get the creepy little man out of his life forever. He opened the kitchen drawer and picked up the first pack of money. Five thousand, he thought, could go a very long way with his modest lifestyle. He stood there for a few minutes in silence, just holding the money before he returned it to the drawer and walked back to the sitting room.

"Good news, Mister Jones. I've decided to take you up on your offer."

"Splendid," Jones replied. He opened his briefcase and took out a thick sheaf of papers.

"What's that?" asked Aronson.

"Why, it's the contract. We are talking about large sums of money and want to make sure that everything is on the up and up." Jones handed the papers to Aronson who began flipping through the pages.

"Why is it so long?"

"Just all the legalese," Jones said with a grin. "Would you like to have your lawyer look it over?"

Aronson paused as he looked the contract over. While it made sense to seek legal advice on this, he honestly did not have the money to waste on lawyers. "No, I'm good. Do you have a pen?"

Jones reached into the jacket of his coat and pulled out a shiny golden pen. "Here. You can use mine."

Aronson took the pen from Jones. It felt warm to the touch and seemed to tingle beneath his fingertips. He signed the contract and handed it back to Jones who quickly put it back in the briefcase. He then pulled out another sheaf of papers and handed it to Aronson.

"What's this?"

"Your script, Mister Aronson," Jones said. "Please learn it and be ready for tomorrow night. I will send over the address later today."

"I can't do this," Aronson said as he flipped through the script, "I don't have the puppets for this."

Jones reached into his coat and pulled out a puppet and handed it to Aronson. He pulled two more puppets from his coat and gave them to the confused puppeteer. "These should be exactly what you need."

"How did you have three full sized puppets in your coat?" Aronson asked.

Jones just smiled. "Learn the script and get comfortable with the new puppets. I will send over the address later today. See you tomorrow night." He turned and walked out the door without another word.

Aronson read through the script and was horrified by what he read. It was a love triangle gone bad, complete with rape and then the violent murder of the young woman, followed by her boyfriend violently stabbing the man who had killed her. This was no child's performance and Aronson felt sick as he thought of what kind of twisted person would enjoy watching such a depraved performance.

The next day he drove out to the address Jones had sent over. It was an old warehouse and he was directed by a security guard to drive around back. Aronson parked and saw Jones standing there, as if lying in wait. He walked over to greet him.

"Aronson, it's a pleasure to see you. Are you ready for your performance?"

Aronson nodded, but his heart wasn't in it. Jones led him inside and had him set up on stage. With the overhead lights, he couldn't see back into the audience. The only reason he knew anyone was there was due to the subdued whispering and occasional cough from the darkened theatre.

He ran through the script with the puppets that Jones had provided. They were a lot more realistic than the ones he was used to and even shed fake blood when stabbed. Aronson's deft touch made the puppets seem lifelike and the performance passed before he knew it. When done, he was greeted by thunderous applause. He stood to take his bow, but also to get a glimpse of the crowd. The overhead stage lights lit up and momentarily blinded him. He turned his back to the lights and waited a moment for his sight to come back into focus. By this point, he was alone in the theatre and packed up his gear in silence.

Aronson loaded his truck and was about to drive away when he heard a knock at the driver's window. He turned to see a grinning Jones standing there. He lowered the window and looked at the little man in disgust. "Can I help you, Jones?"

"Why yes, you can," Jones replied. He handed Aronson an envelope. "Here is your payment for today." He then procured another envelope from his jacket pocket. "Here is the script for your next show."

"I don't understand, Jones," Aronson said while flipping through the new script. "This is nothing but death and killing for the sake of killing. It's not very good and not very entertaining. Why in God's name would you even want this performed, let alone pay me so much to do the show?"

"Why, indeed," Jones replied. "We have our reasons." He reached into his jacket and pulled out four more puppets, this time of children, followed by an adult puppet. "Please use these for the next show. I will send you the address by the end of the week. As before, please make sure you memorize the script." He smiled and walked back into the darkened theatre, blending into the darkness.

Aronson drove home and looked morosely at the script. It was far worse than the last one. This time, four young boys go to see an old man putting on a puppet show, not knowing that they are being followed. Once they exit the theatre, the man who had been following them lures the boys into his van and takes them to an abandoned warehouse where they are systematically tortured and murdered.

Aronson threw the script down in disgust. There were limits and he didn't care what kind of twisted individual would find this type of performance entertaining. He was done. He was about to call Jones when he realized that he didn't have any way to reach the strange little man. It didn't matter. He just wouldn't go. He hadn't spent much of their initial payment. He'd give it all back and walk away.

The days came and went and no word from Jones. As they got closer to the date of the next performance, Aronson began to worry. Maybe he should just leave. He had no family or close friends. He had few possessions aside from his beloved puppets. There was nothing holding him to this apartment. As much as his instincts warned him to leave, he knew that, for better or worse, he was an honorable man. He would do the show and then tell Jones that he was done.

The day of the show came and he drove to the address that Jones had sent him. It turned out to be a school in a small town at the other end of the state. Once again, he was directed to drive around back and, as before, Jones was there to greet him.

Jones broke into a huge smile when he saw the elderly puppeteer. "Ah, Mister Aronson, how good it is to see you. Everyone is eagerly waiting on your next performance." He led Aronson inside and to the back entrance of the school's auditorium.

Aronson set up his stage and performed the show without error. It made him ill to hear the cheers as the puppet children were brutally killed one by one. He finished the performance to thunderous applause. He stood quickly and peered out into the crowd. Once again, the overhead lights came on and he was momentarily blinded by the bright glare. He cursed, hating himself for his greed and for succumbing to the lure of wealth.

When his eyes cleared up, Aronson went looking for Jones. He found him, as before, waiting by the side of his van. Jones handed him an envelope which he said was payment.

After taking his cash, Aronson looked over to Jones and said, "I'm done. This was my last show."

Jones looked shocked. "I don't think so, Mister Aronson.

Our contract does not give you a clause to opt out. We have the rights to opt out of the contract, of course at our discretion. You have the sworn duty to perform to the best of your abilities for one year or unless we so choose to rescind." He smiled, showing his teeth, but there was nothing warm about his smile. Aronson stepped back in fear. "And we do not rescind."

"I'm a puppeteer with next to nothing to my name. Sue me. You'll find it's not worth your while."

Jones chuckled. "I am a reasonable man, Mister Aronson. Watch the news tonight. I will return tomorrow and we can take this up where we left off." He turned and walked back into the school, leaving Aronson standing there shivering.

He drove home and realized that Jones had not given him a new script or puppets. Perhaps he would simply let him go. At home, he heated up a frozen dinner and took a soda from the refrigerator. He sat down to eat and remembered Jones's comment to watch the news. He was sure the little man was more than a little crazy but, if he intended to get out of this raw deal, he'd need to see what Jones was up to.

As he ate dinner, he watched the news. Same as always, the world was going to Hell in a hand basket. Just more stories about terrorist attacks, problems in the Middle East, more politics and partisan crap. They were just about to break before they got to sports when a local story came on about four boys who had gone missing that afternoon. They showed recent photographs of the boys and Aronson froze. His four puppets were the spitting image of the missing children. The announcer asked that anyone with any information as to their whereabouts contact his local police station immediately.

Aronson felt sick. Four children were missing and somehow he was involved. He picked up the phone and was about to call the police when he heard a voice behind him.

"Please hang up the phone, Mister Aronson."

Aronson turned and saw Jones standing there. He seemed to glide across the floor until he was face to face with the terrified puppeteer. "How did you get in my house? I want you to leave right now."

"And if I decide that I don't wish to leave, Mister Aronson? What will you do then?" Jones asked, keeping his voice low and guttural.

Aronson started to dial 9 – 1 – 1. This had gone far enough. He managed only the first two digits when Jones clamped his hand on Aronson's arm. Jones began to squeeze and Aronson screamed as the little man applied a crushing, vise-like grip. He dropped the phone to the ground and Jones let go of his arm.

Jones bent over to pick up the phone and gently placed the receiver back in the cradle while Aronson stood there rubbing his arm.

"What happened to those children?" Aronson asked.

"I think you know."

Aronson looked imploringly at Jones. "How does my putting on a puppet show have anything to do with this?"

"It has everything to do with it, Mister Aronson. It's why we chose you."

"I'm done, Jones!" Aronson shouted. "I don't care. I won't put on another show for you!" He walked to the kitchen and collected the money he had been paid. "Take your blood money, you bastard. I don't want it."

"Keep it," Jones hissed. He pulled a sheaf of papers from his coat. "You will do one more show as per the script."

"And if I don't?" Aronson said defiantly.

Jones pulled a puppet from his pocket.

How does he keep doing that? Aronson thought.

Jones took the puppet and held it in front of Aronson. It was a young woman, likely in her early twenties. Fair skinned with chestnut colored hair and hazel eyes. "Her name is Emily," Jones said with a snarl. "She is married with two children, a boy and a girl, both under six. She teaches elementary school and, in her spare time, volunteers at the senior center a mile from her home." He gave the puppet's head a sharp twist and Aronson heard the crack. A red, blood-like liquid oozed out of the broken stump of the puppet's neck. "She was an innocent. Now she is dead. I will kill one person at random who lives within ten miles of you every single day until you agree to perform the last show."

Aronson felt the tears well in his eyes. "You monster," he said softly and took the script. He read through it while Jones watched carefully. Finally, he put the script down. "If I do this, you will never ask me to do another show again?"

"After tonight, you can consider our contract finalized. I will see you tonight."

The day passed slowly, with Aronson checking his watch every fifteen minutes, dreading the time he'd have to leave. Tonight's script was by far the worst, but Aronson knew he had no choice. He had no proof that Jones had killed that young woman when he snapped the puppet's neck, but he had a damn good idea that he had.

Eventually, it was time to go. Aronson drove to the address provided by Jones which turned out to be a mansion in the nicer part of town. He was directed to the front and a valet went to park the van while Aronson walked in through the open front door. Jones hadn't provided any of the puppets, and insisted that they would all be provided at the house.

Aronson was speechless at the sheer opulence of the home. He wondered who he'd be performing for. Jones emerged from a door and walked over to Aronson.

"You made it, and right on time," Jones said.

"I always honor my word," Aronson replied, and added, "I expect you to do the same."

Jones looked at the old puppeteer and patted him on the back. "I always keep my word, Mister Aronson." His voice lowered and took a more menacing tone. "I just want you to understand that."

The implicit threat was not lost on Aronson. With a heavy heart, he followed Jones to a large ballroom. A puppet theatre was set up in the middle of the floor. There were dozens of puppets, each one beautifully designed and crafted to look just like a human being.

There was a large black leather chair in the middle of the floor. A man of indeterminate age sat cross-legged in the chair. He had a slim build and wore tight jeans over black cowboy boots. He wore a black silk shirt with the sleeves rolled up. His face was lean and angular; his black hair was cut short and brushed forward with the front slicked up. There were streaks of silver in the hair which lent a more distinguished air to his appearance. His eyes were hazel and twinkled in the dim light of the room. He stood up and strode over confidently to where Aronson was preparing for his show.

"Mister Aronson," the man said, "I am honored to meet a man of your skills."

Aronson stood and stared at the man. *Why does he look so familiar?* "Thank you. Do I know you?"

The man chuckled and extended his hand in greeting. "Forgive my manners. My name is Smith. I am your partner in this venture. Mister Jones is in my employ."

Aronson saw Jones standing off in the corner. It was clear that he felt uncomfortable in his employer's presence and was content to stay on the periphery.

"Why did you choose me to do these shows?" Aronson asked bluntly.

"I do like a man who speaks his mind," Smith said. "I chose you, Mister Aronson, because you not only are a very talented man, but you are also an individual who would be willing to step outside your comfort zone for the right amount of money. You are a good man who was willing to stray off the path with the right incentive. Those were all characteristics that I was looking for."

"You are aware that tonight is my last show?" Aronson asked.

"Of course I am. After tonight, your services will no longer be required."

Aronson smiled. "Thank you. Although I probably don't want to know, what happens next?"

Smith looked confused. "I'm afraid I don't follow."

"I doubt that I was the first person you...hired for your pleasure. I doubt that I will be the last."

"You are quite astute, sir," Smith said. He added, his voice low and taunting, "The lure of good money is always enough to attract plenty of eager souls." Without another word, he returned to his seat. The lights were dimmed and an overhead light shone down on Aronson's puppet theatre.

Aronson set to work putting on the show. He hated doing this, but Jones's threat from the night before was frozen in his memory. Better to take the lesser of two evils then add to the body count that Jones had hinted at.

The performance was short, but brutal. Aronson ran his puppets masterfully. He guided the lead puppet, a young college student named Jack, to a party at a local fraternity. The frat brothers played a nasty prank on Jack and humiliated him in front of all the party guests, including his date. Jack fled in tears while the partygoers all laughed. Jack then came back later with several tanks of gasoline. He locked all doors and doused the frat house with fuel. Starting on the doors, the house quickly went up in flames, killing all partygoers, including the young woman Jack had taken as his date. Jack then turned himself in to the police and was arrested. Later, he hung himself in his cell.

Aronson finished the show and stood up. Smith was on his feet, applauding.

"Brilliant, as always," Smith said. "I believe that our arrangement is at an end. Mister Jones will see you out and make sure you get what you are due." He extended his hand which Aronson reluctantly shook. "I look forward to when we meet again."

Aronson, having no gear to pack, walked out to where Jones was waiting for him. Jones handed him an envelope with his payment and gave him a curt bow.

"It's been a pleasure, Mister Aronson."

Aronson took his money and left without another word. He decided to treat himself to a nice dinner, a celebration to being free of Jones, Smith and the whole sordid ordeal. He did feel remorse for his actions, but managed to justify them by reasoning that if he didn't do the shows, someone else would have, and perhaps more people would have gotten hurt.

He drove downtown, parked on a side street and walked until he found a bistro where he could enjoy a nice meal. A night out, he decided, to celebrate his retirement. He had made more money doing three shows than he had in the prior two years. With his social security checks coming in, and his conservative lifestyle, he decided he could get by with this extra money for several more years.

Dinner was pleasant, but the whole time Aronson's thoughts kept drifting back to the last show. So many wasted lives…He decided that he had had enough and just wanted to go home. He had the rest of his meal boxed up and walked to his van.

The air was crisp and Aronson wished he had brought a heavier coat. He started the van and pulled out into the street when the engine sputtered, coughed and then died. Cursing, he managed to get it to roll to the curb and put the vehicle in park. Aronson popped open the hood and got out. He looked at the engine and realized that he had no idea what to look for. He checked his watch and saw that it was ten-thirty. It was far too late to call a tow truck. AAA would have come in handy but, on his fixed income, it was a luxury that he decided he didn't need. I guess I picked the wrong horse, Aronson thought glumly.

Aronson had some money on him and decided to take a taxi. He would address getting the van towed and repaired in the morning. He pulled out his cell but saw that there was no service. Bundling up against the chill night air, he walked back to the restaurant hoping they would let him use their phone. He tried the door and found it locked. The restaurant was dark and deserted.

It doesn't make any sense, Aronson thought. I left here no more than fifteen minutes ago. Where were the other customers? Where was the staff?

Not only was the restaurant deserted, but nothing else appeared open either. There wasn't a single other car on the road. The sidewalks were empty. It was as if he were alone in the world.

He started walking. It was too far and too cold for him to try and walk home. Besides, at his age, it would be foolish to even try. Someone has to be open, he thought. Aronson walked for another ten minutes and didn't see another soul. All the shops were closed, including gas stations and convenience stores, even the ones which advertised as being open twenty four hours a day.

The night was certainly getting colder and Aronson wished he had brought a heavier jacket. I can't spend the night out here, he thought with a growing sense of panic. He turned the corner and saw the police station across the street. He thanked God for his good fortune and hurried over.

The door to the police station was locked. He peered through the glass doors but didn't see anyone inside.

"Open up, God damn it!" Aronson screamed as he pounded on the door. He found that his voice sounded thin and pleading in the crisp air. Frustrated, Aronson sat down on the stone steps and put his head in his hands.

"Hello, Mister Aronson. It appears we meet again," a voice from across the street said in a deep baritone.

Aronson looked up and saw a man standing in the shadows across the street. The figure stepped forward and began walking towards him, the shadows clinging to him as he walked.

"Who are you?" Aronson called out.

The stranger chuckled and the shadows which surrounded him seemed to bleed back, revealing a smiling mister Smith. "How good it is to see you again, Mister Aronson. It seems we have one last bit of business to transact."

Aronson stared at Smith who calmly stood there while the darkness swirled about his ankles. Every instinct told him to run. He may have been getting on in years, but he was fond of saying that his parents didn't raise a fool for a son. Aronson started walking down the steps of the police station towards

Smith. Then, without warning, he turned and bolted, running as fast as he could from the mysterious Smith.

He ran a block and felt his heart pounding in his chest. He stopped for a moment to catch his breath. Aronson looked back and saw Smith purposely striding towards him, all trace of civility gone from his features. Even though Smith appeared to be out for a casual stroll, he was rapidly closing the gap between the two men.

Aronson turned and started running. His chest hurt and he prayed that he wasn't having a heart attack. He looked back and saw that Smith was getting closer. Aronson knew that he was kidding himself if he hoped to outrun Smith. His only hope was to evade him long enough to lose him.

At the first cross street, Aronson turned. It was a short street and cut through to the next block. He turned right and ran across the street, cutting in to an alley. He looked back and didn't see Smith. Perhaps I lost him, the old puppeteer hoped. Stopping in the doorway of a second-hand bookstore, he hoped to catch his breath. His felt a tightness in his chest and a tingling in his left arm. If he wasn't having a heart attack, any more exertion would certainly push him over the edge.

Aronson stepped out of the doorway and saw that Smith was standing there. He looked around in a panic and saw there was nowhere to run. Smith pulled a packet of papers from his jacket.

"I have your contract, Mister Aronson," Smith said with a scowl. "As per the terms of our agreement, it is time for us to collect our restitution."

"I don't understand," Aronson said. "What could I possibly owe you?"

Smith flipped through the pages and pointed to a certain clause in the agreement. "Let me paraphrase. It says that if you do not honor your full commitment, then I, as the employer, am entitled to recover damages from you, the employee."

"I may be a simple puppeteer, Smith, but I didn't just fall off the turnip truck. Your associate Jones agreed to cancel our contract as long as I did one more show. I did the show, as agreed, and now we are done."

Smith roared with laughter. He flipped through the pages. "Look here, Mister Aronson. Once again, I will paraphrase. It says that the full commitment is a year of service. If you were to fail to perform the full year, we do allow you the right to end our agreement, but there is a cost to opt out."

"Then sue me, Smith. Other than the money you paid me, I have nothing. Good luck getting blood from a stone. Good day, Mister Smith." Aronson turned and started to walk past Smith towards the street. Smith grabbed Aronson by the arm and pulled him close.

"Don't you dare try and walk away," Smith said in a low and menacing growl. "I think you haven't grasped what is going on. You do have something I want and I'm here to collect."

Aronson stared at Smith and saw the man's features waver. He caught a glimpse beyond the illusion. It wasn't the golden hue to his skin or the massive wings that froze Aronson's blood. It was the two horns. Smith let go of Aronson's arm, and the old puppeteer took a hesitant step backwards.

"Please…" Aronson said drily, "I'm nobody. I'm just a puppeteer."

Smith grinned and said slowly, his voice full of malice. "So am I. In fact, I'm the greatest puppeteer of them all." He then advanced on Aronson. Payment was due and he intended to collect in full.

Shadow Play

The night is cool under a clear, starlit sky. A slight breeze blows, its touch leaving frosty prints on all it passes. A man walks down the deserted alley in the early hours of the morning. He is well aware of the darkness and takes comfort in the scant amount of light offered from the stars above. The screech of a cat as it knocks over a garbage can sets his heart racing as he looks around in terror, trying to discover the source of the noise. His brow is soaked in a cold sweat and his hazel eyes are glazed over in fear. He begins to shiver and feels the fine hairs on the back of his neck begin to stand on end.

Deeper and deeper the man ventures into the alleyway. He wishes he were anywhere else, but he feels compelled to move on. The clock in the church tower on Main Street strikes twice, and the sound echoes and reverberates in the still air. He hugs himself, partly for warmth, but also to give himself a perceived sense of safety.

He softly whispers to himself, "These are only the sounds of a sleeping city. Everything will be all right."

The man knows in the core of his being that things aren't right. There is a different feel to the night. It feels closer and somehow more suffocating. The wind blows a numbing draft across the man and he shoves his hands deep into his pockets in a futile attempt to keep warm. He senses that someone is nearby and he spins around, ready to confront whoever might be following him. The alley looks deserted, but the man knows better. Someone is close. Some*thing* is close. He feels it in his bones. The darkness begins to slowly creep in, stretching tendrils of inky black toward the man

"The forces of evil are at work tonight," he mutters to no one in particular.

The air around the man gets noticeably colder and he sees the darkness creeping ever closer from the shadowy corners of the alley. The darkness glides up the walls beside the man, taking on distinct, individual shapes. The shadows get taller and seem more menacing as they move around the man. The man looks at his dark tormentors and stands transfixed in terror. The shadow beings seem to feed off his fear and grow larger still. They rise and sway, and begin a darkly hypnotic dance. The man tries to scream but finds that he's paralyzed with fear and can barely manage a hoarse whisper. He fights to regain control of his senses and looks about for a means to get out of the alley and back to the well-lit downtown street. The shadows close in on the man, smothering him in their icy grip and begin to feed.

The man snaps awake, his heart hammering in his chest. He is soaked in perspiration and it takes him a few minutes to realize that he is back in his bedroom. He climbs out of bed, throws on his robe for warmth, and then paces back and forth, trying to get the horrible dream images to fade away. He looks over at his clock radio and sees that it is only three- twenty in the morning. The long night still has plenty of time to wreak its havoc.

"Insomnia and nightmares every night for weeks, you say?" Doctor Harris Trenton remarked soothingly. "Well, I'm glad you decided to give me a call, Mister Donaldson. I do think that we can get to the root of the issue and, through a series of sessions, we can hopefully find the means to resolve this conflict." Trenton was reputed to be one of New York's best psychiatrists, and boasted many of the city's A-list celebrities as his clients. His services were not cheap, but his track record for success spoke for itself. He was well published, with over a dozen books on the market, his latest having spent close to a year on the New

York Times best seller list. If anyone could help, Trenton was the person who could.

"I hope you can, Doctor Trenton. The last few weeks I've been having nightmares and they've gotten so bad, I'm actually afraid to go to sleep. I'm exhausted and I'm falling asleep at work, while driving, and even sitting down for a simple dinner. I can't take this anymore. That's why I decided to call you."

Donaldson took a deep breath. He was in his mid-thirties with dirty blond hair cut short and brushed in a stylish and professional manner. He stood at five feet ten and, while still in good shape, he was showing the signs of softening around the middle that often accompanied approaching middle age. Until recently, Donaldson had been fine with his physical and mental well-being. It was only recently that he had begun to have concerns for the latter.

"Lately, it seems as if I have the nightmares every time I go to sleep," Donaldson continued. "It's always the same. In each nightmare, I find myself in a dark alley being stalked by shadowy beings until they attack and devour me. Every night it's the same thing"

"That's why you're here, James," Trenton replied. "We will dig into these nightmares of yours and see if we can root out the cause of the dreams and find some way to resolve this. Now then," he said, while cupping his hands together, "I'd like to go back to the beginning. First, let's try an exercise to help you relax."

"Sure, Doctor Trenton, what do you want me to do?"

Doctor Trenton led Donaldson over to the couch and motioned for him to lie down. "Okay, James. Let's start with a simple exercise. Please close your eyes and listen to the sound of my voice. I want you to concentrate on my voice and nothing else. You are feeling calm and serene. All your worries are gone and you feel incredibly peaceful. Your breathing is calm and you feel like you have no cares in the world."

Trenton continued to speak soothingly to Donaldson

until he felt the man's breathing was slow and regular. "James," Trenton said, "can you hear me?"

"Yes," Donaldson replied.

"Thank you, James. When I snap my fingers, you will open your eyes. All your anxiety will be gone and you will remember with prefect clarity everything that happened the day your nightmares began." Trenton snapped his fingers and Donaldson opened his eyes. "How do you feel, James?"

Donaldson smiled. "I feel good."

"So, let's start at the beginning. Let's start with the day you first started having the nightmares."

Donaldson took a deep breath. "I remember the day it all started. I was in my yard, digging a hole where we were planning to plant one of the three fruit trees that we had bought at a local nursery. It was a hot day and the digging was slow going. My wife..." Donaldson swallowed hard, desperately trying to hold back the tears.

"Please take your time, James," Trenton said in a calm and reassuring voice.

Donaldson nodded and continued. "My wife wanted the fruit trees. We have a good sized yard and she admitted that ever since she was a little girl, she had wanted to have fruit trees like apple, pear and peach in her yard. I learned early in our marriage that a happy wife meant a happy life. So I bought the trees and set about digging the holes to plant them. I was perhaps a few feet down trying to get a hole big enough for the roots when my shovel struck something hard.

"At first I thought I had hit a rock, so I stopped digging and peered into the hole. I had to brush away the dirt with my hands, and I saw soon enough that it was not a rock. It was a box of some kind. I began shoveling again, this time being careful around the box to make sure that I didn't do any damage to whatever it was. At this point, my mind was racing. As a kid, I always dreamed of finding buried treasure and, there it was, in my own backyard, a box that could have contained anything. What was interesting was that my home was only two years old and, while where I was digging was my lawn, three years earlier it had all been densely packed woods. I cleared enough of the dirt and saw that it was a good sized box made out of a gleaming black wood, polished to a high shine. I'm telling you, Doctor Trenton, as God is my witness, I was sure that there, buried in the moldy earth, was a treasure chest."

Trenton saw that Donaldson was getting agitated and was trembling as he spoke. "Would you care for a glass of water, James?" Donaldson nodded and Trenton got him a glass from the bubbler. "Please continue. So you found a chest in your yard. What happened next?"

Donaldson gulped down the water and put the empty cup on the table. "Well, I dug around the chest and saw that it was huge. I spent the next few hours digging around it, but realized that I'd never be able to just pull it out. So I jury rigged a rope around the chest to a winch and used that to pull the chest from the ground. It must have been damn heavy because the winch was straining to the point of smoking. I was sure it would break and drop the chest back into the hole. I guess luck was on my side because I managed to get the damn thing out of the hole and onto my lawn. The chest was about two feet long by a foot wide and a foot high. It was a solid, well-polished black where I could feel myself being drawn into its inky depths. It was a black so rich that, if I stared at it long enough, I'd find myself adrift in it."

Trenton jotted down some notes in his pad and looked up at Donaldson. "That's a very visual description, James. Why did you feel it was important to describe the chest like that?"

"I suppose that I wanted you to really understand how unusual this chest was. If I just said it was black, then something would have been lost in my retelling of what happened."

"That makes perfect sense. Please continue, James."

"At first I thought the chest was a solid glossy black but, upon closer inspection, I saw that I was wrong. The chest was covered in strange markings, like runes or glyphs. The only way

I could actually see them was to stare directly at the chest. In the center of the lid was a hollow five-pointed star within a golden circle. At each point of the star were these little red gems. The strangest thing was the golden bands that wrapped around the chest, maybe half a foot or less from each side. These bands didn't seem to have a beginning or end, but rather were a continuous loop of gold around the chest. Whoever forged them made them to keep the chest closed and deter others from ever opening it. I was becoming even more convinced that the chest held some kind of treasure."

"So what did you do next?" Trenton asked.

"Well, I borrowed a metal cutter and carefully removed the bands. I tried lifting the lid, but it wouldn't open. It was then I noticed the tiny lock set in to the lid. Like the runes which covered the lid, the lock was hard to see and only became clearly visible was when I stared at it. So I called my friend, Rick, who is an experienced locksmith. If anyone could get the chest open, it would be him. All it took was the promise of a cold six pack and he said that he'd be right over."

Trenton got up and refilled Donaldson's glass. "Please continue."

Donaldson drank some more water and continued. "Rick arrived close to an hour later. As you can imagine, I wasn't too happy. He did apologize, and blamed traffic, but I suspect, like everything else, Rick simply got a late start or got distracted by something else. Once he arrived, he set about trying to get the lock open. I'm telling you, Doctor Trenton, I've never seen him so frustrated. He spent well over an hour trying every trick he knew, and still it wouldn't open. It got so bad that he was actually cursing and slamming his fist on the lid of the chest. Now, here's where it gets strange. Rick was ready to give up and, once again, punched the lid in frustration. He cursed loudly and showed me the gash across his knuckles. Something on the chest's lid must have cut his hand. That in itself was strange because the surface was as smooth as glass. We both saw his blood pool on the lid then roll down the chest into the tiny lock. When all the blood was absorbed, there was a clicking sound and then the gold bands seemed to melt into the wood of the box and disappear."

Doctor Trenton shifted uncomfortably in his chair. He took a few more notes and tried to compose himself. "James, let's pause here. Are you telling me that your friend Rick could not open the chest until his blood filled the lock, and that once the lock snapped open, the gold bands that circled the chest simply disappeared?"

Donaldson nodded. "I know it sounds like I'm making it all up, and we were having a few drinks, but it's the honest to God truth. And let me tell you something, the weird shit didn't end there."

"What do you mean?" Trenton asked.

"Do you remember how I told you that the chest was too heavy to lift and that I had to use a winch to get it out of the hole?"

Trenton nodded.

Donaldson wiped his brow and continued. "Well, judging from how heavy the chest was, I was convinced that it was full... perhaps gold or something else of value. We opened the chest and looked inside. It was empty except for a small black bag. Like the chest, the bag was ebony in color with a gold trim. It was tied with a golden cord. I grabbed the bag and fumbled with the cord. Rick was behind me, telling me to hurry up, going on about what his share would be. It seemed as if every sound around me became amplified to the point that I was sure my eardrums would burst. I finally got the cord open and everything got deathly silent. I wondered if I hadn't gone deaf. I looked over at Rick, but he seemed frozen in place, as if time had stopped for him. I tried calling his name, but I couldn't even hear my own voice.

"I reached into the bag and there was only a single item inside, a beautiful gold ring with a black gem mounted on top. Ochre veins ran through the gem and I swear that if I looked long enough, the veins were moving. As suddenly as everything had come grinding to a halt, things reverted back to normal. Sounds came back and I no longer felt as if I were in a frozen tableau."

Trenton took a few more notes. "Let's recap, James. You were expecting a treasure and instead you found a ring. Tell me what you were feeling"

Donaldson stood up and walked the length of the office before returning to the couch. He seemed to stare at his hands for a moment, as if he were composing his thoughts. "How I was feeling? Let me say that I was feeling a lot of things. I felt really angry because I had gone to all this effort for a ring, but I was also disappointed because I was deeply hoping for some kind of treasure. Instead, I ended up with a lousy prop that looked like it was ripped off from *The Lord of the Rings*. It was then that my wife got home from shopping and saw the huge hole in our yard and the chest sitting on our lawn. She asked me what the Hell was going on. All I could do was show the ring to her and see what she thought."

"Did you tell your wife about all the strange things that happened?"

Donaldson smiled. "Of course I didn't. I was there and I didn't believe it myself. My wife, Janice, said the ring looked valuable and we should take it to a jeweler to get it appraised. The whole ride down, Janice was yelling in my ear to go fast-er and wondering what we should do with the money that we could get if we sold the ring. It was like someone took my sweet and quiet wife and replaced her with someone else entirely."

"Was it possible that she was just excited about maybe finding something really valuable?"

Donaldson sat up and took another drink of water. "I'm sorry Doctor Trenton, but I know my wife. In twenty years to-gether, she has never told me to go faster while driving. She's very cautious and would rather take longer to get somewhere than take unnecessary risks. And as for the ring, she does not have a materialistic bone in her body. While she does enjoy hav-ing nice things, like anyone else, she is not driven by greed.

"The jeweler took a look at the ring and, while he couldn't give me an exact price, he did say that it was very old and likely very valuable. He said that he'd never seen a gem like the one on the ring and if we wanted a more accurate assessment, they could send the ring out to an expert who could price it properly. My wife grabbed it from his hands and told him that we'd figure out what we wanted to do with it. She put the ring on her finger and we drove home in silence, each of us lost in our own thoughts."

Trenton glanced at his watch and frowned. "James, I'm confused. The jeweler said the ring is likely valuable, yet it sounds like you both were unhappy for some reason. Why is that?"

"I can't answer for my wife. Since I had found the ring, she had been acting strangely. I think I was having mixed feelings. On one hand, it seemed like a valuable piece of jewelry, yet, on the other hand, there was something about the ring that unsettled me."

Trenton shifted uncomfortably in his chair. "What made you feel that way?"

Donaldson sighed. "I honestly don't know. I only had held it in my hand for a short time but, when I did, it was as if I were holding something…vile. I wish I could explain it, but touching the ring felt foul. And that worried me, because my wife seemed quite comfortable wearing it.

"Over supper, we didn't really say much. After, as we were cleaning the dishes, she suggested we go to the mall for some shopping. It was a Saturday afternoon and I didn't want to waste it walking around the mall. Besides, money was tight enough. The thought of her pissing away our hard earned money just for the sake of spending didn't sit well with me. As usual, I said nothing and told her that I was tired, but that she should go. She kissed me goodbye and, when she put her arms around me, the ring on her finger came in contact with the back of my neck. I got a jolt that sent a numbing pain down the entire left side of my body. I watched her drive off and then I went to the den to sit by the fire. For the life of me, Doctor Trenton, I could not get warm and sat there shivering before the flames until I fell asleep."

Trenton nodded and took a few more notes. "Did you believe that your inability to get warm was caused by the ring?"

"At the time, I did," Donaldson replied. "I must have been dead to the world because when the telephone woke me up, it was already morning. I reached over to the desk and picked up the receiver, still groggy from being awakened. It turned out to be the police. Apparently, my wife had been in an accident and was at a hospital in Manchester, New Hampshire. The officer refused to divulge much information, but urged me to come down right away."

"Was your wife alright, James?"

Donaldson wiped away a tear. "I drove down to the hospital right away. The entire way down I was wondering what the Hell she was doing in New Hampshire, hours from home. As far as I knew, she never even ventured into New Jersey, let alone drove by herself to New Hampshire. By the time I arrived, I was a wreck. Not knowing whether she was okay, let alone what in God's name she was doing all the way out in New England, was killing me. I ran to the front desk and I'm sure I yelled at the receptionist on duty until she told me what room my wife was in. I certainly wasn't prepared for the condition that Janice was in."

"Was she badly hurt, James?" Trenton asked.

"I swear to God that if I had known what was coming, I'd have gone with her when she went shopping. Perhaps I could have avoided what happened."

Trenton waited while Donaldson collected his thoughts. He sensed that they were getting closer to the root of his issues and wanted to keep Donaldson talking. "Please continue, James."

Donaldson's lower lip trembled slightly and he seemed to be holding back the tears. "My wife was lying there in the hospital bed and, for a brief moment, I wasn't sure who it was. It certainly didn't look like my wife. Her skin appeared to be translucent and I could see all her veins and arteries. She also looked much thinner than she had the night before and her features were drawn and gaunt. Ever her lustrous black hair was grey and brittle. It was as if someone had siphoned out her life force. Know what's interesting, Doctor Trenton? As horrific as her condition was, my eyes were drawn to the ring she wore on the ring finger of her right hand. The gem seemed to be emitting a dark aura and the red veins in the stone were pulsating. I couldn't allow the ring to be on Janice's hand a minute longer, so I went over to the bed and took her hand.

"Her skin was like ice, although the ring felt warm. I twisted the ring and pulled it off her finger and slipped it into my pocket. I don't know why, but I felt that the ring was behind my wife's accident. I suspect that it had been buried for a reason and I should have left it where it was. I felt that, in order to save my wife, the ring had to be destroyed."

"Hold on a minute, James," Trenton began, "but did you ask the doctor what had happened to your wife?"

Donaldson narrowed his eyes. "Of course I did, Doctor Trenton. The physician on duty said likely had blacked out while driving and flipped the vehicle, causing all the blood loss. I was stunned. I'm not a doctor, but it was blatantly obvious that she didn't have a single wound on her body. If she didn't have any wounds, then how did she bleed out as badly as she had? It had to be something else, and my money was on the ring. It took blood to open the chest. It didn't seem so far-fetched that the ring could have been drawing out her blood from the moment she put the damned thing on."

"Did you ever find out why she was in New Hampshire?" Donaldson asked.

"That's the thing that is most perplexing," Donaldson said. "She said she was going shopping. My wife was a lot of things, but she wasn't impulsive. It wasn't in her nature to do something like this."

"James," Trenton said in a gentle, soothing tone, "is it possible that she might have been leaving you?"

"What?" Donaldson screamed, as he leaned in towards Trenton. "Are you serious, Trenton? Sure my wife and I had our issues, as all couples do, but there is no chance she was leaving me. I'm sure that, if she were, she'd have waited for a day I was at work and might have considered taking some of her clothes and possessions."

Trenton put his hands up in a calming gesture. "I'm sorry. I need to ask questions from all perspectives if I want to get a clear picture of what is going on. Some of the questions might seem either personal or uncomfortable, but it's necessary to help with your cure."

Donaldson sat back on the couch, his hands still balled into fists. "I suppose you're right. But having you imply that our marriage was broken, especially after what happened to my wife, really cut me deeply."

"I understand. Let's get back to what happened."

Donaldson took a deep breath and continued. "Seeing my wife hovering near death, without even a mark on her, made me see that the ring was cursed and that it needed to be destroyed. I got into my car and all I could think about was disposing of the damned thing. I knew of some companies that boasted industrial furnaces in the city and my goal was to pay them to melt the ring down until nothing remained. I can see the way you're looking at me, but I'm not crazy."

"I assure you, James, that I do not think you're crazy," Trenton said softly. "This is a safe place where we do not judge."

"It doesn't matter, Doctor Trenton," Donaldson continued, as if he didn't even hear Trenton, "because I never made it back to New York. On my way back, as I merged onto Route 90 from Route 495, some maniac ran me off the road. I lost control of my car and rolled it a few times before ending up in a ditch by the side of the road. The asshole never even stopped to see if I was okay. I was lucky a passing motorist saw my car in the ditch and called the police. If he hadn't, I might have died."

"So what happened next?"

"Well, my car was totaled and the police called an ambulance for me. Thankfully, my injuries were not too bad...mostly superficial cuts. They released me the next day. I was still a few hours away from home and had to rent a car just to get back. I don't need to tell you that I was terrified. I was convinced that the ring's curse had now been passed on to me. I decided to go into hiding."

"I'm sorry, James, but why didn't you just get rid of the ring at that point? If you were so convinced that it was cursed, then wouldn't throwing it away sever the curse?"

Donaldson let out a small laugh. "Don't you think I tried that, Doctor Trenton? Right after the accident, I decided to throw the ring into the woods. I was done with it. But I couldn't get it off my finger. It seemed to have fused itself to my flesh. Even worse was that night at the hospital was when the dreams of being stalked by the shadow creatures began. It all made sense. They were coming for me and the ring was some kind of a conduit for them.

"Once at home, the first thing I decided to do was burn the chest. It was too heavy to move so I doused it with gasoline and covered it with wood. I set it ablaze and watched the fire rage for over an hour. The damn thing not only didn't burn, but there wasn't one bit of damage to it. Unfortunately, in my desire to burn the wretched thing, I lost track of time. It was dusk and I could see the shadows building at the edge of the woods and around the corners of my house. The darkness began creeping across the lawn toward me, flowing like liquid. I skirted the shadows and was about to go inside when I saw the darkness pooling under the back deck, its tendrils snaking up the stairs. I couldn't go that way. They would get me. I ran around to the front and rushed inside. The first thing I did was throw on every light I could find, sending the shadows screeching back to the corners and under the furniture and giving me safety.

"Things got worse. I saw that, if I let my guard down, the shadows would reach for me, trying to draw me into their dark embrace. I couldn't let that happen, so I'd spend my nights in my den, with all the lights on, watching television. I couldn't risk sleeping until the daylight hours where I could open all the blinds and, with every light on, manage to get a bit of sleep. But there wasn't any rest to be had. The shadows came after me every time I closed my eyes. Each night was the same. I would find myself walking down a dark alley in the city and then be attacked by the shadow creatures who wanted to devour me."

"Didn't you leave the house, James? What about your job? Did you check on your wife?" Trenton asked.

"I'm not a monster, Trenton," Donaldson hissed. "I would call the hospital twice a day. The doctors always said the same thing, that her condition was unchanged but that my presence could only be beneficial. She might be in some kind of a coma, but comatose patients have responded to the presence of their loved ones. I told them I would try and visit. After two weeks, they stopped asking. I called in sick to my job the first day. After that, I didn't bother. I honestly didn't care. If I went in to work, I'd be too tired to stay up all night and the shadows would get me. I suppose I've been fired by now."

"What did you do for food? Surely you had to eat?"

Donaldson smiled. "Of course I ate. I would order something to be delivered mid-to-late afternoon after I awoke, but before it started to get dark. I'd try to order enough for a few days just to save on delivery charges.

"After two weeks, the dreams suddenly changed. I was still in the alley but, this time, my wife appeared out of the shadows and walked toward me. She approached and smiled and I had to take a step back. Her eyes were gone and, in their place, was inky darkness. She opened her mouth and it exploded out of her, wrapping its icy tendrils about my body. Wherever it touched, I felt a burning sensation as if acid were being poured on my skin. I tried to run, but the shadows were too strong and began pulling me toward their stygian depths. I was sure that I was going to die. If it wasn't for the ringing of the phone..." Donaldson stopped and wiped a tear from his eyes.

"What happened, James? Who was on the phone?" Trenton asked.

Donaldson reached for a tissue and proceeded to blot the tears. "It was the hospital," he said at last. "They called to tell me that my wife had passed and that I needed to come down to the hospital to claim her effects and sign some paperwork. I checked and saw that I'd never make it there and back before sundown, so I promised to drive up the next day. I left the house at daybreak and took the rental car up to New Hampshire. I didn't get there until noon, but that was fine. I figured I had enough time to get back.

"The nurse gave me my wife's personal belongings. I took them, but couldn't look at her. The doctor came by and offered his condolences. I asked him what had happened and he told me that she was starting to show signs of improvement when she suddenly sat up in bed, threw her head back and shrieked until she fell lifelessly back to the bed."

"And what were you feeling when the doctor told you this?" Trenton asked.

"Do you want to know if I cried, doctor?" Donaldson screamed. "No, I didn't cry. I suppose I was numb because I didn't feel a damn thing. I didn't have time to mourn because the doctor started changing right in front of me. His eyes seemed to dissolve and become inky pools of nothingness. He opened his mouth and the darkness came pouring out of him. I didn't stick around. I turned and ran. I took the stairs two at a time and managed to get down to the lobby far faster than I would have in the elevator. I ran to the door and saw a woman standing there with the darkness swirling around her. I didn't stop and threw her out of my way. I heard screams behind me, but I couldn't stop. The darkness was coming for me. I needed to get home."

"James, please sit down. I understand this is very difficult, but let's try to keep calm," Trenton said in a placid tone. He saw that Donaldson was getting very agitated and he wanted to ensure that he didn't cross over to violence.

Donaldson sat back down. "I'm sorry, doctor. Revisiting that day brings back a lot of awful memories."

"I understand. So what happened after you left the hospital?"

"Well, I drove home as fast as I could. As I got close to New York, I hit traffic. By the time I pulled into my garage, it was starting to get dark. I barely made it inside. The shadows were leaping out at me from every corner. Several of them managed to reach me and I felt my skin burning everywhere they touched. When I turned the light on, I was able to send them back to the nooks and crannies and knew I was safe once more."

"James, I'm glad you came to me," Trenton said. "We need to start with the root of your issue and work out from there. The shadows you see are most likely a manifestation of the stressors that you endure on a daily basis. As you deal with the issues that seem beyond your control, you are feeling smothered. The shadow creatures are what your mind is making you see as your means of labeling everything that is happening around you."

Donaldson stood up and saw that Doctor Trenton began shimmering and changing. His eyes dissolved and were replaced by shadowy nothingness. He opened his mouth and dark tendrils extended, whipping around as they tried to reach Donaldson. "You're one of them!" Donaldson cried out. "You got me here and allowed me to lower my guard."

The darkness spread out around Trenton, twisting and spiraling in all directions. Shadows flowed outward from him and glided across the floor and up the walls. Trenton raised his arms and reached out for Donaldson who stood there paralyzed by fear.

Donaldson roared with rage and swung as hard as he could at the shadow-thing that used to be Trenton. His fist connected with the creature's face and sent it sprawling back into a wall. The shadow being lay still and the darkness pulled back in to Trenton's body. Donaldson turned and bolted from the office. He had to get home to where he was safe. The darkness was closing in.

Trenton stood up and gently rubbed his chin where Donaldson had struck him. He called for his receptionist, who rushed in. When she saw Trenton, she froze.

"Doctor Trenton, you're bleeding," she said softly. She reached for a Kleenex and gently applied it to Trenton's lip. "I heard some noise but I remembered your strict instructions to never interrupt a session. But when Mr. Donaldson ran out, I didn't know what to do."

Trenton smiled and winced from the pain. Donaldson was certainly a lot stronger than he looked. "I appreciate your concern, Hanna. I really am fine. Sometimes the patient isn't quite ready for the treatment."

Hanna smiled. Aside from being quite strict and completely devoid of any sense of humor , Doctor Trenton was a good boss who treated her fairly and paid quite well. She wanted to make sure that she didn't do anything to jeopardize this job.

Trenton walked back to his desk and sat down. He looked up at his receptionist. "Hanna, could you please call Elliot Hospital in Manchester, New Hampshire and ask for as much information as they can provide on James Donaldson's wife's accident and passing?" He glanced down at his notes. "Yes, here it is. Her name was Janice Donaldson. Also, please print out James Donaldson's profile and employment history from Linkedin and anything else you can find on other social media platforms."

"I'll get right on it," Hanna said and left the office.

Donaldson looked back through his notes. There is a piece missing to this story, he realized. He would find it. He suspected that Donaldson was getting close to the edge and knew that time was short.

Donaldson made it home just before dusk. He ran to his den, closed all his blinds, and turned on all the lights in the house. He then turned on his television and computer, grabbed his camping lantern and sat in the middle of the floor where it was brightest. He said a silent prayer and hoped that God would keep the darkness away for another night.

Time passed and Donaldson was getting tired. He kept the air conditioning on high, hoping the chill air would keep him from nodding off. He needed sleep, but to do so at night, when the shadow beings were strongest was suicide. He looked at his watch. It was only eight- thirty. He had several hours before sundown. He was just about to make some coffee when the doorbell rang. He wanted to see who it was, but that meant opening the door and letting the darkness in. He stayed still and hoped whoever was at the door would leave.

The doorbell rang again, with three consecutive chimes. He got up, still holding his lantern and peered out. Doctor Trenton was standing there.

"James, I can see you at the window," Trenton called out. "Please let me in."

"Go away!" Donaldson screamed, "You're one of them."

"Let me in, James," Trenton replied. "Shine your light on me. It will prove I am who I say I am."

"It's a trick. You just want to get in and make me let my guard down."

"I have a way to make the shadows go away forever, James. You just have to trust me."

Donaldson didn't know what to do. If Trenton was still human and not tainted by the shadow beings, then it would make them both safer against attack. On the other hand, if this was a trick, he'd be caught. Deciding to chance it, Donaldson opened the lock on the front door and shone the bright halogen lantern directly at Trenton.

Trenton came in and shut the door. "Could you please not shine that thing in my eyes? I would like to see."

Donaldson led them to the kitchen where he motioned for Trenton to sit at the table. "I was just about to make some coffee. Would you like some?"

"I'd love a cup."

Donaldson brought Trenton a cup and set it down in front of him. He took another cup and sat on the opposite side of the table. The men drank their coffee in silence. Finally, Donaldson spoke up. "What are you doing here, Doctor Trenton? I wasn't aware that shrinks made house calls."

"I usually don't, James. But I felt I had to see you right away."

Donaldson looked at Trenton suspiciously. "Why?"

"I was worried that you might harm yourself or someone else. After the incident at the hospital, and then your attack on me at my office, I realized that it was time to address this head on."

Donaldson let out a short chuckle. "This is way above what a shrink does for his patients. And besides, I've come to realize that my problems are not going to go away if I talk about them. This is way above your pay grade."

Trenton frowned. He could tell he was losing control and that Donaldson was rapidly slipping into his delusional world. He had to act quickly. "I'm here to give you a reality check. I'm going to prove that you are not cursed by the ring that's on your finger."

Donaldson stood up and hurled his coffee cup across the room where it shattered against the far wall, spraying coffee and ceramic shards everywhere. "I am cursed!" he screamed. "The damn thing was on my wife and now I can't get it off my finger. It's bonded with my skin."

Trenton pulled a jar from his pocket and applied a large glob of the paste on his hand. He grabbed Donaldson's hand and spread the paste over the ring and finger. Donaldson began thrashing and pulling, trying to get away, but Trenton held firm. He twisted and pulled and soon the ring slid off the finger. "There," he said triumphantly. "All it took was a dab of Vaseline." He took the ring and slipped it into his pocket before Donaldson could say anything.

Donaldson stared in shock at his finger. "How the Hell did you get it off?"

Trenton held up the jar. "Your finger got a little swollen from the ring which was too tight. I noticed it at my office and would have suggested this if you hadn't hit me and run out."

"What about my wife?" Donaldson asked. "She was wearing the ring and got into some crazy accident up in New Hampshire. Explain that."

Trenton sighed. "I did some checking into what we discussed. The reason your wife was up in New Hampshire was that she was looking to rent a ski lodge for your anniversary. She was on her way to Waterville Valley when she must have had a minor stroke. It happens to people a lot younger than you. She flipped her car and lost a lot of blood from internal bleeding."

"I don't buy it!" Donaldson yelled. "You didn't see my wife. I did. She looked like she didn't have a mark on her."

"James, listen to me. She was on the bed with a sheet up to her waist. You did not pull the blanket down to expose her injuries. She did, in fact, get hurt in the crash, including a cut to her femoral artery. The only reason she didn't bleed out entirely was due to the accident itself. The way the paramedics found her, there was enough pressure on the leg to staunch the bleeding."

"It wasn't an accident. The shadows took her."

"Explain to me why you can't accept that she died of an accident."

"Easy, doctor. The day she died, I had a horrific dream of her death by the shadows. Even the doctor at the hospital told me she had sat up and shrieked before falling over dead. Why would that happen unless she was taken by the shadows?"

Trenton sighed. "Listen to me, James. I'm a doctor. What your wife had was a cerebral hemorrhage. She must have woken and been in excruciating pain when the blood vessels in her brain burst. I'm sorry, but she died from injuries sustained in her crash. As for the dreams you had, think of all the stress you've been under. Your job in advertising is as high pressure as it gets. I had my receptionist call your office and they told us that you've been working on one of the largest accounts your firm ever had when you stopped showing up. Factor in your wife in a hospital at death's door and it's a guarantee that some of your waking world will carry over into your dream world."

Donaldson looked confused. "You have an answer for everything, Doctor Trenton, but I guarantee that you can't explain why the chest was so heavy or wouldn't burn."

"Actually, I do. I drove to your house and saw the chest in your yard. I scraped the black coating off the chest. Underneath, it was made of cast iron which was three inches thick all the way around. Do you know how heavy a thick cast iron chest would be?"

"Then why did it take blood to open it?" Donaldson asked.

"It would have taken any liquid," Trenton replied. "The lock was old and there was dirt in it. The blood softened the dirt to allow the lock mechanism to work."

Donaldson sat down. He looked completely deflated. "I guess it's over, then."

Trenton shook his head. "Unfortunately, it isn't over just yet. There is the matter of the day you went to the hospital to collect your wife's remains. You said that there was a woman possessed by the shadows that you threw out of the way. Well, it was an old woman and your pushing her caused her to fall down the stairs and break her hip. She doesn't remember who struck her, but the hospital did notify the police and they are looking for the woman's assailant. That was you, James. You need to turn yourself in. I am willing to go with you and attest to your state of mind. I'm pretty sure due to the circumstances we can get all charges against you dropped."

Donaldson nodded and followed Trenton to his car. The two men drove to the local police station where the officer on duty directed Trenton and Donaldson to an interview room to discuss what had brought them there.

Donaldson sat there in silence as they waited for the police detective to join them. Trenton stood in the corner taking stock of their surroundings. The room looked pretty much what he expected one of these rooms would look like. He had watched enough police dramas on television. The room was small with a sturdy, but plain, table set in the center. On each side of the table were two metal chairs. There were hooks on the table which Trenton assumed would be to cuff a prisoner if need be. Three of the walls were cinder block painted slate grey. The fourth wall had a large mirror which was almost certainly a two-way mirror where other officers could observe from outside. A video camera was mounted on the wall in the corner near the ceiling above the door.

After an hour of waiting, Trenton was getting frustrated. The officer on duty said they'd be in shortly. Trenton frowned. In what universe is an hour considered shortly.

Without warning, the lights suddenly turned off and the door to the interview room swung open.

"They're coming," Donaldson muttered solemnly.

"Who are you talking about?" Trenton asked.

"The shadow-beings from the dark ring are coming. I told you that they are after me. We can't stay here."

"It's all in your mind, James," Trenton said. "We discussed this. I'm sure there is a simple explanation like a power outage. Wait here. I'll see if I can find one of the officers on duty."

Trenton left Donaldson who sat huddled in the corner in wide-eyed panic. He returned a few minutes later.

"Well?" Donaldson asked.

Trenton shook his head. "I don't understand it. We're all alone here. All the officers are gone. I found coffee cups on desks with hot coffee in it. It's like everyone just disappeared. What the Hell is going on?"

"Do you believe me now, Doctor Trenton?" Donaldson asked, practically spitting out Trenton's name. He chuckled. "Now you're involved as well and, trust me, it won't end well."

"There must be an explanation," Trenton said. He didn't want to let Donaldson know, but there was something unsettling about the sudden disappearance of all the police officers. He reached into his jacket to make sure that the small Smith Wesson AirLite snub nosed .22 was still there. He had bought the gun two years ago after a vicious mugging and, even though he abhorred guns, having it in his pocket gave him a sense of security.

"Come on," cried Donaldson, "we need to get out of here or they will get us. It's far too dark. We need to get somewhere well lit."

Trenton followed Donaldson out of the deserted police station. The air outside was noticeably colder than before and had a frosty feel to it. The streets were dark and deserted and Trenton noted, with growing unease, that there wasn't a single sign of anyone out on the roads. The streetlights which were still on began turning off, one by one, as they approached. The wind picked up and blew icy daggers around the two men, tearing the warmth from their bodies.

"They're here!" Donaldson screamed. He looked around in terror, trying to decide where to run.

"There has to be an explanation," Trenton muttered. He looked skyward as if in prayer. "Please let this all be just a coincidence."

With the streetlights out, the darkness poured out of every gloomy recess. It glided toward the men, sentient and hungry. The shadows rose up, swaying in a rhythmic dance. Donaldson stared in terror at the macabre dance before turning and fleeing down the darkened street.

"James, wait. Don't run off. There has to be an explanation," Trenton called after Donaldson. Behind him, the darkness began swirling together. It grew and then shrank back again, merging together with other shadows and then pulling apart as if completing a dark ritual. They formed shapes both familiar and utterly alien, and began converging on the terrified psychiatrist. Trenton stared as the darkness circled around him until he had nowhere to turn. A tendril of darkness reached out and caressed his cheek, leaving a burnt sear where it touched. He screamed as the shadows closed in. Even though the air was frosty and crisp, he thought he smelled freshly baked bread. Another shadow swirled around his face and he saw myriad faces from his life.

He saw past loves, friends and colleagues. He felt a flood of emotions rushing past. Pain from wounds long forgotten brought tears to his eyes, only to be replaced by feelings of love, lust, fear, anger, hatred, joy and humor. He saw death take form in front of him, first those of parents, friends, beloved pets and, finally, his own impending demise. Death smiled at him and beckoned him to abandon all hope and welcome her cold, eternal embrace and then drown in it for eternity.

Trenton fell to his knees, the tears flowing from his eyes. "Damn you," he whispered. He wasn't sure who he meant that for. Was he cursing the shadows or the feelings of leaving behind so many uncompleted aspects of a rather mundane existence? He remembered the gun he carried for protection and pulled it from the pocket holster. He fired all eight rounds into his shadowy tormentors, screaming in rage as he did. The bullets passed harmlessly through the ethereal demons. He swore he saw one of the shadows smile before it grew larger, engulfing all the others. Trenton looked on in terror as the shadow being wrapped him in darkness. He was surprised that he felt nothing but warmth as the darkness welcomed him home.

Donaldson was still running when he heard the sounds of gunfire. He pitied Trenton. He was a good man who meant well, but this was out of his league. He should have listened when he had the chance. Donaldson turned down an alley, hoping to cut through to the next block. He kept running until he saw the wall at the end. *Oh God*, he thought, it's a dead end. He looked around and froze when he realized that this was the alley from his nightmares. He turned to head back when he saw the shadows come bleeding into the alley from the street.

Donaldson crouched behind a dumpster, hoping it offered him a modicum of protection against the shadow beings. They were coming for him and there was nothing he could do about it. He shivered as the temperature dropped. He watched the rime rise on the dumpster's metal surface. He saw the plume of frost made by his breath. He thought grimly that, if the shadows didn't get him, he would likely expire from exposure. Trenton was likely dead and there was no one else around who could possibly offer help. Donaldson wondered how the shadow creatures managed to separate him from the rest of the world. *Did they stop time or exist in some world parallel to ours?* He supposed the point was moot. They were coming for him and they would kill him. For what it was worth, this validated everything he had told Trenton. He was not crazy. Sadly, that revelation offered no comfort.

He thought back to everything that had happened. Was the plan to get him to lose his sanity so he'd separate himself from the rest of the herd, making him easier prey?

Donaldson resigned himself to the fact that death was imminent. He peered around the dumpster and saw the darkness flowing into the alley. It glided seamlessly over the filthy ground and up the buildings on either side. One of the shadows took on a humanoid form and moved forward until it was directly in front of Donaldson. Donaldson stared deeply into the endless void and felt stripped down to his very soul. He felt cold and alone as the thing in front of him teased out his memories and feelings and left him drained and empty. Donaldson saw the end of his own existence and, with that, the end of all life as he knew it. He began to fear for more than his life. His soul and the billions of others in the world were what the shadows were after.

The shadow being then drew back to the others and they began circling Donaldson, swaying and moving in a bizarre dance. He tried to flee, but they were everywhere. One of them extended a shadowy limb and grasped his arm. Donaldson screamed in agony as the creature's touch burned through his shirt and then his skin. Another one grabbed his other arm and they held him tight. He screamed again and the darkness poured into his open mouth. He tried to shut his mouth, but was unable to stop the flow of darkness into him. He felt himself die as the darkness destroyed him from within.

Donaldson bolted forward, straining at the woolen blanket that covered him. He wiped his eyes and looked about groggily.

"I'm home?" he muttered, still trying to claw the cobwebs from his brain. He looked over to see his wife, Janice sleeping peacefully beside him. She looked beatific in sleep and had a small half-smile as if she were enjoying a pleasant dream. Then he saw it. On his wife's night table was the damned ring. He stared at it and shuddered at how the ochre veins seemed to pulse in the rich black gem. He remembered that they had found the chest that morning and inside had been the ring. *Had it all been nothing more than a dream?* Donaldson couldn't believe the clarity of the nightmare. It had felt so real.

Donaldson got out of bed and walked around to his wife's side. He picked up the ring and looked at it closely. It felt cold to the touch, but other than the weird pattern in the stone, it was nothing more than cheap costume jewelry. So why did it make him feel so unsettled?

He leaned over and gave his wife a quick kiss and quickly dressed. He threw on a light coat and headed outside. The street was deserted, but that was to be expected. It was a quiet, upper middle class neighborhood where most people were more apt to be asleep in the middle of the night. Donaldson walked for a few blocks, not encountering a soul. The air was crisp and cold and he hugged himself for warmth. Winter was around the corner and soon their quiet little town would be blanketed by snow. He eventually came to the end of the block, took one last look at the ring and then dropped it down the sewer. Contented, he returned home where he fixed himself a hot chocolate to try to take the edge off the chill from outside. He couldn't believe his foolishness and knew he'd have a Hell of a time explaining to Janice why he had thrown away her ring.

Donaldson returned to his bedroom, stripped down, pulled back his covers and fluffed up his pillow before climbing back into bed. Within minutes, he was fast asleep, a sleep both calm and dreamless.

The air began to grow colder. Their nightlight flickered and then winked out. Shadows began to spread from the darkened corners to deeper in the room. It flowed from under the bureau and nightstands as well as from under the bed. Long, sinewy tendrils of darkness snaked up the bed from all sides, slowly covering the sleeping couple. The darkness entered them and began to feed from inside. During the entire ordeal, neither of them stirred. Before long, nothing remained of the Donaldsons except for their bedclothes. On the nightstand next to where Janice used to sleep was the ring. It twinkled in the darkness, pulsating and waiting.

The Horseman

The storm clouds rolled in, forming a thick canopy overhead and casting a dark pall over the desert. This was accompanied by a bone chilling wind that howled and whipped sand and detritus in chaotic swirls through the air. Tumbleweeds rolled by, propelled along by the storm's fury. Thick drops of rain fell at sharp angles, as if trying to defy the force of the winds. In the midst of this onslaught of nature was a lone figure mounted atop a powerful black Spanish Mustang. The figure sat straight in the saddle, seemingly oblivious to the elements which assaulted him from all angles. He pressed his steed onward, never stopping, never deviating from his path.

The rider was dressed entirely in black. He wore a full length coat over a black shirt. His slacks were tucked into his worn leather boots. Around his waist were twin black leather gun belts which holstered two silver, ebony-handled pistols. He wore thick black gloves, and tightly grasped the horse's reins. His black Stetson was angled forward, obscuring his features in shadow. He gritted his teeth as he rode, and thought of the man he was riding to see. It had been ages since they had last parted and the horseman was looking forward to their long overdue reunion.

It had been twenty years since the dark rider had seen Henry Plummer. They had been inseparable friends back then. They had been close since Henry's family had moved to Bannack from Boston. Henry did not adapt well to the change in life from that of the civilized East to the wild, untamed West and was the frequent target of beatings from the other boys at school. It wasn't until one afternoon when the horseman had been walking home after classes when he came upon three of his

221

classmates mercilessly beating on Henry. While he wasn't one to interfere, the idea of three against one struck him as unfair. The fight was short and the horseman got his ass handed to him, but the boys soon tired over what was a lot closer to a fair fight and left. Henry and the horseman walked home after that, got to talking, and found they had a lot in common. A friendship followed and, by the time they were in their twenties, they had parlayed that friendship into a partnership in a thriving saloon in town.

The town of Bannack was still a half day's ride, but the horseman's anticipation would not allow him to rest. He stopped only to give his tired steed some water and then continued, pushing the horse hard across the Montana wilderness. He noticed something off in the distance, just at the edge of the horizon. It seemed to be heading his way. The horseman's preternatural sense caused him to realize that trouble was approaching. He saw that it was a pack of grey wolves, probably close to a dozen, and if they were this far into the desert, they were surely starving and very dangerous.

The horseman had to quickly weigh his options. He could backtrack and ride east before heading back toward his original destination. This way he would avoid coming anywhere near the pack. That detour would cost him hours though. His other option was to keep riding. He kicked his horse and spurred it forward. After all these years, nothing would keep him from his rendezvous in Bannack.

As he rode, the dark rider pulled out his guns. He inspected the chambers to ensure they had bullets. His pistols were custom Smith & Wesson Schofields, with hand crafted black inlaid handles. The horseman was no stranger to guns and these had been his weapon of choice for years.

Before long, the horseman reached the wolves. They circled his horse, growling and snarling, but cautious enough to keep far enough back from the horse and rider. He quickly looked the wolves over. Their grey fur was thin and patchy and they appeared to be gaunt. Their eyes blazed with a feral hunger and they bared their teeth at the rider. The horseman pulled the reins, forcing the horse to a stop, took aim and fired at the two largest wolves. With a yelp, both animals fell to the ground. The other wolves paused and backed up a step, unsure of what to make of this new development. He took advantage of the wolves' indecision and fired twice more from each gun. With uncanny accuracy, four more wolves fell dead.

The remaining six wolves rushed the dark rider so he kicked his heels to his horse's ribs and the Mustang galloped forward with the wolves in hot pursuit. He turned in the saddle and shot the two at the head of the pack and they, too, fell dead. Three of the remaining wolves leaped for the rider. The horseman managed to shoot two but the third knocked him off the horse. He fell back to the hard ground, the wolf snapping at his throat. He calmly took aim and fired, the bullet blowing a fist sized hole out the back of the wolf's head. It collapsed on top of him. He pushed off the dead animal in time to see the last wolf approach. The wolf leaped on him and managed to clamp its teeth around his arm. The dark rider reached out with his left arm and grabbed the wolf by the throat. The animal tried desperately to free itself, trying to bite down on the horseman's arm. He gritted his teeth and tightened his grip. The wolf released its hold on the rider's arm and lunged forward, reaching for the horseman's throat. He could smell the wolf's foul, fetid breath as it struggled to free itself. He stared into the frightened animal's eyes as he tightened his grip on the wolf's neck. The wolf began thrashing even harder, desperate to get free. Its eyes opened wide and, even with its limited intellect, it realized that it was about to die. The wolf tried one last desperate lunge in an attempt to get free, but was unable to escape from the horseman's vise-like grip. The horseman snapped the wolf's neck and tossed the carcass to the side. He stood and slowly climbed back onto his horse which was standing there, awaiting his master. He didn't brush himself off nor did he check his arm for any damage caused by the wolf. This diversion had wasted enough time and the horseman sensed that time was running short. He couldn't risk falling behind. Not now when he was finally so close.

The sun had set and, with nightfall, the temperature in the Montana plains had plummeted. The harsh winds had abated and the rain had stopped. The air was now still and cold and the horseman noticed the plumes of frost from his steed's ragged breathing. The horse's body was perspiring heavily, in spite of the cold. The dark rider realized that if he pushed his horse much harder, it would die. He clenched his teeth and gently pulled back the reins, putting a reassuring hand to the horse's side. The horse slowed to a stop and the horseman climbed down to feed the horse a dried carrot and pour some water into a shallow bowl, which the horse greedily lapped up. He then climbed back on the horse and continued on his journey. After another hour, he could see, off in the distance, the lights of Bannack.

Bannack.

The horseman's thoughts drift back the two decades to when he had last been in the small Montana town. The saloon that he had started with Henry was a huge success. As the only place in town where people could meet, listen to live music, get a decent meal and, of course drink, they soon found themselves very wealthy. They had each bought large homes in town on sprawling properties. In order to keep up with demand, they hired a woman from town to help as a barmaid. The horseman remembers that day quite clearly. When she walked in to the saloon for the first time, he felt like the world around him had stopped moving and only she existed.

The woman came into the saloon mid-day, and walked confidently up to the bar where the horseman was busy drying some glassware. She said her name was Rose and that she was looking for work. She extended a delicate porcelain hand which the horseman cautiously shook, fearful that he'd harm such a delicate flower. After a short conversation, he realized that she was bright, charming and very warm. He knew right away that she would be a perfect hire for their saloon. He told her that he thought she was great but wanted her to meet his partner, Henry, before they extended an offer.

The horseman brought Rose through to the back where Henry was in the office, going over the ledger. Henry looked up and saw his partner and Rose standing in the doorway to the office.

"Henry, I'd like to introduce you to Rose. She's looking for work and I think she'd be a great fit as our new barmaid."

Henry stood and extended his hand which Rose quickly shook. "It's a pleasure to meet you, Ms?"

"Cavanagh," Rose added. "It's a pleasure to meet you as well, Mr. Plummer."

Henry smiled his most infectious grin, and Rose instantly warmed to it. "Please, call me Henry."

The horseman felt a momentary pang of jealousy. Henry was a smooth talker, quite charming and had a way with the ladies. He quickly dismissed the thought. Rose was a prospective employee and Henry was just being friendly.

"So, Rose," the horseman began, "the position is not that complicated. The majority of your duties would involve you taking food and drink orders, and then bringing them to the customers either at their tables or the bar. Most people who come here are local and, while we allow a nightly tab, we do expect payment by the end of the night. Any tips are yours to keep plus a nightly rate. Henry, do you have anything to add?"

Henry shook his head. "No. It seems like you have this covered."

"When can I start?" Rose asked. Both men smiled and the horseman indicated that the next night would be fine.

The horseman gazes ahead. The town seems to beckon to him, calling him home. He urges his horse forward and rides into town. The town of Bannack is built around a hard packed dirt road that bisects the town. A barbershop, general store and brothel are some of the stores that line the main street. The saloon stands at the edge of the road, a large two- story structure with wooden swinging doors out front. The sound of piano playing and raucous cheers can be heard.

The horseman slowly guides his horse to the front of the saloon. He dismounts and ties his steed to the wooden post. He walks up to the swinging doors, pauses, then confidently steps through. The saloon looks exactly as he remembered it. The room is dimly lit, with an overhead chandelier and kerosene lamps on each table. Several men are sitting around the tables playing faro or poker. In one corner of the room, a man in a bowler hat plays on the player piano while dancing girls entertain some of the customers who cheer and holler as the women dance. A dozen men stand around the bar drinking. The air is thick with smoke and the room smells of pine, tobacco and alcohol.

The horseman spies an empty table in the corner. He walks through the crowd, causing people to whisper about the identity of the dark stranger. He chooses the chair against the wall and beckons the serving girl over.

He thinks that the serving girl is quite pretty and bears a strong resemblance to Rose. The thought of Rose brings the memories back. He can still remember how her smile lit up a room and how her hair, like spun gold, seemed to catch the light. She had bright blue eyes and a smattering of freckles across her small, pert nose. She was slim and petite, and stood just over five feet tall. In addition to looking like the girl next door, she was an excellent barmaid, and the customers loved her infectious warmth. It wasn't long before both the horseman and Henry fell for her like a ton of bricks.

Henry had been the first to ask Rose out. They dated a few times and, while their dates were pleasant, and Henry was a perfect gentleman, Rose hadn't felt a connection and couldn't see Henry as anything more than a friend.

Rose hadn't planned on getting involved with either of the men, but the horseman's kind nature and easy going manner soon won her over. They started seeing each other and, before long, they were in love. They began spending all their time to-gether and soon began discussing marriage.

All their friends were ecstatic except for Henry, who felt that the horseman had betrayed his trust and stolen Rose's af-fections from him. Watching his best friend and Rose together ate away at him and soon became more than he could bear. One night, at the end of the workday, he called Rose into his office.

"Is everything okay, Henry?"

Henry sighed. "I'd like to take you out again. I think we should give us another chance."

"I'm sorry, Henry. It just didn't feel right between us. You know that Jeremy is courting me now and we are considering marriage. I'm sorry if I gave you any cause to believe otherwise."

Henry stood up, knocking his chair over. "We're meant to be together, Rose. I can't bear to see you with anyone else. You belong to me."

"Jeremy is your best friend. Can't you just be happy for us?"

Henry's features darkened. "You're mine, Rose."

Rose backed up slowly. "You're scaring me, Henry."

Henry lunged for Rose. She ducked and ran for the door. The saloon was dark and empty, but Rose had worked the floor for several months and knew the layout well. She dodged be-tween tables and ran out the front door. She heard Henry run into a table in the dark and his cry of pain.

Rose ran down the darkened streets. She had to get to Jeremy. He would protect her. She turned off the main road and ran down the side street which led to Jeremy's house. She now wondered why he hadn't been at the saloon. *Had Henry done something to him?*

Jeremy's house loomed ahead. She ran as hard as she could and up the walk to the front door. The house was dark. Rose pounded on the door, but no one seemed to be home. She ran around back and found the hidden key under the rock closest to the back porch. She let herself in and ran through the house looking for Jeremy.

Where could he be?

Rose knew she had to get out of there. Henry would be sure to check Jeremy's house for her. She ran to the back door and threw it open. Standing in the doorway was Henry. He glared at her with a burning hatred.

"Hello Rose. What a surprise finding you here."

"Where's Jeremy?"

Henry smirked. "I asked him to ride to Alder Gulch for me. I told him I wanted to invest some of our earnings from the saloon in purchasing a claim. Gold had been found there and seemed like a great opportunity."

"No wonder you tried what you did," Rose yelled. "You'd never have tried anything with Jeremy around."

Henry stepped over the threshold into the house. "You are correct, Rose. That is why Jeremy won't be coming back."

Rose's blood ran cold. "What do you mean he isn't coming back?"

"I hired some men to meet up with Jeremy midway between here and Alder Gulch. I told them to make it look like a robbery."

Rose turned and ran. She heard a loud crack and felt something slam hard into her back, throwing her forward. She tried to turn over and screamed in pain. "Please, Henry. You don't have to do this."

"I don't have to do this?" Henry roared in anger. "You humiliated me in front of the entire town. I am a well-respected member of this community. I have plans to be sheriff in this town. How do you think it looks losing my sweetheart to my best friend? The humiliation is bad enough, but the betrayal you both showed to me is inexcusable."

"Please," Rose sobbed. The pain in her back where Henry had shot her was excruciating. "I never meant to hurt you, Henry. The heart knows what it wants."

"It should have wanted me, Rose. I never meant for it to end this way, but you left me no choice. The wheels have already been set in motion. Your body will be found in Jeremy's house. He will be blamed for your murder. Of course, since he will be dead and buried in the desert, everyone in town will assume he killed you and ran away. I'll be the grieving friend and, in the end, parlay the outpouring of sympathy into becoming sheriff and amassing a very large fortune."

Henry aimed his gun at Rose and fired three shots into her chest and neck. She twitched once and was still.

The serving girl walked over to the man in black. He sat there in the shadows, his hat tilted forward, obscuring his features in the shadows.

"Can I help you mister?" the serving girl asked.

"Yes," the horseman replied, his voice dry and raspy. He pointed to the middle-aged man behind the bar. "Bring me a bottle of whiskey, and fetch the landlord. We have some items to discuss."

The serving girl hurried back to the bar. The horseman watched her with mild amusement as she spoke to the barman and pointed nervously to his table. The barman sauntered over and put a glass down on the table. He poured two fingers of whiskey which the horseman downed in a single pull. The barman poured another and the horseman motioned to the seat across from him.

"Have a seat," the horseman said, and the barman recoiled at hearing the stranger's raw and haunted voice. He sat and looked at the stranger across from him. He tried to make out the man's features, but found that he couldn't in the darkened light of the saloon, and the way the stranger wore his hat.

"What can I do for you?" the barman asked the stranger who sat there in stony silence. "The serving girl said you wanted to speak with me."

The horseman chuckled, and spoke. "I'm here about a killing," he said coldly.

The barman tried to discern the man's features. He could swear he saw a malicious grin but, with the thick shadows in the corner, it was impossible to tell. "A killing?" the barman repeated.

"Yes, it was a murder from many years ago," the stranger hissed. "I'm sure you remember Rose Cavanagh, don't you, Henry?"

The barman froze. *Who was this man?* He thought back to that day with Rose at Jeremy's house. There were no witnesses. It was easy to pin the blame on Jeremy as he never returned to town. He played the part of the loyal friend, claiming unwavering faith in his friend, while sowing the seeds of doubt in town. He organized searches but Jeremy was never heard from again. Henry assumed that he was left for dead in the desert somewhere, buried where no one would ever stumble upon his body. Yet, here was a stranger sitting in the bar and implying his complicity in Rose's death.

"Who are you, stranger?" the barman demanded. "Rose was a dear friend of mine. What business do you have stirring up painful memories?"

"Why, Henry," came the mocking reply, "surely you haven't forgotten your best friend?"

"Jeremy?" Henry asked. He started to reach for his guns. If this was indeed Jeremy, then he needed to handle this fast before things got out of hand.

"Sit down!" the horseman commanded. He started to laugh, cold and malevolent. The stranger slowly lifted his gloved hand to the brim of his hat and eased it back to expose his features, by the glow of the oil lamp, to Henry Plummer.

Henry sat there numbly staring ahead, his eyes fixed on the face of the man who sat before him. While it was clear that the dark stranger was his former friend, there was nothing left of the man he once called friend. Jeremy's skin was desiccated and peeling, exposing the shriveled muscle and skull beneath. The lips were pulled taut, showing grey teeth and blackened gums. His right eye was gone and Henry watched in terror as a maggot crawled out of the socket. The left eye was clouded over, but still twinkled with intelligence. Jeremy's skull was cracked and broken on the right side, and Henry was able to see a bullet hole in the forehead.

"It's good to see you again, Henry. I've waited many years for this day."

Henry wanted to run, but found himself frozen with fear. He moaned softly and rocked slowly back and forth in the chair. "What do you want from me, Jeremy?" he asked. His voice barely rose above a whisper.

Jeremy made a sound like a low growl. "Think back, Henry. You asked me to ride out and purchase a claim. Like a fool, I trusted you and I lost everything. You took from me my life and the woman I loved. Now it's time to balance the scales."

"That's a lie!" Henry yelled, hoping that he could bluff his way out of this. "I never did any of that. I was devastated by the murder of Rose, and your disappearance was something I never got over."

Jeremy laughed again. "You always were slick, Henry. You could sell moccasins to an injun. Unfortunately for you, I have evidence that says otherwise."

"What evidence?" Henry asked nervously.

The horseman poured himself another shot of whiskey which he promptly swallowed. "I remember the day quite well. I was riding out to purchase our claim when I was set upon by three men. At first I thought they were bandits and were looking to rob me. One of the men asked me to toss my pistols aside and then get off my horse, which I did. Two of the men aimed their guns at me while the third transferred my bags to their horses. Then, without warning, they looked at each other, grinned and opened fire on me. They dragged my bleeding body to a hole they must have already dug and buried me alive. Just before they covered me up fully with dirt, one of them said that you sent your regards.

"I died there in the desert, alone and in unbearable pain. It took hours for my life to drain away and I welcomed leaving the agony and drifting into sweet oblivion. I thought that would have been the end of it, but she wouldn't let me."

"She?"

The horseman continued. "It was Rose. She found me in the desert."

"I don't understand?" Henry said. His curiosity was stronger than his fear. "How could Rose have found you in the desert?"

"Maybe it's because you killed her, Henry. How could a dead woman find her dying beau in the vast desert?" the horseman said with a sneer. "It's because we had a connection. She came to me while I lay dying and stayed with me as I took my last breath."

"Cut the crap, Jeremy. Sure, you look like shit, but you ain't dead. I don't know how you're still alive, or why you bothered to come back here, but I'm gonna finish what those three fools failed to do." Henry stood and pointed a gun at Jeremy. "Now stand up slowly and keep your hands where I can see them." He slipped the guns into his jacket pockets. "I've got my pistols trained on you. One false move, I'll shoot you here and now."

Jeremy stood and silently walked to the saloon's exit, followed closely by Henry. He stepped outside and saw that the street was deserted. He walked up to his horse and stopped. Jeremy slowly turned and faced his former friend. "There's one last piece of the story, Henry. Want to know what it is?"

"Not really. I want you to climb on your horse and we'll ride out of town."

"I think I'll tell you anyway. After all, even a condemned man gets to say his piece at the end."

"Make it quick."

"I lied in there, Jeremy. I didn't die. Not there in the desert. I probably would have, if it weren't for Rose. Her spirit kept the spark of life from fading. She helped me heal, for want of a better word. It took me twenty years to find my way back to you. I had no choice, you see. That was the deal. Rose kept me alive, and helped me heal, and I would do one thing for her."

"And what was that?"

"I promised that I'd let her kill you." Jeremy smiled. His grin grew wider until his lower jaw split open. A dark, amorphous shape spewed out of Jeremy's ruined face. The shadowy mass took shape, with appendages extending and a rudimentary head forming. The roiling mass spilled forward, landing on the dusty ground and began twisting and spiraling until it assumed a humanoid form. Blood red eyes appeared in the shade's head and it extended its arms until they wrapped around Henry. The thing's touch was so cold he felt his skin burning beneath his clothes.

Henry began firing, emptying his bullets into the shadow creature. The shots had no effect as the dark form glided across the ground toward him. It began extending tendrils of darkness which spread out across Henry's body. He screamed and desperately tried to pull off the creature. Everywhere the thing touched burned him as if it were made of acid. The darkness extended to his face and worked its way across his features, leaving burns. Henry felt his life force slipping away and was close to blacking out from the pain. He fell to the ground, his body slowly dissolving from where the shadow creature had touched him. He tried to scream, but it only came out as a wet gurgle and then nothing as his throat bubbled away to a pulpy mess. The darkness poured out of Henry and glided across the ground to where Jeremy stood, passively watching. It formed into a humanoid shape once again, this time taking on Rose's features. She looked at Henry with a cold expression and maintained eye contact with him without saying a word until he died. Jeremy and Rose stood there, watching Henry's body dissolve into a thick and bloody mass. They stayed there until there was nothing left but bones. Jeremy then took Rose's hand and they walked off into the darkness.

Knob Lake

The frigid air whipped about in menacing blasts, causing the powdery snow to rise up from Knob Lake as if possessed. It was twenty below and the thermostat was steadily falling as nightfall approached. Above, the sky stood as a slate grey and stretched out ominously across the bleak, snow covered horizon. A storm was coming and most of the locals had already found somewhere safe and warm to ride it out.

Igaluk walked slowly, the hood of his parka pulled over his head and tied tight. He struggled to keep the stinging snow and wind from his eyes. As it was, his eyes began to water. He looked around at the vast emptiness, feeling a strong sense of loss, as if he were alone in the world. Igaluk was used to being alone. He didn't make friends easily and more often than not seemed to attract the unwanted attention of bullies. Today had been one of those days. He attended high school in Schefferville, which was in northern Quebec, near the border into Newfoundland. He was one of the few Inuits who attended the school. Most other families opted for either home schooling or joining the other First Nation tribe, the Naskapi, at their school in nearby Kawawachikamach just north of town. Attending school here had been his idea, and while he hated each day with every fiber of his being, he knew it was the best route to escaping his bleak Northern existence and perhaps finding his way south to Montreal where he could actually make something of his life.

Like most days, Igaluk walked the two miles to and from school each day where he attended ninth grade. His mother worked a late shift at a local diner waiting tables and wasn't even awake when he left for school. His father had been shot and killed years earlier outside a bar that he regularly frequented after a heated discussion with a local francophone about how the Iron Ore Company's mine was leaving industrial waste and polluting the tundra. When local authorities arrived, no one was willing to come forward and Igaluk's father's murder went unsolved. Even though his father enjoyed drinking a little too much, he had been a good man. His death left a void in their family which never healed. That was in 1981, a year before the mine closed. Igaluk had only been five at the time and the thought that he would never see his father again seemed far too abstract a concept for his young mind to process. Now, ten years later, Igaluk barely remembered his father and never really saw his mother in the cramped two bedroom shack they shared and called home.

The town barely had two hundred residents and perhaps fifty students from grades one through eleven. Of that group, there were perhaps a dozen kids roughly his age. Igaluk used to think about the girls in his class, but after the endless beatings and insults from a trio of French boys, he realized that was never going to happen.

Igaluk was so lost in thought that he failed to hear the boys approach.

"I-gloooooo." The voice behind him was high pitched and shrill, and mocking in tone. It carried over the howl of the wind. Igaluk's blood froze. He knew right away who it was. Only one group of kids chose to taunt him by making fun of his name and a symbol of his First Nation heritage. "Iiiiiiiiiiiiii-glooooooo," the voice repeated. "We want to talk to you."

He turned and saw the three boys and knew he was in trouble. Even though they were still a ways off, he recognized Serge Ouellette, Jean-Marc Fortin and Denis Pronovost. Serge was the leader of the little group. He was a year older than Igaluk and probably the most popular boy in school. He was tall and muscular with thick, dark hair and dark eyes. He had almost olive skin, a long, straight nose and full lips. The girls in school all followed him like lovesick seals and the boys all idolized him. Igaluk saw through the façade and actually found his supposedly infectious grin to be more of a cruel sneer. Serge's penchant for cruelty had no bounds. Igaluk knew this well and had suffered many a beating at his hands. He might be able to fool the other kids and teachers, but Igaluk saw the darkness of his soul and made a very conscious effort to stay as far away from Serge as possible. His friends were different stories altogether. Jean-Marc was Igaluk's age and was wiry and devious. A cowardly boy by nature, he enjoyed being in Serge's shadow as it allowed him the privilege of enjoying perceived strength and superiority over others. When alone, he was quiet and meek, but the minute Serge showed up, his nascent cruelty came out in force. Denis, on the other hand, was only fourteen, but was already six-foot-two in height and easily weighed over two hundred and twenty pounds of pure muscle. He was slow-witted and mean and had a reputation for torturing animals. Igaluk saw the boys all held bottles of Molson's ale in their hands and cigarettes dangling from their lips. They seemed oblivious of the storm that raged around them. Yet another day after school for the lost youth of this miserable patch of earth, Igaluk mused.

His thoughts drifted back to class that afternoon. He was minding his own business when Manon Gervais came over and sat down next to him. She was far from a great beauty, but Igaluk felt his heart race nonetheless by her proximity. She smelled faintly of perfume which made him think of summers by the lake. She smiled a shy and friendly smile at him. Igaluk wondered why she would even approach a guy like him. While he kept himself in good shape, he was nowhere close to being considered attractive. His face was a bit too thin, his nose and mouth a bit too wide, and his jet black hair always seemed to hang down limply in every conceivable direction.

Manon had explained that she was having a hard time with her studies and knew that Igaluk was one of the smartest boys in school. She hoped that he would be willing to tutor her and that it wouldn't be too much of an inconvenience. Igaluk was thrilled to get the opportunity to spend time with Manon and nearly blurted out that very fact. He managed to get some of his composure back and actually asked her why him? He was surprised as most people in the school avoided him and did nothing but tease him about his being an Inuit. Manon had laughed then, a rich and hearty laugh that Igaluk found quite pleasant. She told him that the boys in the school were small minded and only teased him because they were jealous of how smart he was.

Igaluk gave it some thought and agreed to tutor Manon starting the next day after school. Manon smiled again and gave Igaluk a quick peck on the cheek, telling him she would see him then. He blushed and the warm feelings in his stomach turn to ice when he saw Jean-Marc Fortin glaring at him from the back of the class. With a swiping motion across his throat, he mouthed the words 'you're dead' to Igaluk.

Igaluk suddenly felt ill. What had he done? He knew that Manon was Serge's cousin and being on good terms with her would not mean his safety from the boys' bullying, but rather would make him an even more visible target for their beatings. His only hope was to disappear after school, walk a new way home and hope to God that Serge and his group did not find him. There was the slim hope that he had actually outsmarted them and was home free and that he could get home in peace. At the very least, he hoped the impending storm would keep the boys away. Being wrong was no longer a viable option. He knew if Serge and his friends caught him out in the open, they would beat him unconscious and he'd freeze to death out in the cold. An icy knot of fear seemed to grow in his belly and realized he was in very deep trouble.

Igaluk glanced back and saw the three boys trotting over towards him. Figuring he had his best chance of escape at that moment, Igaluk turned and ran, heading off towards the old abandoned Iron Ore mine. The mine had closed ten years earlier and had gotten a reputation among the locals for being haunted. Igaluk didn't believe the stories. He had his own reasons for avoiding the mine as they reminded him too much of his father and how much he missed having him as a part of his life.

With the heavy wind and the driving snow, Igaluk reasoned that he might actually lose his tormentors. At the very least, he could hide in the mine itself. He used to play in the tunnels as a child and knew them fairly well. Also, there was a good chance that Serge and his friends would avoid the mine based on its reputation. Behind him, he heard angry shouts and knew without turning that they were in pursuit. This prompted Igaluk to run even faster. If he had just stayed where he was, there was always the chance that they might have only slapped him around a bit. Now that he made them run, they would make him bleed if caught.

Even though his lungs burned, Igaluk kept running. His face was frozen and he felt that he could barely breathe. None of that mattered and he kept running until he saw the old abandoned mine up ahead. Pausing, he allowed himself a moment to catch his breath. The snow was coming down in stinging sheets and even though he couldn't see his pursuers through the snow and wind, he did hear their screams of anger. They were not far behind. He took huge gulps of the frigid air which burned his lungs even more. Hoping to put some more distance between himself and the three boys, he quickened his pace. The entrance to the mine loomed ahead, boarded up and mostly blocked by high snowdrifts. Igaluk realized that he could hide in the mine without Serge and his friends knowing he went in as the snow and wind was blowing so fiercely, his tracks would only be visible from close up, and even then would quickly be obliterated by the raging storm. Then, after his pursuers lost interest or got too cold, he could then safely make his way back home.

Running up to the entrance, he tried the door to the mine. It was locked, but the wooden door was rotted through after a decade of exposure to the wind, cold and snow. He kicked at the door until it snapped open, the sound like a rifle shot in the crisp winter air. Igaluk prayed that the boys did not hear it over the howling of the wind. He peered inside and saw nothing but pitch black shadows. Carefully stepping in, he shut the broken door behind him, plunging him into total darkness. From his jacket pocket he pulled a pack of matches and struck one. The match head seemed unnaturally bright in the near Stygian darkness. Igaluk saw some splintered beams on the ground ahead and grabbed one. They were surprisingly dry and light and had a smell that reminded him of camping in the woods with his father. After a few attempts, he managed to get it lit to serve as a makeshift torch. The flame danced and crackled and cast a warming glow around him.

The light from Igaluk's torch showed a long, downwardly sloping tunnel supported by lichen covered wooden beams at regular intervals. The air was surprisingly warm and felt thick with an earthy smell. Something else lingered in the air, something sweet and ripe and cloying, like fruit left out too long in the hot sun. Reaching out to touch a beam, he found it cold and slimy and quickly pulled his hand back, wiping his fingers on his pants. Igaluk felt light-headed when he saw movement at the end of the tunnel. He lifted the torch and watched as a beautiful woman seemed to glide out of the shadows. She stood tall and slender, completely naked, with alabaster skin and hair as white as freshly fallen snow. Her body was utterly devoid of any color except for her eyes which shone a wet and glistening black. Igaluk stared, captivated by her alluring beauty. He couldn't take his eyes off the inviting thatch of downy white hair between her legs. She smiled lasciviously, beckoned for him to follow, and then turned and melted back into the shadows.

"Wait," Igaluk called to the woman. "Who are you? Do you need any help?" When no response came, he set out in pursuit. Outside of the few magazines that circled amongst the guys at school, he had never seen a naked woman. He felt himself growing painfully aroused. Hurrying down the tunnel, he reached the end which branched off in a T-intersection. There weren't any visible tracks in the earthen floor of the tunnel or anything else which could provide evidence that the woman had ever passed in either direction. He cocked his head down towards the right and didn't hear anything. From the left, there came a faint sound like sticks being alternately rubbed together then snapped. The same sweet smell, which seemed to linger on the air, seemed to be getting stronger. Walking cautiously forward, the growing sense of fear began getting in the way of any immediate needs or desire. The noises which came from further ahead in the near absolute darkness seemed to grow louder. At the end of the tunnel, it widened and opened into a large, natural cave. Stalactites lined the cavernous ceiling and stalagmites littered the ground. A shallow, fetid pool of an oily and dark looking liquid covered a good section of the cavern floor. Igaluk saw the girl near the rear of the cavern, beckoning to him. Without hesitation, he hurried over towards the woman. Blinded by desire, he did not pay attention to his footing and slipped, landing hard on a stalagmite which jutted out from the ground. The stalagmite pierced Igaluk's shoulder and waves of intense agony washed over him until everything went black.

Igaluk came to, his head pounding and his left shoulder completely numb. A dry, pasty feeling filled his mouth and he wished he at least had some water. The air was thick with a damp and rotten earthy smell. The same scraping and clacking sounds noted earlier in the tunnel could be heard, coming from all around him. He tried to sit up and found that he couldn't move. A stalagmite had him pinned to the ground. The darkness wasn't all encompassing, at least. Off to the side, the torch still burned and cast a dim but very welcoming light.

Igaluk felt something crawl over his chest and he screamed as the thing moved into his peripheral vision. It had the appearance of a cross between a crab and a cockroach. The thing was large, at least as big as a baseball that seemed to end at sharp angles. From the main body extended six thick multi-jointed biramous appendages, each one ending at sharp, barbed points. Its carapace was a mottled mix of green and rust. The thing stopped, reared up and rubbed its long-jointed appendages together, making the scraping sound he'd heard earlier. He noticed that its underbelly was a series of ribbed bands of chitin that glistened wetly.

Gordon Anthony Bean

It had a long, triangular head with black, liquid eyes that seemed to be studying him. He didn't know why, but the way those dark eyes stared at him gave him the sense that the creature was highly intelligent. It had a double set of mandibles which extended from its mouth, twitching furiously. The smell coming off the thing was incredible, a heady and overpowering scent of decaying earth and fruit.

The roach-thing slowly crawled forward and tentatively put two legs on Igaluk's chin. He felt revulsion as the thing's touch sent shocks through his skull. It moved closer, standing directly over Igaluk's mouth. The roach-thing then began secreting a foul liquid from between the chitin bands on its belly. He held his lips tightly, but several of the drops had already gotten in and felt like they were eating away at the walls of his mouth, throat and tongue. Igaluk screamed and the creature secreted even more of the foul mixture into his mouth. It then turned around and a clear, viscous fluid was excreted from an aperture on the back of the thing.

Igaluk tried to dislodge the creature and shook his head vigorously. His thrashing had no effect as the fluid on his neck stretched forward, taking on a snake-like appearance. To his horror, Igaluk watched as the creature seemed to dissolve into a jelly-like substance which became absorbed in the writhing gel-like mass. It slithered slowly up his cheek, whipping and flagellating its tail end to allow for forward mobility, leaving a slight acidic burn in his cheek. Igaluk screamed in pain as it crossed his face and slithered up his nose. The worm-like thing burrowed behind his eyes and then back to his brain. Igaluk felt the thing moving around in his head and he sobbed in helpless terror as he realized there was nothing he could do to get it out. It grew as it worked through his head, absorbing Igaluk's memories and knowledge as it went. He relived every painful moment of his life, from his sheer loneliness, to his father's passing, to his own mother's indifference. He felt his memories, and what made him who he was, being torn away as the thing worked its way through his brain. Soon Igaluk felt a detached sense of self, as if he were now a passive passenger in his own mind.

Igaluk felt the presence of hundreds others around him, their thoughts shared with his own. He heard their screams and almost went mad as his head was filled with hundreds of the others' thoughts, crowding out his own and threatening to lose himself amid all the chaos.

The thing in his brain made him stand up. He stood, with movements that were slow and jerky, and pulled his shoulder free of the stalagmite with surprisingly little pain. Igaluk felt the muscles and tendons stitching themselves back together in his wounded shoulder. Soon, feeling actually returned to his wounded arm. He took a tentative step forward, then another and another. It was as if it had never walked before, but he sensed the thing in his brain was a quick learner. Moving slowly, and taking deliberate steps, it was as like learning how to walk all over again. With slow, plodding steps, he made his way down the mine's tunnel and came to the door leading outside. With a new found strength, he swung the door open and came face to face with Serge and his two friends.

Igaluk was about to say something when Denis grinned and savagely punched him in the face. His head snapped violently back, but his body didn't move and stood there stiffly. With a careful slowness, he lifted his head up, snapping broken vertebrae in his neck back in place as he pushed his head forward until he was face to face with the boy. Denis was clearly stunned, looking at Igaluk, who stood there with a sinister grin spreading across his face. Igaluk felt his arms reach out and grab the bewildered boy by the ears and pull his face in close. Still grinning, he then spit a thick viscous wad of gel in Denis' face. Denis screamed and clawed at his face as the skin bubbled and dissolved. The other two boys stood there transfixed as they watched the skin and flesh began to slough off Denis' skull

"What the fuck did you do, Igloo?" Jean-Marc cried out as he looked over at Denis in horror. Denis stood there pawing at his ruined face, screaming in pain, as a whisper of smoke rose from the rapidly dissolving flesh. Igaluk smiled broadly and ripped out Jean-Marc's throat in a single swipe. Jean-Marc stared in disbelief as his blood sprayed out from his ruined throat. He collapsed without saying a sound.

Serge stared in shock at Jean-Marc who lay there on the ground with his life blood pooling around his still body and then at Denis whose dead hands still clutched his ruined face which was still being steadily eaten away by the acidic mess that Igaluk spat at him. He didn't need to be told twice that things were not turning out as planned. He turned and ran as fast as he could away from Igaluk and the mine.

Igaluk watched the boy run away, barely discernible with the wind and blowing snow. He was already sickened by what the thing in his head made him do to the other boys. He wanted to let this one go. As much as he hated Serge and his friends, the idea of killing them was not something he would have ever considered.

The thing in his head had other ideas.

He felt himself stiffen and then get down to all fours. Rushing out of the mine, he bounded after the boy through the snowy landscape, leaping and running along with speed and grace like an animal instead of a man. It did not take long for Igaluk to catch up to Serge and he landed hard on the boy's back, driving him face forward into the frozen ground. Igaluk stood and grabbed Serge by the hair and pulled him back towards the mine. Serge thrashed and kicked and screamed for help. Igaluk had to smile. Out here, past Knob Lake, at the entrance of the old abandoned mine in the middle of a raging winter blizzard, help would not be coming anytime soon.

At the mine, Igaluk grabbed Serge and dragged him down the tunnels until they found themselves back in the natural cave. With a surge of strength fueled by fear, Serge tried to get up and run, but Igaluk was too fast, grabbing him by the collar and slamming him back to the ground, impaling him through the chest on a stalagmite. He shuddered once and then was still. Igaluk returned to the mine's entrance and dragged back the body of Jean-Marc. He then returned a third time for Denis.

Igaluk laid the three boys out on the floor. Serge had regained consciousness and found that he could no longer move. "Why?" he asked weakly, his eyes filling with tears as a trickle of blood fell from his lips.

"Because we need you," Igaluk replied, his voice both deeper and coarser, and with a subtle echo, as it came from the thing in his brain. He whistled and from all corners of the room, a clacking, chittering sound could be heard. The first creature came out of the shadows, a miniature version of the thing that had climbed on top of Igaluk a mere hour earlier. Then another creature came forth, then another. Soon, hundreds of the crustacean-like creatures poured forth from the shadows, and Igaluk felt them in his head. He felt their raw need and it sickened yet excited him at the same time. He couldn't do anything but be a spectator in his own body.

The creatures scurried over to the three boys and within moments had them completely covered. The clacking sound intensified, and drowned out the rending and tearing sounds. Within minutes, the creatures left the skeletal remains of the boys and blended back into the shadows.

Igaluk smiled and walked back to the entrance of the mine. He looked out at the snowy landscape and breathed in the frosty air. He liked this body, despite all its imperfections. It was firm and coursed with raw vitality. The children were now well fed, thanks to those three foolish boys. He knew the town of Schefferville lay off in the distance. He smiled as he thought of the two hundred people who lived there.

He started walking purposefully towards town.

He was so very hungry. The town would satisfy him and the children for a long time to come.

About the Author

Gordon Anthony Bean was born in Laval, Quebec but now lives and works in New England. He is married with one daughter. He has published the short stories 'From a Whisper to a Dream' in the *Sinister Landscapes* anthology, 'Out of the Corner of His Eye' in the *From Beyond the Grave* anthology and 'Knob Lake' in the *Forgotten Places* anthology. His debut novel, *Dawn of Broken Glass*, was released in 2013 by Guardian of Forever Publishing. *Bloodlines*, his second novel was released in 2015, also by Guardian of Forever Publishing. He is hard at work on his third novel, *Shadowspawn*, due out in 2016 by Off the Beaten Path Press. He is also a member of the New England Horror Writers Association.